"A descendant of Agatha Christie."*

## Praise for
# SLAY BELLS

"A true holiday gem . . . An amazing accomplishment."
—*Mystery Scene*

"The author draws as much from *Fawlty Towers* as she does from Agatha Christie, crafting a charming . . . cozy delicately flavored with period details of pre–World War I rural England." —*Publishers Weekly*

"A charming cozy . . . Entertaining." —*Midwest Book Review*

"Charming . . . Its straightforward writing and tight plotting are reminiscent of Agatha Christie's books . . . *Slay Bells* is the fourteenth in Kate Kingsbury's Pennyfoot Hotel mysteries—having thirteen more of these delicious stories will give new readers something to cheer about." —*Cozy Library*

## Praise for the Pennyfoot Hotel and Manor House Mysteries of Kate Kingsbury

"[Kingsbury's] books are lighthearted and serious, amusing and well plotted." —*The Salem (OR) Statesman Journal*

"Clever and cunning . . . Delightfully unique and entertaining. A most delicious teatime mystery with just the right atmosphere and a charming cast of characters."
—*The Literary Times*

"Delightful and charming." —*Painted Rock Reviews*

"Likable characters, period details, and a puzzle that kept me guessing until the end . . . Very enjoyable." —*Mystery News*

## Visit Kate Kingsbury's website at www.doreenrobertshight.com

## Berkley Prime Crime titles
## by Kate Kingsbury

*Manor House Mysteries*

A BICYCLE BUILT FOR MURDER
DEATH IS IN THE AIR
FOR WHOM DEATH TOLLS
DIG DEEP FOR MURDER
PAINT BY MURDER
BERRIED ALIVE
FIRE WHEN READY
WEDDING ROWS
AN UNMENTIONABLE MURDER

*Pennyfoot Hotel Mysteries*

ROOM WITH A CLUE
DO NOT DISTURB
SERVICE FOR TWO
EAT, DRINK, AND BE BURIED
CHECK-OUT TIME
GROUNDS FOR MURDER
PAY THE PIPER
CHIVALRY IS DEAD
RING FOR TOMB SERVICE
DEATH WITH RESERVATIONS
DYING ROOM ONLY
MAID TO MURDER

*Holiday Pennyfoot Hotel Mysteries*

NO CLUE AT THE INN
SLAY BELLS
SHROUDS OF HOLLY
RINGING IN MURDER

# RINGING IN MURDER

## KATE KINGSBURY

BERKLEY PRIME CRIME, NEW YORK

**THE BERKLEY PUBLISHING GROUP**
**Published by the Penguin Group**
**Penguin Group (USA) Inc.**
**375 Hudson Street, New York, New York 10014, USA**
Penguin Group (Canada), 90 Eglinton Avenue East, Suite 700, Toronto, Ontario M4P 2Y3, Canada
(a division of Pearson Penguin Canada Inc.)
Penguin Books Ltd., 80 Strand, London WC2R 0RL, England
Penguin Group Ireland, 25 St. Stephen's Green, Dublin 2, Ireland (a division of Penguin Books Ltd.)
Penguin Group (Australia), 250 Camberwell Road, Camberwell, Victoria 3124, Australia
(a division of Pearson Australia Group Pty. Ltd.)
Penguin Books India Pvt. Ltd., 11 Community Centre, Panchsheel Park, New Delhi—110 017, India
Penguin Group (NZ), 67 Apollo Drive, Rosedale, North Shore 0632, New Zealand
(a division of Pearson New Zealand Ltd.)
Penguin Books (South Africa) (Pty.) Ltd., 24 Sturdee Avenue, Rosebank, Johannesburg 2196,
South Africa

Penguin Books Ltd., Registered Offices: 80 Strand, London WC2R 0RL, England

This book is an original publication of The Berkley Publishing Group.

This is a work of fiction. Names, characters, places, and incidents either are the product of the author's imagination or are used fictitiously, and any resemblance to actual persons, living or dead, business establishments, events, or locales is entirely coincidental. The publisher does not have any control over and does not assume any responsibility for author or third-party websites or their content.

PRINTING HISTORY
Berkley Prime Crime trade paperback edition / November 2008

Library of Congress Cataloging-in-Publication Data

Kingsbury, Kate.
  Ringing in murder / Kate Kingsbury.—Berkley Prime Crime trade pbk. ed.
    p. cm.
  ISBN 978-0-425-22399-4
  1. Baxter, Cecily Sinclair (Fictitious character)—Fiction.   2. Pennyfoot Hotel (England :
Imaginary place)—Fiction.   3. Murder—Investigation—Fiction.   4. Christmas stories.   I. Title.

  PR9199.3.K44228R56   2008
  813'.6—dc22                                                                                  2008022222

PRINTED IN THE UNITED STATES OF AMERICA

10   9   8   7   6   5   4   3   2   1

*To Bill,*
*for all that you give and all that you are.*

# ACKNOWLEDGMENTS

Writing can be a lonely business—days spent in front of the computer with no one to talk to but the dog, and let's face it, those conversations tend to be clearly one-sided. There are, however, many compensations, and I have been blessed with more than my share.

First and foremost are the people who help me put my books together. I have had many editors over the last twenty years, some of whom have been exemplary, and others—not so much. My current editor, Sandy Harding, surpasses all others. Always helpful, always cheerful, always encouraging, always there. I enjoy our lengthy chats, and my creative output has benefited from her skills and her friendship. My sincere thanks.

Paige Wheeler came into my life late in my career, and this outstanding agent has been a constant source of encouragement and inspiration. She's efficient and knowledgeable, and most of all, accessible. I haven't always had that and I deeply appreciate her efforts on my behalf. Many thanks.

Ann Wraight is a friend of long-standing, who keeps me constantly supplied with research and memorabilia. Thanks for always thinking of me, and for sending me those heavy magazines that keep me in touch with the UK.

My sincere thanks to Judith Murello and her wonderful team in the art department. My covers are amazing—eye-catching, intriguing, and beautiful, down to the last detail.

My thanks also go to my incredible fans, who never fail

to let me know when they have enjoyed one of my books. It is because of them that the Pennyfoot Hotel Mystery series survives. I, along with the entire staff and guests of the Pennyfoot Hotel, wish you and yours a joyous and peaceful holiday.

And, as always, thanks to my patient and understanding husband. He gives so much of himself, and I hope he knows how much it means to me.

Happy holidays, everyone.

# CHAPTER
## 1

"I still find it hard to believe that your wedding is only a few days away." Cecily Sinclair Baxter examined a crystal bell for cracks before handing it to the slender woman perched on a stool in front of the Christmas tree. "I truly did not think the day would ever dawn."

Madeline Pengrath's tinkling laugh seemed to echo in the high ceiling of the library. "You have to agree, I am well past the age of a blushing young bride. I can imagine what people are saying—what is a respected doctor like Kevin Prestwick thinking, marrying that old witch? She must have cast one of her dastardly spells on him."

Cecily would have laughed, too, except Madeline was closer to the truth than she cared to acknowledge. "Piffle," she said briskly. "I'm quite sure the people of Badgers End are happy that the doctor has found not only a good wife, but a beautiful one, no less."

"Why thank you kindly, my friend, but I think it's more likely they are plotting how to get rid of me."

In spite of the leaping flames in the fireplace, Cecily shivered. The Pennyfoot Country Club had dealt with more than its share of misfortunes over the past Christmas seasons. So much so that she couldn't find humor in any hint of disaster, no matter how remote.

To change the subject, she murmured, "Yet another year has flown by. It really doesn't seem that long since we were celebrating the turn of the century."

"Well, things have certainly changed since King Edward took over the throne."

"They certainly have. I often wonder if the late queen is turning over in her grave. She was such a stickler for protocol. Her son has no such restraint, I'm afraid."

Madeline grinned. "And the country is much happier for it. Come Cecily, surely you don't begrudge people some levity in their lives? You must admit, Queen Victoria was a priggish tyrant who frowned upon the slightest hint of revelry. No wonder Edward is such a libertine."

"Levity is one thing. Promiscuity is something else entirely."

"But so much fun!"

Madeline's eyes twinkled with mischief, and sensing she was deliberately trying to shock her, Cecily changed the subject again. "How is your friend Miss Danbury enjoying our little seaside town? It was good of her to come in for your wedding, though it's quite a change from London, I'm afraid. I trust she's not finding it too cold and damp for comfort?"

Madeline stretched an arm to hang the bell near the top of the tree. Her long black hair, which she refused to bind up, reached almost to her waist, and swung back and forth as she moved. "Not at all. Grace is quite enjoying the recent snowfall. It doesn't snow that often in the city."

"It does make everything seem more festive." Cecily dug into the large box on the floor and came up with a bag of white lace angels. "I noticed she wasn't at the midday meal yesterday. I do hope she's not under the weather?"

"She's perfectly well." Madeline took an angel from her and examined it with a frown. "She met a friend from London. I believe they planned to go gift shopping in Wellercombe."

Cecily stared up at her friend. "Goodness. I would have thought shopping in London would have been far more productive. After all, the choice is somewhat limited in a small town like Wellercombe."

"But the prices are a good deal more reasonable. Grace loves to find bargains, and she said her friend was delighted to spend a day at the seaside."

"Ah." Cecily nodded. "A man friend, I presume."

"Not at all. Grace doesn't much care for male companionship."

"Well, I hope she will attend the banquet this evening."

"I'm sure she will. She's looking forward to it. As am I." Madeline handed her back the ornament. "I think I'll put these angels on the tree in the foyer. They looked very nice there last year."

"They did indeed." Cecily smiled, remembering how lovely the tree looked. "Will you make those pretty little sugar bells again?"

"I already have." Madeline waited while Cecily dug deeper into the box. "Did Phoebe manage to finish your gown for the wedding?"

Cecily paused. Phoebe Carter-Holmes Fortescue was an excellent seamstress who, before her marriage to Colonel Fortescue, out of financial necessity had sewn her entire wardrobe. She had offered to make the bridesmaids dresses as a wedding present for Madeline.

Phoebe and Madeline were Cecily's very best friends, but both could be somewhat unpredictable. "Phoebe assures me the dresses will be ready for the wedding on New Year's Eve," Cecily said, praying that was true. "She plans to do the final fitting right after Christmas."

"Well, I hope she doesn't let us down. I would hate to see my maid of honor walking down the aisle in a tea gown."

Cecily laughed. "This will be my first time attending a wedding as maid of honor. I promise you, I will make sure that Phoebe has us all properly attired."

"Yes, much as I dislike the idea of being married in a church, I am happy that you and Grace will be my attendants. I can't say as much for the other bridesmaid. I've never met Emily Winchester, but from what Kevin tells me about her, I have a feeling I won't like her."

Since Madeline's predictions tended to be remarkably accurate, Cecily felt a small qualm. She had been the one to persuade Madeline to marry her handsome doctor in the sanctity of the Lord's house, and in deference to her friend and her future husband, Madeline had reluctantly agreed.

Knowing quite well that her friend would much rather have been married privately in the woods with only the birds and woodland creatures in attendance, Cecily wanted so much for the wedding to be perfect in every way.

Picking out a green glass ball inlaid with gold filigree, she murmured, "I happened to bump into Mrs. Winchester yesterday morning. She seems pleasant enough, though a little put out. Her husband had to return to London for the day. An emergency with a patient, I believe she said. He's Kevin's best man, isn't he?"

"Yes. Dr. Winchester studied with Kevin in London. They have remained best friends, even though they haven't seen much of each other since then."

"Well, I'm sure you and the doctor's wife will become the best of friends, too." She handed the ball to Madeline. "You have such a sweet nature, Madeline. Everyone who knows you loves you."

"Not everyone. Phoebe, for instance. She will never forgive me for not inviting her to be a bridesmaid."

"On the contrary, I do believe she was quite relieved. I

know she was most pleased that you had accepted her offer to sew the dresses."

"Well, I felt obligated to allow her to be part of all this fuss. After all, her son will be performing the ceremony." Madeline sighed. "I suppose her cuckoo husband will have to be there."

Cecily hid a grin. "I can't imagine Phoebe being there without him."

"Well, we can only hope that he behaves himself and refrains from attacking imaginary enemies or I'll be forced to turn him into a toad."

Cecily's grin vanished. As well as she knew Madeline, she could never be quite sure that her friend wasn't actually capable of carrying out her outlandish threats.

"At least we shall have one dependable member of the wedding party," Madeline murmured. "It was so very gallant of Baxter to agree to give me away." She raised herself on her toes to reach an upper branch, her floral skirt swirling around her bare ankles.

Madeline often declined to wear shoes or stockings while indoors, which had raised more than one aristocratic eyebrow in the halls of the Pennyfoot.

As for the local residents of Badgers End, they were well used to Madeline's odd habits. Though the women tended to fear her and kept out of her way, unknown to most of them, their husbands flocked to Madeline's house for a supply of her special potions. Many of them owed their continuing virility to Madeline's magic touch with herbs and flowers.

"I do think that's enough on the tree for now." Cecily gazed in admiration at her friend's handiwork. "It looks quite dazzling. "Besides, I'm becoming quite nervous watching you dance around on that narrow stool."

Madeline laughed, and leapt lightly down from her perch. "Dear Cecily. You know you worry entirely too much."

"Perhaps." Cecily closed the lid of the box. "Then again, while running an establishment as popular as the Pennyfoot, I have a lot to worry about."

"You should insist that Baxter help you more. After all, he used to be manager of the Pennyfoot before he married you."

"Baxter has his own business to worry about. Though he does help me a great deal when we are busy. Which reminds me. He should be home from the city by now. I need to talk to him about the Christmas Eve ceremonies."

"And I must finish the decorating if I am to attend the banquet tonight." Madeline bent down and with surprising ease hoisted the heavy box in her arms. "Christmas is only two days away. There is still so much to do before the wedding." She hurried over to the door. "We will see you at the banquet, then. It was good of you to invite Kevin and me."

"It will be your last Christmas as a single woman." Cecily followed her to the door. "I want all of us to share at least part of it."

Madeline made a face. "Including that insufferable Phoebe and her deranged husband?"

"Of course." Cecily gave her a gentle poke. "You can complain about Phoebe all you like, Madeline, but I know quite well that you are fond of her."

"As a horse is fond of flies," Madeline muttered. She waited for Cecily to open the door for her then squeezed through with the box in her arms. "Ah well, beggars can't be choosers, as they say."

She drifted off down the hallway, her breathless "Goodbye" floating behind her.

Gertie McBride stomped down the hallway to the kitchen, muttering to herself under her breath. *Christmas.* Nothing but a big fuss and a lot of hard work. She slapped open the kitchen door so hard it swung back, bounced off the wall and smacked into her as she barged through.

"Bloody hell!" Rubbing her nose, she glared at Mrs. Chubb as if it were her fault.

The housekeeper dug her fists into her ample hips and shook her head at her chief housemaid. "Gertie Brown McBride! What's got into you lately? You're like an elephant loose at a vicarage tea party, crashing and banging around like that."

"I bumped me nose, didn't I." Gertie stalked over to the sink and turned on the tap. "I think it's bleeding."

"Here, let me look." Mrs. Chubb peered at her face. "No, it's not bleeding. Now you'd better tell me what's got you in such a dither."

"It's that Lady Clara on the top floor. Blinking miserable, she is. She's been complaining ever since she got here two days ago. Her window doesn't have a view of the ocean, and the fireplace isn't big enough, and the bedclothes aren't silk and she wants fresh roses on her dresser."

Mrs. Chubb raised her eyebrows. "Roses?"

"Yeah." Filling her palm with the ice cold water, Gertie splashed some on her sore nose. "She says as how she heard about the rose gardens here and was expecting roses in her room. Talk about potty. Who ever heard of roses growing in the winter?"

Mrs. Chubb dusted flour from the bib of her apron and went back to her table. Picking up her rolling pin, she began flattening out the lump of pastry on the large wooden board. "Maybe you should have a word with madam. She'd want to know if one of her guests isn't happy. Especially the wife of an important member of parliament like Sir Walter Hetherton."

Gertie sniffed, dug in the pocket of her apron for a handkerchief and dabbed her wet nose. "What's so blinking important about him, anyway? He makes me sick, strutting around like he's Lord Almighty. Not like he's royalty, is it."

"He might as well be, seeing as how he's the speaker in the House of Lords."

"So what?"

"So he's blue-blooded, that's what."

"I bet if he nicks his chin with a razor his blood is as red as yours or mine."

"You know what I mean."

Gertie tossed her head. "Well, hoity-toity Lady Clara ain't the only wife of an MP. What about that Mrs. Crossley in room twelve? She's the wife of an MP, too."

"Roland Crossley might be an MP, but he's in the House of Commons. There's a world of difference." The house-keeper reached for a pie plate and slapped the pastry onto it. Taking a knife, she deftly trimmed the edges, leaving strips of the dough lying all around the plate.

"They both work for the government, don't they?" Gertie walked over to the massive dresser and pulled out a drawer. Taking out a tray of silverware, she closed the drawer again with a nudge of her hip. "Anyhow, he ain't no bleeding saint, neither. Went off hunting yesterday, he did, and left his wife all alone. What was she supposed to do all day all by herself?" Carrying the tray over to the table, she muttered, "All a bunch of gormless twerps if you ask me."

"Nobody's asking you, my girl, so hold your tongue." Mrs. Chubb gathered up the strips of pastry and squeezed them into a ball. "Talking like that about our guests will get you into trouble with madam, if you don't watch out."

"Madam would agree with me." Gertie picked up a fork and started rubbing it with a soft cloth. "She don't have no time for the government, seeing as how they treat women. Throwing them into jail and doing horrible things to them when all we want is the right to vote like the men."

Mrs. Chubb sighed. "Don't get started on that again, Gertie McBride. Once you get on your high horse over women's rights it takes a stick of dynamite to get you off."

"What ees this I hear about dynamite?"

Gertie looked up as a wiry man in a white chef's cap strode into the kitchen. "Nothing to do with you, Michel," she said sharply, "so you can keep your blinking nose out of it."

"It is to do with me if you blow up my kitchen, *non*?" The chef marched over to the stove and started rattling the saucepan lids—a sure sign he was upset about something.

Wisely, Gertie kept quiet. She loved to get Michel going in a good fight and usually got the best of him, but she knew when to leave him alone and judging by the way he was throwing stuff around on the stove, this was one of those times.

Instead, she caught Mrs. Chubb's eye and silently mouthed at her. *What's up with him?*

The housekeeper lifted her shoulders and let them fall. Shaking her head in warning, she said sharply, "Stop arguing and finish polishing that silverware. We'll be serving supper in less than two hours and the tables aren't even laid yet."

Gertie raised her chin in protest. "The banquet's being held in the ballroom, remember? The tables have been laid since the crack of dawn this morning."

"Not with the silverware they haven't. Before you do that, though, find madam and let her know that Lady Clara isn't satisfied with her room. She wouldn't want anything to spoil a guest's Christmas visit."

"I don't know what's so bloody special about Christmas, anyway." Gertie rubbed the cloth viciously on a dessert spoon. "Work ourselves to death, we do."

Mrs. Chubb frowned. "You love Christmas. You know you do. You get as excited about it as those twins of yours."

"Yeah, well, sometimes I get tired of all the fuss."

Michel slammed a saucepan down on the stove. "I know what is making her so meeserable. She misses her sweetheart, *non*?"

Gertie sent him a ferocious glare. "Just goes to show what you know, Mr. Bleeding Know-It-All. I don't miss him at all, so there."

She barely resisted the urge to stick out her tongue at

him. Nothing was going to make her admit that she missed Dan Perkins dreadfully. It was about this time last year when she first met him, and all the Christmas preparations reminded her of those exciting days.

Mrs. Chubb looked worried. "You're not pining after Dan still, are you, Gertie? I don't know why you turned him down, I really don't. He's got money. Lots of it. He could have given you and the twins a wonderful life."

"In London," Gertie said sharply. "I told you all this before. He wanted us all to go and live with him in the city. Can you see the likes of me trying to fit in with the people he mixes with every day? All those toffs sticking their noses in the air because of the way me and my little ones talk? No bleeding thank you."

"You could have learned to talk better," Michel offered.

Gertie turned on him. "Why should I bloody talk better? It's not how I talk but how I bleeding behave that makes me what I am."

"Exactly," Mrs. Chubb said, shaking her head at Michel. "Dan knew that."

"Well, his friends wouldn't." Gertie threw down the last fork in disgust. "Sooner or later they would have turned him against me. I've been through enough bloody heartache with men. I'm not going to let another one break my heart, so there."

"Just because the twins' father didn't let on he was married when he got you pregnant doesn't mean all men are like that." Mrs. Chubb dusted more flour from her apron and slapped her hands together to dislodge it from her fingers. "Look at Ross McBride. He loved you enough to marry you and take on another man's children, didn't he. Not many men like that."

"Yeah, and then he went and died on me, didn't he. Left me all alone and broke my children's hearts."

"He couldn't help dying, Gertie."

"Yeah, well, I'm through with men. As far as I'm concerned, me and my twins are better off without them." Gertie headed for the door.

"You say that all the time," Michel called after her. "Until the next one, *oui?*"

"Bugger off," Gertie said rudely, and swept out into the hallway.

By the time she'd climbed the stairs to madam's suite she was feeling a little less cranky. The gorgeous fragrance of pine from the Christmas tree followed her, and in spite of her bad mood she felt a tug of excitement at the thought of the twins on Christmas morning when they saw what Father Christmas had brought them.

James and Lillian were her life, and she'd move heaven and earth to make them happy. They had been through so much, losing Ross—the man they'd adored and looked upon as a father.

Thank heavens they'd never known their real father. Gertie pulled a face as she reached madam's door and raised her hand to knock on it. Ian Rossiter was never no good and never would be.

Hearing madam's voice from within the room, Gertie squared her shoulders, pushed open the door and went inside.

# CHAPTER

## ❁ 2 ❁

"Was that Gertie's dulcet tone I heard?" Baxter came out of the water closet and closed the door behind him.

Seated on the davenport in the window of their suite, Cecily smiled at her husband. "She wanted to tell me that Lady Clara is dissatisfied with her accommodations."

Frowning, Baxter tugged at his tie. "What's wrong with the room? It's one of the best we have."

"Among other things, apparently the dear lady had heard of our beautiful rose gardens and would like fresh roses on her dresser."

"Then tell her to come back in the summer when the roses are in full bloom." Baxter removed his tie and starched collar. "For heaven's sake, the more you do for these people the more they seem to want."

"Not all of them," Cecily murmured. "And I do my best to accommodate them. I'm afraid that Lady Clara will have to do without the silk sheets, however."

"Silk sheets! Good Lord! What does she think this is—Buckingham Palace?"

"Hush, dear." Cecily glanced at the door. "She is only two rooms away from us. She might well be able to hear you."

"Jolly good job if she does." Baxter threw his tie and collar down on the windowsill and sank down next to his wife. "Sometimes I wonder if all this is worth the trouble." He waved an arm in the direction of the door. "Always at the beck and call of finicky guests, never having any time to yourself—don't you ever get tired of it?"

Cecily looked down at her hands clasped in her lap. "Sometimes—but I missed it so badly when we lived in London. I don't think I could be truly happy were I not here taking care of the Pennyfoot."

"Well, I certainly could."

Cecily laid a hand on her husband's arm. "You are just tired, my love. You have had a hard week at the office. I often think all that traveling back and forth to London is terribly taxing on your health."

Baxter sighed. "No doubt, but that's where all my clients are and I have to be accessible to them."

Cecily suppressed a stab of guilt. True, Baxter had not been in favor of her taking over the management of the Pennyfoot Country Club and moving back to England's windy southeast coast. It was her decision to make, however, and as a strong supporter of the women's movement she had clung steadfastly to her right to choose her own destiny.

Baxter had at least understood that, even if he had not condoned her decision. Their lives had been disrupted by the move, and at times Cecily questioned whether she had taken the position because she had truly wanted it, or because Baxter had not.

Shaking off her doubts she said brightly, "I shall have Madeline order fresh roses from Covent Garden and have them sent down here. That should keep Lady Clara happy."

Baxter grunted. "Won't that be terribly expensive?"

"Perhaps, but worth it to please the wife of such a prominent visitor as Sir Walter Hetherton. We are indeed honored to be entertaining the illustrious Speaker for the House of Lords."

Baxter grunted even louder. "The man is nothing but a puffed-up popinjay blowing hot air. I can't abide the way he prances around with that dashed walking stick as if he's superior to everyone he meets. Same with that Crossley chap. Those MPs are nothing but stuffed puppets—certainly not fit to run the country."

Cecily gazed at her husband in surprise. "I had no idea you had such strong adverse opinions of our government."

"I don't. Just some of the numskulls who run it." Baxter rose to his feet, snatched up his tie and collar from the windowsill and stalked back to the boudoir.

Gazing after him, Cecily shook her head. Only two days left until Christmas. She certainly hoped that by then Baxter would have recovered his good humor. She had enough to worry about attending to the preparations, without concerning herself with her husband's bad mood.

Sighing she got up and headed for the door. Much as she loved the Christmas season, she did not relish the problems that sometimes came with it. All she could hope was that this Christmas would be a little more peaceful than those in years past.


"Look! Someone's built a snowman out there." Pansy Watson pointed at the tall windows of the ballroom. "Did your twins do that?"

Gertie craned her neck to see where the young housemaid was pointing. The windows overlooked the bowling green and on the far side, close to the trees, she could see the snowman. It wore a black hat and a red scarf, and had a broom stuck in its side.

"Look," Pansy said again, "there's your kiddies. I can't see Daisy, though."

"Neither can I." Gertie frowned. She didn't like the idea of the twins running around the grounds on their own, even though they knew well enough not to go into the woods. She'd have to have a word with the nanny about that, she decided.

"They look like they're talking to the snowman," Pansy said, laughing. "I wonder what he's saying to them."

"Probably telling them to behave, more'n likely." Gertie turned back to the table, where she carefully laid out the silverware in the proper order. "Seems as if I'm telling them that all the time."

"Oh, there's Daisy. She must have called them. They're running over to her."

Relieved, Gertie surveyed the cutlery in its neat pattern. Soup spoon on the outside of the place setting, then butter knife, then fish knife and fork, then dinner knife and fork, then dessert fork and spoon laid across the top.

That morning she and Pansy had arranged the glasses at the top right of each place setting, with sherry, wine, champagne and brandy glasses in order. They'd also placed a shiny Christmas cracker on the left of each setting.

"It's nice that the banquet is being held in the ballroom instead of the dining room." Pansy picked up a cracker and shook it. "It gave us plenty of time to get the tables laid. We got most of it done this morning so now all we have do is put the cutlery out. We don't have to rush around at the last minute like we usually do."

"There's still plenty left to do." Gertie moved a knife a little closer to the soup spoon.

"I do love Christmas crackers." Pansy gazed fondly at the golden paper tube in her hand. "They are always so much fun to pull."

Gertie merely sniffed. Carefully she moved a red candlestick to a safe distance from the arrangement of fresh holly and mistletoe.

She still wasn't in the mood for Christmas yet and that worried her. Even though her twins were singing carols and talking nonstop about Father Christmas and opening their presents.

"Don't you like crackers?"

Gertie made an effort to answer her. "They're all right, I suppose. That's if you don't have to clear up after them. They make too much blinking mess for my liking. All them paper hats that come out of them end up on the floor, then there's bits of paper and cardboard all over the tables—takes forever to get it all cleaned up in here."

"But they're so pretty!" Pansy held up the gleaming tube. "All these sparkly gold leaves and swirls on the pretty cream paper. I bet that's real silk ribbon around the ends, too. Mrs. Chubb says they were handmade especially for the Pennyfoot. Look, they have P.C.C. written on them in gold. That stands for Pennyfoot Country Club."

"It's a stupid idea if you ask me." Gertie picked up a cracker and frowned at it in disgust. "First you have to find someone who'll pull one end while you pull the other, then try not to have a heart attack when it makes a bang and splits apart, then you have to take out the paper hat and put it on your head, then read the silly joke inside. What's more, they're never funny."

"But they have presents inside, too." Pansy held the cracker close to her ear and shook it.

"Yeah, cheap, useless things that everyone leaves on the table for us poor blinking maids to clean up."

Pansy pouted. "I like cleaning up after them. I like to keep the presents. Even if they are only cheap things."

"Yeah, well I know one present you won't get, that's for sure."

"What's that?"

Gertie shrugged and moved onto the next table. "I'm not supposed to say. It's a secret. At least, it was when Mrs. Chubb told me about it."

Pansy put down the cracker and followed Gertie. "It can't be much of a secret if you know about it."

"Well, I suppose it won't make any difference now, seeing as how the guests will be pulling these tonight." Gertie picked up one of the crackers and raised it in the air. "If you must know, one of these crackers has a big surprise. There's a real pearl brooch inside one of them."

"Go on with you. I don't believe it."

"It's the truth." Gertie laid the cracker down next to a row of forks. "Mrs. Chubb told me. She said that madam thought it would add some excitement to the banquet. She's going to announce it at dinner. Nobody knows which cracker it's in. Not even madam."

Pansy opened her eyes wide. "Mrs. Baxter doesn't even know who's going to get the brooch?"

"Nah, no one does."

"Wouldn't it be lovely if there were crackers left over and one of us got it." Pansy looked wistfully around the festive tables.

Gertie uttered a scornful laugh. "Not much bloody hope of that happening. These crackers must have cost a barrel of money. I heard that madam only ordered enough to give one to each of the guests."

"Well, two of them are going to be disappointed."

Gertie raised her chin. "Whatcha mean?"

Pansy pointed across the room. "Look over there. Two of the crackers are missing."

"Nah, they can't be." Heart hammering with anxiety, Gertie skirted the tables, bumping her hips against the chairs in her haste. "Bloody hell." She halted at the far table, one hand over her mouth.

Pansy appeared at her side. "What do you think happened to them?"

"How the heck do I know? Unless they fell under the flipping table."

She stuck her head underneath the edges of the tablecloth

and received a sharp crack from Pansy's head as the maid ducked under the table with her. Uttering a curse, she stood up. "They're not there. Madam's going to be really, really upset about this."

"P'raps she's got some spare crackers after all."

"Well, we'd better be quick and find out. Dinner's going to be served in an hour or so and there'll be hell to pay if everyone doesn't have a cracker to pull."

"P'raps someone heard about the brooch and stole it. After all, them crackers have been sitting out here on the tables all day."

Gertie turned on her. "Don't be daft. How would they know which one it was in? In any case, you keep your blinking mouth shut about that brooch, you hear me? No one's supposed to know until dinnertime."

She didn't wait for Pansy to answer but barged across the room to the door. She had to tell Mrs. Chubb about the missing crackers right away, though what the housekeeper could do about it now she couldn't imagine. All she could hope was that Pansy was right and madam had a couple of spare ones.

A few minutes later she burst through the door of the kitchen, wincing at the usual hubbub of crashing saucepans, rattling bottles and Mrs. Chubb and Michel screeching at each other.

"You're supposed to be a chef," the housekeeper yelled, her fists dug into her well-padded hips. "How could you put pepper in the trifle?"

"Eet ees not my fault!" Michel yelled back. He waved a large wooden spoon in her flushed face. "Someone move ze mixed spices jar and put pepper in its place! *N'est-ce pas?*"

"No one moved the pepper." Mrs. Chubb picked up the pepper pot and shook it at him. "You've been at the brandy again, that's what. You can't see past the end of your rosy red nose."

Michel flung the spoon across the table. It bounced off a

jug of cream and clattered onto the tiled floor. "It is not the brandy, imbecile! It is my eyes. They are failing."

"Then get yourself some specs. And for heaven's sake make some more trifle. We have to serve it in the ballroom in a couple of hours."

Michel muttered something unintelligible in his fake French accent, and the housekeeper turned away in disgust. Catching sight of Gertie, she snapped, "What's the matter now? You look as if the world is coming to an end. Did you get the tables laid?"

"Yes, I did." Gertie picked up the spoon and took it over to the sink. Turning on the tap, she held it under the chilly water and rinsed it off. "I've got some bad news."

Mrs. Chubb groaned. "Don't tell me. The Christmas tree in the library is on fire again."

"No, course it's not. It's the bloody crackers." She faced the housekeeper again and held out the spoon.

Mrs. Chubb snatched it from her. "How many times do I have to tell you to watch your language. One of these fine days I'll wash your mouth out with soap, that I will."

Gertie paid no attention to the threat. It had been administered too many times to bear any weight. She'd been trying to stop swearing since she was a kid but habits like that were hard to break.

Still scowling, Mrs. Chubb tossed the spoon to Michel. Unfortunately he'd turned his back on her and it caught him right between the shoulder blades before landing on the table.

"Sacre bleu!" The chef spun around, eyes blazing. "Why you do that to me, huh?"

"Because I felt like it, didn't I." Ignoring him, Mrs. Chubb looked at Gertie. "What about the crackers?"

"Two of them are missing, that's what."

The housekeeper's look of horror wiped Gertie's smile from her face. "They can't be."

"That's what I bloody said. But they're gone all right. Me

and Pansy looked everywhere. Someone must have heard about the you-know-what and blinking stole them."

Mrs. Chubb threw up her hands in despair. "Now what are we going to do?"

"Maybe madam has some up in her suite?"

"I don't think she does." Mrs. Chubb cast an anxious look at the kitchen clock. "Run upstairs and ask her. If she doesn't we'll have to send Samuel into town to buy some."

"They won't match."

"I know they won't match, but I don't know what else we can do."

"Samuel will be busy stabling the horses and motor cars. Everyone's arriving now."

"Gertie McBride, will you *please* stop wasting time arguing and get upstairs to madam's suite!"

"*Oui*," Michel echoed, brandishing the wooden spoon at her. "For pity's sake stop that squealing at each other. It is *très* bad for my nerves."

Gertie glared at him. "I'll give you something that will really damage your nerves in a minute, you besotted twerp."

"Ger-*tay*!"

Gertie jumped. "All right, all right, I'm going." Grumbling under her breath, she rushed out the door, just as Pansy reached it. The two of them collided in the corridor, sending Gertie's white cap over her eyes.

Pansy's slight build was no match for Gertie's chunky girth, and the young girl slammed into the wall with a yelp of pain.

Gertie shoved her cap back in place and muttered, "Crikey, what a start to Christmas week. I wonder what the flipping heck is going to happen next."


Seated at her dressing table, Cecily dabbed a spot of rouge to the center of her cheek and then gently spread it around with her forefinger. "I'm really getting too old to use this any more," she murmured. "It tends to settle in the wrinkles."

Her husband, seated on the end of the bed behind her, snorted. "Wrinkles? What nonsense. You are far too young to have wrinkles."

That being exactly the answer she was angling for, Cecily smiled. "I'm so happy you think so."

Baxter got up from the bed and wrapped his arms around his wife. "I do, indeed, think so. You will always be the beautiful woman I fell madly in love with years ago."

She leaned back against his chest. "Not so many years ago. And now we are almost at the end of another one. I do adore this time of year. This Christmas will be especially enjoyable, now that we have a wedding to include in the celebrations. It certainly adds to the excitement."

"Not to mention the extra work. I really—" Baxter straightened as a loud rapping on the door interrupted him. "Oh, Lord. I do hope this isn't a problem."

Cecily rose from the embroidered stool and smoothed the skirt of her gray heavy silk gown. "There will always be a problem of some kind or other. That's what makes being the manager of a country club so interesting."

Baxter grunted. "I would hope the staff would be able to take care of their pesky problems and give you some respite during the Christmas season."

Cecily smiled fondly at him. "Dearest Baxter. You know quite well that most of the problems occur when we are at our busiest. Every room in the club has been taken, so I expect a glitch or two over the next few days. That's all part of my responsibility."

"Well, pox on responsibility, that's what I say." Muttering to himself, Baxter strode across the carpet as yet more rapping invaded the room.

In spite of her apparent levity, fabricated for her husband's sake, Cecily watched anxiously as Baxter tugged the door open. It was rare for the staff to disturb her while she was dressing for dinner, unless it was for something of great importance.

The sound of Gertie's voice did nothing to reassure her. "May I have a word with madam, please, Mr. Baxter?"

"If you must." Baxter drew back to allow the chief housemaid to enter.

Cecily produced a smile for the young woman. Except for a few brief months in Scotland with her late husband, Gertie had worked at the Pennyfoot since it was a fledgling seaside hotel in the waning years of the previous century. Along with Mrs. Chubb, Samuel, the Pennyfoot's reliable stable manager, and the fiery chef, Michel, she had become family to Cecily, as had every subsequent member of the Pennyfoot staff.

This time of year, in particular, the festivities seemed to augment that feeling of closeness she had to the people who served under her.

"I'm sorry to disturb you, madam," Gertie said, as she hurried into the room, "but we have a problem in the dining room."

Baxter raised his chin and glared at the ceiling. "Of course you do."

Cecily sent him a reproachful glance before asking, "What kind of problem, Gertie?"

"Two of the Christmas crackers are missing, m'm." Gertie plucked at the skirt of her white apron. "Me and Pansy looked everywhere, even under the table, but they're gone. Someone must have took them."

"Someone being a member of the staff, no doubt," Baxter muttered.

Gertie spared him a quick glance before saying, "I never told no one about the brooch, m'm, but I suppose word could have got out."

"Of course word got out," Baxter said, without bothering to hide his irritation. "I've heard people all over the place talking about the Christmas cracker surprise."

"Really?" Cecily frowned. "I'd hate to think someone working for me has stolen them. Are you quite sure they're not merely misplaced, Gertie?"

"Quite sure, m'm. I don't suppose you have some spare ones?"

"I'm afraid not." Cecily sighed. "We'll have to send someone into town to get some more. I suppose Samuel's busy stabling horses?"

"Yes, m'm."

"Then tell one of the footmen to take a carriage into town. Show him the crackers and tell him to find some as close to that design as possible." Cecily shook her head. "Though if he can do that at this late date it will surely be a miracle."

"Perhaps the woman who made them can make you two more," Baxter suggested.

Cecily shook her head. "I understand it's quite a complicated process. I know she buys those little strips that make them burst open from a company in London. I really don't see . . . oh!"

Her words had ended on a gasp, muffled by a boom that seemed to shake the floor. Ears ringing, all she could do was stare at the shocked face of her husband.

Dear heavens, surely disaster could not be happening again?

# CHAPTER

## 3

For a moment no one spoke as all three of them stared at each other. Then both Gertie and Baxter spoke at once.

"Bloody hell, what was that?"

"What the blazes?

Her ears still ringing from the noise, Cecily stared into her husband's worried face. "Whatever it was, I think we'd better make haste to find out where it came from. I didn't like the sound of it at all."

Gertie rushed for the door, nearly knocking Baxter over in her haste to get outside. Swearing, he followed close on her heels.

Cecily drew in a long breath to steady her nerves, then lifted her skirts and hurried out after them.

The smell of burning greeted her as she stepped into the corridor. Farther down, smoke coiled from under one of the doors and wafted toward her.

Baxter raced past Gertie and reached the door first, just

as other doors opened along the corridor and curious faces peeked out.

"Stand back!" he ordered, waving an arm to reinforce the order. He paused for a moment, then took hold of the door handle.

"Be careful, my love!" Cecily glanced at her chief housemaid, who seemed rooted to the spot. "Gertie, please go and tell Philip to ring for the fire brigade."

Gertie stared at her, her dark eyes huge in her chalk white face.

"*Now*, Gertie! And find Clive and send him up here immediately."

"Yes, m'm."

The housemaid leapt for the stairs, and Cecily turned back, just in time to see a cloud of smoke from the open doorway envelop Baxter's head.

Coughing and spluttering, Baxter drew back and slammed the door shut. "Everyone! Quickly! Downstairs as quickly as possible!"

Smoke drifted in an ugly black cloud down the corridor, chasing the guests hurrying toward the staircase.

Baxter waited until the last of them had disappeared, then slowly opened the door again. "We need buckets of water up here," he said, his voice hoarse from the choking smoke. "As fast as possible."

"I'll see to it." Cecily held out a hand to him. "Don't go in there. Please, Bax."

"It's all right. There's not too many flames." He disappeared inside the smokey room before she could protest further.

Half stumbling down the stairs, she pushed her way past two straggling guests and muttered an apology as she plunged down ahead of them.

Others were gathering in the foyer, exchanging anxious questions. A quick glance assured her that Philip, the elderly desk clerk, manned the reception desk as usual. Holding the mouthpiece of the telephone in one boney hand, he talked rapidly while he kept smoothing back the sparse hair that insisted on falling across his eyes.

Just then Clive Russell pushed through the crowd toward her. The sturdy maintenance man towered head and shoulders above everyone else, and the guests parted for him as he crossed the floor. He reached her side, his craggy face creased in concern, his dark eyes questioning.

"We need water," she told him. "Get the footmen to help you bring buckets up to the top floor."

Nodding, he turned away, and she stepped out into the middle of her uneasy guests. Raising her voice to capture everyone's attention, she announced, "I must apologize for this unfortunate turn of events. Apparently we have a small fire in one of the rooms on the very top floor. Rest assured it is being taken care of and no one is in any immediate danger."

A chorus of garbled questions and comments answered her and she raised her hand. "I haven't time to answer all your questions now, as I'm sure you can appreciate. I must ask all of you to retire at once to the ballroom for the time being. I will see that aperitifs are served as soon as possible. I must ask you all to remain there until it is safe to return to your rooms."

Gertie appeared at her side just then. "I'll get them all in there, m'm," she said. "Philip's rung for the fire brigade and they're on their way."

"Thank you, Gertie. Be sure to take in hors d'oeuvres and dry sherry." Anxious to see what was happening to her husband, Cecily left her housemaid to usher the unsettled patrons into the ballroom and fled once more up the stairs.

Panting and puffing, she reached the top, thankful that all the guests from that floor appeared to have escaped safely down the stairs.

Just to make sure, she rapped on each door as she rushed

past, though how anyone could have failed to hear that awful boom she could hardly imagine.

The door of the smoke-filled room still stood ajar and she paused in the doorway, afraid of what she might see. Relief tore through her when she saw Baxter's shadowy outline savagely beating the scorched davenport under the window.

"Wait!" he shouted, coughing as she stepped forward. "Stay right there and don't take another step."

Normally she would have bristled at being ordered about by her husband. The panic in his voice, however, convinced her that he was merely watching out for her well-being, so she obeyed his command.

The sound of footsteps behind her took her attention away from him, and she turned to see Clive rushing toward her, slopping water over the sides of a pail he held in each of his powerful hands.

"Strewth," he muttered, as he reached the open doorway. "What happened here?"

"I imagine it was a gas leak," Baxter said, beckoning to him. "I think I've put out all the flames but just in case, you had better soak everything in sight."

More footsteps pounded along the hallway as three young footmen carried more buckets of water to the room. Above the commotion, Cecily caught Clive's exclamation. "Holy cow, what's that!"

"Ah, yes," Baxter said, his voice grim. "I'm afraid we have somewhat of a problem on our hands."

"What is it?" Determined to see what had shocked Clive so, she stepped into the room. She just had time to glimpse what appeared to be piles of singed clothes on the floor before Baxter strode toward her and hustled her out into the hallway.

Sick with apprehension, she pulled away from him. "Don't tell me that's what I think it is."

Baxter pulled her close. "I'm sorry, Cecily. It appears that two of our guests have met with a grave mishap. I'm afraid they perished in the explosion."

Staring up into his face, Cecily drew a troubled breath. "Heaven help us. The Christmas curse is on us again."

"I was rather hoping," P.C. Northcott said, "that h'I would not be called 'ere again at Christmastime."

He stood with his back to the leaping flames in the fireplace that graced the west wall of the library, and rocked back and forth with a look of pure displeasure on his round, ruddy face.

"Rest assured," Cecily said, resisting the temptation to knock the police helmet off his head, "that I was hoping exactly the same thing." Sam Northcott was not known for his genteel manners, but even the most unrefined man should know to remove his hat while indoors.

"Yes, well, I suppose it can't be helped." As if reading her mind, he dragged his helmet off and laid it on the seat of the blue velvet chair at his side. Twisting his head, he looked at the clock on the mantelpiece. "I am off to London for my h'annual visit to my wife's relatives shortly. Everyone's waiting for me at home, so I hope we can get this business over and done with as soon as possible."

"By all means." Cecily gritted her teeth, knowing that the second he left the library he'd be on his way to the kitchen for a sampling of Mrs. Chubb's mince pies and sausage rolls. Which no doubt was the real reason for his haste.

She waited while the police constable pulled a creased notebook from his breast pocket, then dug in the pocket again for a stubby pencil.

"Now then," Northcott said, doing his best to sound officious, "tell me exactly what 'appened up there in that there room."

Cecily drew in a deep breath. She would have much preferred her husband to be present when dealing with the constable. Baxter, however, together with several of the staff, was conducting a thorough examination of all the gas lamps in the entire hotel.

"As far as we can tell," she said carefully, "there must have been a gas leak in one of the lamps. We assume Sir Walter Hetherton lit a match to his cigar, thus causing a rather nasty explosion. I'm afraid both he and his wife died as a result."

The constable licked the end of his pencil then proceeded to write in the notebook. "Sir . . . Walter . . . 'Etherton," he murmured, scribbling the name down as he repeated it. Frowning, he gazed at the page. "Funny, that name sounds awfully familiar to me."

"Most likely because Sir Walter is . . . was . . . the Speaker of the House of Lords."

"Go on with you! That's going to cause a stir in Westminster all right. Let's see . . . what was his wife's name again?"

"Lady Clara."

"That's it. Lady Clara." He scribbled some more. "Poor blighters. I take it they were guests in this here establishment?"

"Yes." Cecily cleared her throat. "Unfortunately there are no witnesses. Mr. Baxter was first on the scene, if you would like to speak with him?"

Northcott studied his pencil, then with a flourish, licked the end of it again. "I don't think that will be necessary, Mrs. B. I shall rule this as an accidental death, due to a gas leak. Not the first time it's happened, by any means." He started scribbling again.

"It's certainly the first time it's happened at the Pennyfoot."

"Yes, well, quite." Once more Northcott licked the end of his pencil and continued to write. "I take it you've summoned Dr. Prestwick?"

"Yes, I have." Cecily glanced at the clock. "He should be here by now."

"And the fire brigade?"

"They were here, yes. Mr. Baxter had already put out the fire, but they inspected everything in the room, just to make certain the danger had passed. They also advised us to inspect the remaining lamps."

"Which you are so doing, I certainly trust?"

"As we speak."

"Right." The constable closed his notebook and tucked it back in his pocket. "Then I'll toddle along." He picked up his helmet and crammed it on his head. "Dr. Prestwick can give me his report after I return from my holiday. Happy Christmas, Mrs. B."

"I rather doubt that now, Constable, but thank you. My regards to your good wife."

Cecily waited for the door to close behind him before sinking into her favorite chair.

The library was her favorite room in the entire building. Especially when it was decorated for the holidays. Madeline had wrought her usual magic with the towering tree in the corner.

The crystal bells hung among shiny red and green glass baubles and delicate red velvet roses. The scent from the tiny white silk sachets of lavender mingled with the fresh fragrance of pine. A nice touch, and so typical of Madeline.

Cecily leaned back and stared at the glowing coals in the fireplace. At one time her late husband's portrait had hung above the mantelpiece.

James had been her first love. It had been his idea to take the neglected mansion and turn it into one of the finest hotels on the southeast coast of England. A bout of malaria had taken him from her too soon, and her faithful manager, Baxter, had stepped in as her advisor and protector, obeying James's dying wish.

Cecily smiled as memories crowded her mind. Her first dance with Baxter, and the moment she realized his attentions had become personal. His long and arduous courtship, complicated by the desperate need to maintain a professional image in front of the staff.

Their efforts to keep their deepening affection a secret, while all the time everyone was aware of, and delighted by, the delicious romance going on right under their noses. Then, at long last, Baxter had asked for her hand in marriage.

Those were heavenly days, and sometimes she missed the excitement of it all. Her smile faded as she thought about the untimely death of the couple upstairs.

What a tragedy, and it couldn't have happened at a worse time. Christmas was supposed to be a time for joyous celebration. There would be no celebrating this year for that poor family. What's more, each Christmas would bring back dreadful memories. How sad.

She lifted her head as a tap on the door disturbed her thoughts.

"Cecily? Are you in here?" A handsome face crowned with graying brown hair peered around the edge of the door. "Oh, there you are. Thank goodness you're alone."

Cecily rose to greet her visitor, Dr. Prestwick. Madeline's husband-to-be was always a welcome sight. "Kevin! How good to see you. Everyone is in the ballroom, waiting for the inspection to be completed."

"Yes, I know. I thought that fool Northcott might still be with you."

"As usual, P.C. Northcott has pressing business in London."

Kevin Prestwick smiled as he advanced into the room, though his blue eyes reflected the grim task he'd just completed. "The pressing business of plum pudding and a glass of strong ale, I assume."

Cecily proffered her hand and allowed him to lift it to his lips. "You assume correctly. Sam Northcott is off for his annual Christmas visit to his wife's relatives."

"And we shall see neither hide nor hair of him until the New Year."

Something in his voice worried her. "Is something wrong? Have you examined the dead couple yet?"

"Yes, I have." Kevin moved closer to the fireplace and held out his hands to the flames. "Those poor devils never stood a chance."

"Oh, dear. They must have been standing right under the lamp." Feeling a little queasy, Cecily decided it would be prudent to sit down again.

"That's the odd thing." Kevin turned to face her. "The bodies were on the other side of the room. I suppose the explosion could have blown them there, though judging by the moderate amount of damage, I wouldn't have thought the blast had that much force."

Cecily frowned. "On the other hand, I would think if there'd been enough gas building up in the room to reach across it, one of them surely would have smelled it and raised the alarm."

"My thoughts exactly. In any case, had the room filled with gas to that extent, you would have most likely lost half the top floor."

Cecily shuddered. "Such a terrible thing to happen right at the beginning of the Christmas season. The holiday does seem to attract misfortune at the Pennyfoot."

"You've had more than your share of bad luck, I have to admit."

"Indeed. At least we have your wedding to take our minds off the tragedy. How is Madeline? Is she ready for her big day?"

Kevin shrugged. "You know how Madeline can be. She refuses to tell me anything about the preparations. Says she doesn't want to invite misfortune." He shook his head. "I despair of her ever letting go of her ridiculous superstitions."

Cecily regarded him gravely. "They are far more than superstitions, my dear Kevin, as you well know. Try as you might to ignore them, your future wife has very special

powers that none of us understand. You would do well to re-
spect them if you want to enjoy a harmonious marriage."

"I am a doctor, Cecily. A man of science. It is difficult for
me to accept Madeline's . . . ah . . . unusual abilities. I have
learned not to voice my doubts in her presence, and I'm
afraid that's the best I can do. I love her enough that I'm
willing to overlook her lapses into mysticism, but there is
no possibility whatsoever of my participation in her beliefs."

"What will you do then when someone comes to your
surgery to ask Madeline for one of her virility potions?"

Again he shrugged. "While I shall never allow that these
potions of hers actually produce medical results, I do not believe they cause any harm, either. They are mostly derived
from herbs, plants, seeds and such, and if they bring some
sort of psychological relief then who am I to object?"

"Well said, Kevin." Cecily rose to her feet. "Madeline has
suffered in her past, and has fought hard to overcome her
troubled life. She has taken a very long time to trust her
heart to you. She is my dearest friend. I trust you will take
good care of her."

Kevin reached for her hands and held them to his chest.
"Rest assured I will, my dear. You are a good friend to both
of us. We are lucky to be blessed with your kindness."

Before Cecily could answer in kind the door flew open
and Baxter marched into the room. She stepped back as
Kevin let her go, wincing at Baxter's fierce scowl.

Her husband could never forget that at one time Kevin was
her ardent pursuer and quite persistent in his attentions. Although Cecily had never entertained any amorous thoughts
toward the handsome doctor, Baxter never quite trusted Kevin
Prestwick anywhere in the vicinity of his wife.

Cecily could only hope that Kevin's marriage to Madeline
would help allay Baxter's fears, since none of her assurances
seemed to do so.

Baxter gave Kevin a curt nod, then turned to his wife.

"We have tested every lamp in the building. There appear to be no gas leaks in any of them."

He still sounded hoarse and she gave him a worried look. "Well, that's a relief."

"It is indeed." Kevin headed for the door. "I must get back to my surgery. I've arranged for the bodies to be removed to the morgue."

"I trust you and Madeline will be joining us at the banquet this evening?" Cecily glanced at the clock. "I'm afraid we will be a little late, but we should be ready to sit down by nine o'clock."

He paused, one hand on the door knob. "I wasn't sure if you would continue with the banquet, considering the unfortunate circumstances."

Cecily glanced at her husband. "We have no choice. Our guests have to dine, and the meal has been prepared. The news will be terribly upsetting to everyone, I'm sure, but the best thing to do is carry on as usual, and try to establish some sense of normalcy. This is the Christmas season, after all. Our guests expect and deserve the usual amenities for which they have handsomely paid."

"Of course." Kevin smiled. "Then I shall bring Madeline back with me in an hour."

"And do tell her not to worry about anything. This unfortunate incident will not change our plans for the wedding in any way."

"I'm sure she'll be happy to hear that."

"We are so looking forward to the wedding." Cecily tucked her hand under her husband's elbow. "Aren't we, Baxter."

"More than you can imagine," Baxter said dryly.

"Not nearly as much as I am, old boy." Pure devilment gleamed in Kevin's eyes. "Be sure to take that medication I gave you. It will help soothe your throat. Contact me if it isn't better in a day or two."

Baxter merely nodded in reply, then, as the door closed behind the doctor, muttered something under his breath.

Cecily frowned. "I don't know why you two can't be more sociable with each other."

Baxter raised his eyebrows in exaggerated surprise. "I haven't the slightest idea what you mean. I'm completely civil to the chap."

"So I've noticed." Cecily moved closer to the fireplace. "It's the underlying jabs that are so immature. The silly part is, you like each other. Why do you try so hard to pretend you don't?"

"I don't want him to form the idea that he is welcome to drop in at any time unannounced. If allowed to do so, he could well become a pest."

"Piffle. You're jealous of him, that's all. You always have been."

Baxter gave her a patronizing smile. "If you say so, my dear."

Giving up, she held her hands out to the fire. "I must have that room cleaned as soon as possible. The smell of smoke is horrible."

"I'll see to it." He came closer and laid a hand on her shoulder. "Are you quite all right, Cecily? I know this has all been rather traumatic for you."

She reached up to cover his hand with her own. "I feel so sorry for the families of those poor people. And for our guests. It's not the best way to start out the festivities."

"Indeed not. I had the devil of a time convincing everyone that the building was safe and the likelihood of another explosion was extremely remote."

She gave him a worried glance. "Is everyone settling down again, do you think?"

He shrugged. "Hard to tell. There were at least three couples who considered returning to their homes, but I think I managed to reassure them. After all, it's rather late to make new plans for Christmas now."

"Oh, dear." Once more she held out her hands to the fire, rubbing them together to spread the warmth through her fingers. "I do hope they decide to stay. It would put such a dampener on things if half our guests were to leave."

"I'm sure things will return to normal once the bodies have been removed."

"I hope so." She looked up at him. "I just can't help the feeling that this isn't the end of it. That there's more unpleasant surprises to come."

Baxter squeezed her hand. "You are thinking too much in the past, my dear. This was a simple accident. Unfortunate, to be sure, but unavoidable. These things happen."

"That's what Sam Northcott said."

"There you are then." He planted a quick kiss on her cheek then strode to the door. "I'll find someone to clean up the room."

"Thank you. Could you also tell Mrs. Chubb to continue with the meal? I must go to the ballroom and announce the new arrangements."

He lifted his hand in acknowledgment and disappeared.

She waited a moment before following him. His words had been reassuring, but she wished she could rid herself of the uneasy feeling. Madeline would have called it a premonition. She wished her friend were there at that moment. Madeline's peculiar insight might have given her some relief.

Shaking off her apprehension, she made for the door. There was work to be done, and no time for such impractical concerns. The Hethertons' deaths were a distressing accident, but she owed it to her guests to continue with the traditions that had given the Pennyfoot its enviable reputation.

Her main objective was to provide an enjoyable, festive Christmas for her guests. She could only hope that there would be no more ugly surprises to thwart her well-laid plans.

# CHAPTER
## 4

"It's too bad we're not off tonight," Pansy said, as she scooped a crumb-filled plate off one of the breakfast tables the following morning. "After all, it's Christmas Eve."

"We're never off Christmas Eve." Gertie stacked yet another empty milk jug onto her tray. "I have to scramble every year to get my kiddies' pillow cases stuffed before they wake up."

"You got it off last year. You went out with Dan Perkins, remember?"

"Of course I remember." She paused, gazing into space as she relived that magical night. She could feel again the thrill of excitement as she'd followed Dan into the orphanage. He'd crept around the beds in the dark, leaving all those toys for the poor little orphans. Paid for them all with his own money, and never a word to anyone. He'd sworn her to secrecy, too. Said it wouldn't mean anything if anyone found out it was him. It was right then that she'd realized what a special man he was.

Gertie stifled the ache in her heart. Everything about Christmas reminded her of Dan. She'd really, really liked him, and he'd been so good with her twins. It was a shame they came from different worlds. He would have made such a good father.

"Well?"

Pansy's impatient voice brought her back to earth.

"Well, what?"

"Why did you get Christmas Eve off last year? What made you so special?"

Gertie sighed. "I got it off because we had the grand ball on Christmas Eve instead of the carol singing. This year we're going back to the carols in the library tonight. That means we'll have to be in there to keep handing out the food and drinks."

"Well, Samuel wanted to go down the pub tonight to celebrate. Now we'll have to wait until tomorrow to go down there."

Gertie looked at her in surprise. "You're going down the pub on Christmas Day?"

Pansy shrugged. "There's nothing else to do. Everything's shut down for a week."

"Well, I bet if I had a boyfriend I'd bloody find something better to do than sit in a smokey pub drinking beer." She slapped another milk jug down on the tray. "Look at the bleeding mess on this table. You'd think a bunch of kiddies had breakfast here instead of a posh toff and his wife."

Pansy glanced over at the patch of spilled oatmeal and tea stains marking the white linen tablecloth. "He's a doctor," she said. "Not a toff. He's going to be Dr. Prestwick's best man at the wedding."

"Yeah? Well, I hope he's a bit more careful at the wedding breakfast, or madam will be after him. She wants everything to be perfect. I heard her telling Mrs. Chubb."

"Well, I wish her luck with that." Pansy balanced the final plate on her arm. "Seems to be something's always going wrong at weddings."

"Well, there'd better not be at this one. Miss Pengrath could get cross and turn everyone into a toad."

Pansy giggled. "She can't really do that, can she?"

Gertie gave her a dark look. "Do you really want to find out?"

Shivering, Pansy shook her head. "I like Miss Pengrath, but sometimes she frightens me."

"Yeah, well, she frightens everyone at times." Gertie picked up the tray. "Come on, we'd better get back to the kitchen with these or Chubby will be having a bleeding heart attack."

Pansy giggled again. "Don't let her hear you call her that. She'll have your kidneys for the meat pies."

"Nah." Gertie headed for the door. "You don't know Chubby like I know her. She'll scream and yell at you but it's all show. Underneath she's as soft as a marshmallow."

She reached the door just as Pansy let out a loud gasp. Frowning, she turned to look back at the housemaid. "What's the bloody matter with you?"

Pansy stood transfixed in the middle of the dining room, the pile of plates wobbling on her arm as she stared at the window.

Worried, Gertie hurried over to her, still carrying the heavy tray. Following Pansy's gaze, she stared at the window, but could see nothing but the snowy grounds outside. "What? I can't bleeding see nothing."

"The snowman," Pansy said, pointing with her finger and making the plates wobble even more precariously.

Gertie shook her head in bewilderment. "So what? We saw it yesterday, didn't we?"

"Yes, we did." Pansy's voice sounded strange. "But it was in a different place."

"What?" Gertie narrowed her eyes, trying to remember

where she'd seen the snowman the day before. "Blimey, you're right. It was over by the bowling greens."

"And now it's over by the rockery." Pansy stared at Gertie, her eyes wide. "And last night when I was saying good night to Samuel, we saw it by the tennis courts."

Gertie shook her head. "They must have been different snowmen. My kiddies must have worked themselves to death building three of them."

"It's the same snowman," Pansy insisted, still in that hushed voice. "Same hat, same pipe, same scarf, same broom. See them lumps of coal buttons down the front? They're crooked. Just like on all the other snowmen we saw."

Gertie squinted. "How can you see that far?"

"I got good eyes, don't I." The plates rattled on Pansy's arm, and she rested a hand on them to steady them. "I tell you, it's the exact same snowman. I bet if we go to the ballroom and look where the other one was, it won't be there."

Gertie felt a chill, and did her best to shake it off. Pansy was imagining things, that was all. "Well, let's go and see." She dumped the tray on the nearest table. "Come on, put them down and we'll go right now to the ballroom."

Pansy obediently lowered the plates onto the table and followed her out into the hallway. "By the way," she said, hurrying to keep up to Gertie's long stride, "who won the brooch last night?"

Her mind still on the mysterious snowman, Gertie mumbled, "It were that MP. Mr. Crossley. He gave it to his wife."

"Lucky blighter." Pansy sounded puffed as they reached the end of the hallway and Gertie pushed open the ballroom doors. "That was terrible what happened to that other MP and his wife. Made me scared to turn on me gas lamp last night, it did. Fancy it blowing them up like that."

Gertie murmured an absent, "Yeah. Terrible. I'm just glad we weren't the ones what had to clean up the flipping room after them."

"Oo, I know. That must be awful!"

"Bloody awful." She glanced over her shoulder at Pansy. "I'm surprised you weren't told to do it, seeing as how the other maids had all their rooms to clean."

Pansy shrugged. "Just lucky, I s'pose."

Crossing the ballroom floor, Gertie stared through the window. Pansy was right. There was no sign of a snowman.

She went right up to the glass and pressed her nose to it, unwilling to believe what she couldn't see. "They must have knocked it down," she muttered. "And then used all the stuff to build another one."

"Yeah?" Pansy pointed a shaky finger in the direction of the bowling lawns. "Then where's the pile of snow? Don't tell me they carried it all the way over to the tennis courts, then all the way back to the rockery. Your little ones must have arms of steel. Besides, how would they have time to build three snowmen? They were indoors. Remember? Daisy said she was reading to them all afternoon."

Gertie pulled back from the window. "There has to be a bloody explanation somewhere. I'll ask the kiddies when I see them."

"There is no explanation," Pansy whispered, her eyes wide with fear. "I tell you, that snowman moves."

This time Gertie couldn't shake off the chill. "Don't be bleeding daft. Snowmen can't move."

"Then you tell me where that one went."

"We don't have time to worry about it now. We have to get the dirty dishes back to the kitchen before Mrs. Chubb raises merry hell." Gertie turned her back on the window and marched back to the doors. "My James and Lillian can tell us what happened later."

"I hope they can," Pansy said, as she followed her out into the hallway. "I'd really like to know the answer to that mystery."

So would she, Gertie thought, as she hurried back to the dining room. Just as soon as she got an opportunity, she was

going to talk to her twins and find out exactly what was going on. Moving snowmen. Bloody ridiculous, that's what.


"I really should be getting down to the office." Cecily gazed at
the newspaper hiding her husband's face. "I have so much to
catch up on. Once Christmas is over we'll be caught up in the
wedding preparations and I won't have time to do much else."

Without lowering the paper, Baxter murmured, "Are you
suggesting I come down and help you?"

Cecily smiled. "That would be very nice, dear."

The newspaper rattled in Baxter's hands. "And incredibly optimistic."

"Come now, my love. You know you enjoy digging into
the business side of the Pennyfoot. You're always coming up
with brilliant suggestions on how to improve the way it is
run." She felt a small glow of triumph when Baxter lowered
the paper and met her gaze.

"You should be well enough acquainted with me by now
to know that humoring me with all that false flattery will
get you absolutely nowhere."

"It got your nose out of that newspaper, didn't it."

Sighing, he laid the newspaper on his lap. "Very well.
What is it you would have me do to help you?"

Before she could respond a sharp rap on the door interrupted her. Exchanging a wary glance with her husband, she
called out, "Yes, come in!"

The door opened just a sliver and a deep voice announced,
"It's Clive, m'm. I was wondering if I could have a word with
you."

"Do come in, Clive." Worried now, Cecily watched Baxter get up from his chair. Clive Russell had been working
for the Pennyfoot for only a few months, but he had proved
to be an extremely competent and independent workman.
Never once had he had cause to speak directly to her about a
problem. Apparently until now.

The man's broad shoulders filled the doorway as he hesitated to advance into the room.

"Come in, come in," Baxter said, beckoning with an impatient hand. "You're letting in a cold draft."

Muttering an apology, Clive stepped just far enough into
the room to close the door, then backed up to it. "It's about
the explosion in room eleven, m'm."

Cecily rose to her feet. "What is it, Clive? We're not in
any danger, are we?" Visions of thunderous explosions rock-
ing the building and frantic guests running for their lives
filled her mind.

To her immense relief, Clive shook his head. "No, m'm.
That's just it. I don't think there's any danger at all. Nor has
there ever been. Not from the gas lamps, anyhow."

Cecily frowned at him, while Baxter clicked his tongue.
"What the devil are you talking about? Come on, spit it
out, man."

Clive looked from her to Baxter and back again. "There
never was a gas leak, m'm. I took the whole thing apart and
put it back together. There's no black smoke on it, no scorch
marks. Whatever caused that explosion, it didn't come from
the gas lamp. I'd stake my life on it."

"You could very well be doing that." Baxter stuck his
thumb into the pocket of his waistcoat. "As well as everyone
else's. Are you quite sure?"

"Positive, sir."

"Very well, Clive." Cecily nodded at him. "Thank you for
letting us know." She glanced at the clock. "I don't think
we'll be needing you anymore today. You can leave now and
be with your family for Christmas."

Clive touched his forehead with his fingers. "Thank you,
m'm, but I don't have no family. Only my sister, that is. She
lives in Yorkshire. Bit too far to go for two days."

Dismayed, Cecily glanced at Baxter. "Well, you are certainly welcome to enjoy a Christmas dinner with the rest of
the staff tomorrow evening. They all gather in the dining

room after the guests have left. Gertie will tell you what time."

The maintenance man's dark eyes lit up. "Well, I don't mind if I do. Thank you kindly, m'm."

"Not at all, Clive." She waited until he was halfway out the door before adding, "Oh, and Clive?"

"Yes, m'm?"

"I'd rather you didn't mention anything about the explosion to anyone else for the time being. I don't want talk of what happened to put a damper on the Christmas festivities."

He met her gaze steadily for a moment or two then murmured, "Very wise, m'm. Rest assured, my lips are sealed." With that, he stepped outside and closed the door behind him.

"What was all that about?" Baxter demanded, as Cecily took her seat again.

She gave him an innocent look. "What was what about, my love?"

Baxter's eyes narrowed. "All that about keeping his lips sealed."

"As I said, I don't want everyone rehashing the tragic deaths of two of our guests. It wouldn't exactly enhance the festivities, do you think?" Aware of how easily he read her thoughts, she deliberately avoided his gaze.

"Don't tell me. You sense a mystery here and you're determined to get to the bottom of it. That's why you don't want Clive talking about it."

She sighed. "You have to admit, Bax, it is all rather strange. Kevin says that the bodies of Sir Walter and his wife were on the opposite side of the room from the lamp, and he's quite sure the explosion wasn't strong enough to throw them there. Now Clive is saying that the explosion didn't come from the gas lamp at all. Doesn't that suggest that this may not have been an accident, after all?"

Baxter's grim expression worried her. "No, it doesn't. On the face of it I admit it sounds a little strange, but even if it wasn't a gas leak, that doesn't mean that whatever did blow up wasn't an accident of some sort."

"Such as?"

"I don't know . . . a gun misfiring, for instance."

"Then why didn't you find a gun in the room? I assume you would have told me had you seen one."

Baxter's face hardened even more. "I don't know, Cecily, and I don't intend to find out. If there is any question about the deaths, then it's the constable's job to investigate. Your job is to run this hotel, which, I should remind you, is in need of your attention, as you mentioned a good ten minutes ago."

Cecily pulled in a deep breath. Maybe he was right. In any case, there was no point in arguing with him about it for the time being. "You're quite right, my love. I shall go at once to my office and leave you in peace to finish reading your newspaper."

He stared at her for a moment longer, then, apparently appeased, opened the door for her to leave. "If you need me, I shall be here or in the lounge."

"Don't worry, dear. I'll find you." Blowing him a kiss, she sailed out the door and down the hallway to the stairs.

Baxter was right about one thing, she reflected as she started down. There was definitely a mystery concerning the deaths of Sir Walter Hetherton and his wife, and she would not be satisfied until she knew the answers.

Halfway down the stairs she passed a small, delicate woman wearing a wide-brimmed hat that partially hid her face. Pressed against the bannisters to allow her guest to pass, Cecily murmured, "Good day, Miss Danbury. I trust your shopping trip was successful?"

The woman raised her chin, though she avoided Cecily's gaze. "Yes, indeed, Mrs. Baxter. Most successful, thank you."

"Well, good. Wellercombe has so much more to offer than our tiny Badgers End. Though I must confess, I find those busy streets rather daunting. Especially now that there are so many motor cars dodging in and out among the horses."

"I agree, though the London streets can be even more hazardous, don't you think?"

"Oh, of course." Feeling a little foolish, Cecily felt herself floundering a little. "Ah, I do hope the recent explosion hasn't unsettled you. Since it was in the room next to yours, my staff was exceptionally thorough in the inspection of your room. I'm happy to say that there is absolutely no danger to you or anyone else in the Pennyfoot Country Club."

Grace Danbury appeared to have a nervous habit of wringing her hands. "I'm so relieved to hear that."

"Such a tragedy, of course. A great man has been lost. A terrible loss to society, I'm sure you agree."

"Actually I was not acquainted with the gentleman."

"Oh. Well, as a matter of fact, Sir Walter was the Speaker in the House of Lords. I imagine they'll be quite in disorder without him. Until they get a replacement, that is." Once more Cecily felt at a disadvantage, though she couldn't imagine why. Something about Grace Danbury's reticence discouraged conversation. Cecily had the notion that the woman was not comfortable with strangers. Most likely because she lived alone.

Much as Cecily embraced the women's movement, it was her considered opinion that people were never meant to live alone. A woman needed the challenge of living with a man. Then again, if a woman was fortunate enough to be as happy with her spouse as Cecily was with Baxter, then that was an added blessing, indeed.

"If you will excuse me"—Grace Danbury offered a shy smile—"I really should be on my way."

"Of course." Cecily allowed Grace to scurry by her, then continued on her way.

At the bottom of the stairs she saw Samuel hurrying across the lobby toward her. Catching sight of her, he raised a hand. "I was just coming up to see you, m'm."

Out of all her family of workers, Cecily trusted her stable manager the most. Samuel had shared many an adventure with her, and at times, despite his slender build and youthful appearance, he had proved to be a stalwart protector.

Samuel had accompanied her on paths that her husband would never have allowed her to go, and while at times fearful of the outcome, he had never failed to be at her service.

At the moment he looked somewhat disheveled, with black specks sprinkled in his fair hair and a gray smudge across one cheek. "I've just finished cleaning up room eleven," he said, as he reached her.

Frowning, Cecily demanded, "What were you doing cleaning the room? Don't you have enough work to do in the stables?"

"Yes, m'm. But we were a little shorthanded this morning and Mr. Baxter wanted it done as soon as possible so I volunteered."

"Very commendable of you, Samuel. I shall see you are justly rewarded."

"Thank you, m'm, but it was my pleasure. Weren't no job for the maids, anyway. They can be squeamish, if you know what I mean."

Cecily gave him a hard stare. It was no secret he was sweet on Pansy. The two of them had been seen a lot lately in each other's company. She wouldn't be at all surprised if Pansy had been asked to clean the room.

Her youngest maid was a good worker, but ran at the sight of a spider and absolutely refused to go down into the wine cellar. No doubt she had balked at the gruesome task of cleaning up after the explosion and Samuel had, most likely, gallantly offered to do it for her.

"Anyway, m'm." Samuel held up his hand. "I found this in the room and I thought you should take a look."

The sound of laughter from the hallway drifted across the lobby, and Cecily said quickly, "Come with me to my office, Samuel. This is something we should perhaps discuss in private."

"Right, m'm."

Samuel waited for her to precede him down the hallway as she hurried to reach her office. Something told her that whatever he held might possibly give her some answers to the mystery of the explosion. That was something she very much wanted to see.

# CHAPTER
## ❀ 5 ❀

"I don't know what's wrong with this bloody thing." Gertie shoved her shoulder against the unyielding pantry door and gave it a hefty kick. "Look, it won't shut properly."

"Is that a reason to beat the poor thing to death?" Michel flung a saucepan down on the stove. "How can I concentrate when you make all this noise?"

"Me make noise?" Gertie uttered a harsh laugh. "Gawd, Michel. Ever hear yourself? You sound like a steam engine crashing into a bloody tin factory. You make more noise than a sty full of pigs."

"I have to make noise to shut out the sound of your voice." Michel pinched his fingers against his thumb and kept opening and closing them. "You, Gertie McBride, have a mouth like the Blackwall Tunnel."

Her cheeks burning with resentment, Gertie marched over to him and dug her fists into her hips. "Yeah? Well, you've got a head like a bleeding airship—full of nothing but hot air, that's what."

"That's enough, you two!" Mrs. Chubb's sharp voice cut across Michel's snarling reply. "We've got tables to lay and a midday meal to get out. They'll be singing carols in the library tonight and we have to get that ready before we can start the supper so you'd all better hustle."

Backing away, Gertie dropped her fists. "You bleeding twerp."

Mrs. Chubb waved her wooden spoon in the air. "Gertie! For heaven's sake stop that awful swearing and please leave Michel alone."

"The dirty, smutty Blackwall Tunnel," Michel muttered under his breath.

Gertie swung around, but before she could say anything the housekeeper grabbed her by the arm. "Go and find Clive and ask him to come and fix the pantry door."

Pulling her arm free, Gertie demanded, "Why can't Pansy go and find Clive?"

"Because Pansy is busy, that's why."

"I don't like that bloke. There's something wrong with him."

Mrs. Chubb raised her eyebrows. "Clive? He seems all right to me."

"Well, he don't to me. He's always staring at me, and when I speak to him he don't even answer. Just stands there with a stupid smile on his face."

"That's because he cannot believe what he sees," Michel said, grinning.

"Shut up, twit." Gertie turned back to the housekeeper. "I tell you, there's something wrong with him. I don't think he's right in the head."

"He's shy, that's all."

Gertie snorted. "Shy? He's as big as a mountain and as strong as a bleeding ox. How can he be shy?"

"Just because he's big and strong doesn't mean he's not

shy around women." Mrs. Chubb picked up a tin of custard powder and measured some into a bowl. "He's really polite, I'll tell you that. I like that in a man. Very gentlemanly."

"Well, I don't like him."

"You keep talking about this man." Michel drew his carving knife and sharpener from their holders and started buffing the blade against the steel. "If you ask me, you like him a little more than you pretend."

"Don't talk daft." Gertie headed for the door. "Anyway, if I don't come back soon, you might want to send out a search party. In case he's murdered me or something."

"Gertie McBride." Mrs, Chubb threw her hands up in horror. "Don't you dare talk like that. Isn't it upsetting enough that two people died in this hotel, without you joking about being killed?"

Gertie gave her a dark look. "For your information, I wasn't joking." She didn't wait for the housekeeper's answer. Stepping outside, she let the kitchen door swing to behind her and marched down the hallway.

Nobody ever took her seriously. Nobody. Serve them all bloody well right if she turned up dead like them toffs in room eleven.

Cecily ushered her stable manager into her office and closed the door firmly before turning to him. "Now, Samuel, show me what you found."

Samuel held out his closed fist then slowly opened his fingers. Fragments of paper fluttered from his hand and floated down to settle on the carpet.

"What on earth is that?" Cecily stared at the floor. "Is it a note of some sort?" She bent her knees for a closer look. Some of the pieces were scorched around the edges and had a peculiar sheen to them. Almost like gold.

Her heart skipped a beat. Carefully she pressed a forefinger to one of the fragments and lifted it off the floor. The light from the window made the paper sparkle. She looked up to see Samuel studying her, a look of expectancy on his face. "Is this what I think it is?"

He rubbed the palm of his hand against his hip. "Well, it looks to me like a piece of one of them Christmas crackers you had on the table for the banquet."

Cecily looked back at the tiny scrap of paper. "Yes," she said slowly. "That's exactly what I think it is." Carefully she gathered up the rest of the pieces, her mind working furiously. There had been two crackers missing before the banquet. She'd had to replace them.

Why would Sir Walter, or Lady Clara for that matter, steal two of the crackers? In the hopes of finding the brooch? That made no sense at all.

In the first place, it would be impossible to tell which cracker held the brooch without actually taking them apart. Since none of the other crackers had been opened, that theory held no water at all. In any case, Lady Clara undoubtedly had jewelry far more valuable than anything the Pennyfoot could afford.

No, it was much more likely that someone had given them to the Hethertons. As a Christmas gift to curry favor? That made no sense, either. The Hethertons would know at once the crackers had been pilfered from the banquet tables.

Either the Hethertons had taken the crackers themselves as some kind of souvenir which, knowing the couple as the snobs that they were, seemed highly unlikely, or someone had placed them in the Hetherton's room. Why?

"Are you feeling all right, m'm?"

Samuel's anxious voice broke her chain of thought. "Ah, yes, Samuel. Thank you. I'm sure this means nothing but I'll keep these pieces safe just to be sure."

"Clive said the explosion wasn't caused by a gas leak."

*Drat Clive and his loose tongue.* Cecily nodded. "I don't think any of us really knows what happened. I prefer not to speculate at this stage. I think we should wait until P.C. Northcott returns from his holidays and let him decide."

Scratching the palm of his hand, Samuel leaned in closer and lowered his voice. "Maybe that bloke and his wife was killed by an exploding cracker."

Cecily stared at him, her mind reeling. "What? No, that's nonsense. Crackers don't explode. They just pop."

"What if they had too much of that stuff that makes them pop inside?"

"Yes, well, I suppose that's possible but . . ." She shook her head. "No, I had these crackers especially made for me and I trust Mrs. Lonsdale completely. She's been making crackers by hand for years. I doubt very much that a mistake of that magnitude was made. Besides, if the crackers had been overloaded with gunpowder, or whatever it is that makes them pop, the rest of them would have gone up at the banquet."

"But what if it wasn't a mistake? What if someone had done it on purpose?"

Cecily felt as if all the breath had left her body. Could it be possible that someone had tampered with the crackers . . . maybe added enough of whatever made them pop to cause a deadly explosion?

She would have to ask someone—a scientist. Maybe Kevin. He was a doctor . . . a man of science. Perhaps he could tell her what she needed to know. Until then, she needed to keep this to herself.

With an effort she made her voice sound calm and unperturbed. "Samuel, I really think we should stop speculating before we spoil everyone's Christmas with our overactive imaginations. Now I want you to put this matter completely out of your mind, and please, don't mention anything about this to anyone. Especially Pansy. Am I clear?"

Samuel rubbed both palms against his hips. "Yes, m'm. Perfectly."

"Well, good then. I don't want to start a panic over nothing."

"No, m'm."

"You may go now, Samuel."

"Yes, m'm. Thank you, m'm."

"Thank *you*, Samuel. By the way, is there something wrong with your hands?"

He looked down at his upturned palms. "I've got an itch, m'm, that's all. Must be the new cleaning stuff Mrs. Chubb gave me."

"Let me see." She peered at his reddened palms. "We should have Dr. Prestwick look at that. I'll mention it to him."

"Yes, m'm." Samuel moved to the door, then looked back at her. "You didn't forget there were two crackers missing, did you, m'm?"

Cecily sighed. "No, Samuel, I didn't forget."

"That's good. Because, on the slight chance that someone did fix up a cracker to explode, well, he's still got another one, hasn't he." He quietly closed the door, leaving Cecily to stare after him.

She had assumed that the two crackers had been burned up in the room. If her suspicions proved to be well-founded, and someone had deliberately given a lethal cracker to the Hethertons, there was every possibility, as Samuel said, that the killer still had the second cracker in his possession.

If so, until it was found, everyone in the Pennyfoot was in grave danger.

It took Gertie fifteen minutes to find Clive. The unpleasant odor of paint led her down the hallway on the top floor, where she found him inside room eleven, painting the walls.

Poised in the doorway, she called out, "Mrs. Chubb sent me to find you."

She must have startled him. He swung around, and his elbow caught the ladder propped up next to him. The tin of paint, balanced on the top of the ladder, swayed back and forth then slowly toppled over, spilling thick, cream liquid all the way down to the floor.

Fortunately he'd spread sheets over the carpet to protect it. His boots weren't so lucky. They received a generous dollop across each toe.

Seeing his stricken expression, Gertie fought the urge to laugh. "Oops," she said, one hand over her mouth.

Clive's beet red face looked at her, then back down at his feet. "What would Mrs. Chubb have me do?"

"It's the pantry door in the kitchen. It's sticking and I can't get it to shut properly."

Without looking up, Clive nodded. "Tell her I'll be down there just as soon as I've cleaned up this mess."

He looked so miserable Gertie was beginning to feel sorry for him. "Don't worry, I'll tell her you're really busy and you'll be there as soon as you can."

He was still mumbling his thanks as she backed away then headed for the stairs. Shaking her head, she ran down them. Clive was an odd one, all right. Never spoke unless someone spoke to him first. Always shuffling along with his head down, never looking where he was going. It was a wonder he didn't bump into things more often. Bit thick, he was.

Reaching the bottom of the stairs, she glanced at the clock. Nearly time for her to pay her afternoon visit to the twins. Mrs. Chubb let her slip away about this time every afternoon so she could spend a few minutes with her children.

She reached the kitchen just as Pansy flew through the door carrying the heavy tray of silverware. "Thank goodness you're here," she said, panting a little as she heaved the tray higher in her scrawny arms. "I'm really late with this and Mrs. Chubb is on the warpath. She said to ask you to help me lay the tables."

Gertie sighed. There went her chance to see her twins. Now she'd have to wait until tonight. "All right. Give me the bleeding tray. You look as if you'll bloody break in half any minute."

With a sigh of relief, Pansy deposited the tray in her arms. "I'll go back and get the glasses." With that, she disappeared into the kitchen.

Gertie carried the tray to the dining room and laid it on the nearest table. Just to reassure herself, she wandered over to the window and peered through it in the direction of the rockery. The snowman had disappeared.

Kevin arrived later that afternoon. Cecily was in her office, catching up on the paperwork when she heard his tap on her door. To her delight, when she called out for him to enter, his future wife walked in ahead of him.

"Madeline!" Cecily rose from her chair and hurried to greet her friend. "This is a lovely surprise."

"I was concerned about you." Madeline's lovely dark eyes scanned her face. "You looked quite pale at the banquet last night. Are you feeling better today? You've had all this dreadful business to contend with, just when you are at your busiest."

"I'm feeling much better," Cecily assured her, though she wasn't sure that was entirely true. The possibility that Sir Walter had been deliberately attacked weighed heavily on her mind. Not to mention Samuel's cryptic comment as he was leaving her office. She was anxious to question Kevin Prestwick on the matter, but first he had to attend to her stable manager.

"I'll ring for Samuel," she said, reaching for the velvet pull rope hanging on the wall behind her desk. "He should be here in a minute or two."

Madeline sank onto one of the office chairs and bent down to slip off her shoes. "Well, I brought you one of my potions, just in case you need a pick-me-up."

It was fortunate she couldn't see her future husband's face at that moment. Rolling his eyes at the ceiling, he slowly shook his head.

Cecily caught his gaze and gave him a fierce shake of the head herself. "That's very thoughtful of you, Madeline, dear," she said firmly. "I shall keep it on hand in case I feel in need of it."

Madeline tucked a hand into the pocket of her flowing flowered skirt and withdrew a small white envelope. "Here it is. Just boil a cup of water and pour it on, let it steep for exactly five minutes. You'll feel much better after that, I promise you."

Sensing Kevin's struggle to keep quiet, Cecily took the packet from her. "So tell me, do you have your gown ready for the wedding?"

"It is almost finished. I have yet to sew the silver leaves around the hem but that won't take too long to accomplish."

To Cecily's relief, she heard a tap on the door. Calling out, "Come in!" she went back to sit on her chair behind the desk.

Samuel stuck his head around the edge of the door. "You rang, m'm?"

"Yes, do come in, Samuel. I asked Dr. Prestwick here to inspect your itching hands. He's ready to take a look at them for you."

"Thank you, m'm." Samuel stepped into the room and nodded at the doctor. "I'm much obliged."

"Not at all." Kevin reached for one of his hands and inspected it closely. "It appears that you are having a nasty reaction to something."

Samuel nodded. "Mrs. Chubb is using new cleaning stuff. I used it this morning to clean up room eleven."

"Ah. That could well be the culprit." Kevin nodded, and reached into the black bag he always carried with him. "I'll write out a prescription. You might be able to get it filled at the chemist's before he closes for the Christmas week."

"Make haste and go there, Samuel," Cecily said, glancing at the small clock ticking on her desk. "You don't want to have to wait a whole week before putting medication on that rash."

"Don't worry, Samuel." Madeline stretched her feet out in front of her. "If the chemist is closed I have something that will heal that for you."

"I would prefer that Samuel use the ointment I prescribed," Kevin said stiffly.

Madeline gave him her sweet smile. "Of course you do, dear. I'm merely suggesting an alternative in the event the chemist is closed."

"Then you'd better hurry, Samuel." Kevin's voice was gruff as he held open the door. "Before she slaps on some concoction made of stinging nettles or something."

As Samuel slipped through the door Cecily caught the momentary gleam of resentment in Madeline's eyes. By the time Kevin turned back to her it had gone, to be replaced by her usual serene smile.

Unsettled by the exchange, Cecily quickly sought to change the subject. "I'm so glad you are here, Kevin. I'd like to discuss a matter of some importance with you."

Nodding, Kevin crossed the room to the other vacant chair. "Fire away, then. What is it about?"

"It's about the explosion in room eleven." She looked from one to the other. I'm sure I don't have to ask you to be discreet about our discussion."

"Of course not!"

"Not at all!"

They had spoken in unison, and reassured, Cecily nodded. "Very well." Addressing Kevin, she added, "I need to know if it is possible to put enough explosive inside a Christmas cracker to kill someone."

Kevin's eyebrows rose so high they almost disappeared into his hairline. Madeline uttered a small sigh but mercifully remained quiet.

"Are you suggesting that the Hethertons were killed by a *Christmas cracker*?"

He sounded so incredulous Cecily's convictions wavered.

"I'm not certain, of course, but I think it's a distinct possibility, yes."

"Heavens," Madeline murmured. "Who would have thought something so festive and fun could turn out to be so lethal."

"They'd only be lethal if someone had tampered with them." Cecily looked back at Kevin. "Is it possible?"

He still seemed astounded at the idea. "I—I don't know. I can certainly find out for you." He frowned, rubbing his chin with his long fingers. "Ah, I know who to ask." He got up from the chair. "May I use your telephone?"

Cecily waved a hand at her desk. "Please do."

"Gerald Porchester is a good friend of mine. He's a scientist. He'll be able to tell me what you want to know." He picked up the receiver and waited for the operator to answer.

"I thought it was a gas leak that killed the Hethertons," Madeline murmured, as Kevin asked to be connected to his friend.

"Apparently not." Cecily lowered her voice. "Clive saw no scorching on the lamp that would indicate that it had blown up."

Madeline's forehead wrinkled. "Whatever makes you think it could have been a Christmas cracker?"

"Samuel found tiny scraps of scorched paper from the wrapping on the floor."

"Oh, my." Madeline's body suddenly stiffened, and her eyes glazed over.

Aware of what was coming, Cecily shot a nervous glance at Kevin's back. She didn't know if he had ever seen his future wife in a full-blown trance, and she certainly didn't want to be present if this proved to be an unexpected, and most likely unwelcome, enlightenment for him.

Kevin, however, was earnestly talking to an unseen presence on the telephone, and appeared not to notice the sudden tension in the room.

"Madeline," Cecily whispered. "What do you see?"

Her eyes closed, Madeline moaned, and Cecily hastily coughed loudly to cover it.

"I see smoke, flames, devastation, death," Madeline muttered.

Cecily managed a rather false laugh, hoping to divert the doctor's attention away from his betrothed. "Goodness!" she said brightly. Leaning forward, she added in a whisper, "What else?"

Madeline's eyes flew open, and she reached out to grasp Cecily's wrist. "There's another one."

"Another what?"

"Another lethal cracker. Be on your guard, Cecily. This one could well be for you."

# CHAPTER
## 🏵 6 🏵

"Well," Kevin said heartily, as he clicked the receiver back on its stand. "That answers that question, at least."

"What question?" Madeline asked, in a perfectly normal voice.

Though shaken by her friend's dire warning, Cecily felt relieved that at least for now, she wouldn't have to witness Kevin's reactions to his future wife's uncanny abilities. "So tell me, Kevin, is it at all possible to blow someone up with a cracker?"

Kevin sat down again before he answered. "According to Gerald, loading a cracker with lethal amounts of explosive is entirely possible. He went into a lot of technical details, but basically he said that the compound used to make a Christmas cracker pop open is called silver fulminate. It's actually two chemical elements mixed together to form crystals. In the minute amounts used in a cracker, the compound is harmless, but it's extremely unstable. The weight of the crystals themselves sometimes causes them to self-detonate. In fact, occasionally just adding one single drop of water can cause an explosion."

"Good heavens!" Cecily clutched her throat. "I had no idea they were so dangerous."

"Well, as I said, the compound is harmless in minute amounts." Kevin tucked his fingers into his waistcoat pocket and withdrew a cigar. Fishing in his other pocket, he came up with a small box of matches. "In larger amounts, however, it can quite easily be lethal." He struck a match and held it to the end of his cigar, then puffed furiously to coax it to light.

Cecily shook her head. "But if it's so unstable, how would someone carry it about? I have to assume that if the explosion was caused by a cracker, someone would have to bring it into the building."

"Unless he actually prepared and mixed the compound here in the Pennyfoot. The chemicals are only dangerous when combined." Kevin frowned. "Then he would have had to place the cracker in the Hetherton's room, of course."

"Ah, yes. That's possible, I suppose. Some of our guests can be lax about locking their rooms. The Hethertons would have seen the cracker and might have assumed that there was one in every room. Especially since the banquet was the official start of the Christmas season."

Kevin nodded, his face grave. "So it appears likely that the Hethertons were murdered."

"It certainly is beginning to look that way."

Madeline made a small sound of distress. "But who would want to kill them both, and why?"

Kevin shrugged. "Perhaps only one of them was the intended victim. Sir Walter was a prominent politician. A man like that has many enemies. Whoever wanted him dead could have wanted it badly enough that his wife became expendable."

Madeline gasped. "Are you saying that poor woman died

simply because she happened to be in the same room with her husband?"

Kevin shrugged. "Someone had to pull the cracker with him. No doubt the rumors about a special gift in one of them would be an incentive."

"Oh, dear," Cecily murmured. The thought that her planned surprise could have actually aided a murderer was most disturbing.

Kevin tilted his chin up to blow smoke in a wreath above his head. "Diabolically clever plan. The killer would have been far away from the scene by the time his victim died. Pretty much impossible to trace him, I'd say. Northcott will have his work cut out with this one."

"I'm sorry, Cecily." Madeline patted her arm. "It appears you'll be dealing with Inspector Cranshaw this time."

"Not if I can help it," Cecily muttered through her teeth. "You said the killer could have prepared the compound here in the Pennyfoot. How could he do that?"

"According to Gerald, it's not that difficult." Kevin tapped ash from the end of his cigar into the ashtray on Cecily's desk. "Apparently it's simply a matter of dissolving silver metal in nitric acid and then adding ethyl alcohol to form crystals."

"I would have thought it more complicated than that," Madeline murmured.

"Well, perhaps, but anyone with scientific knowledge could carry out the procedure." He smiled at her. "Even that timid friend of yours, Grace . . . whatever her name is. Isn't she some kind of a biologist?"

Cecily looked at her friend in surprise. "Is she? I had no idea."

Madeline scowled at Kevin, making Cecily nervous. "Yes, Grace is a biologist. A very clever one.

Seeing Madeline's expression, Cecily said hastily, "There's one thing I don't understand. If someone intended to kill Sir Walter in that bizarre manner, surely he would have to know in advance that his victim would be staying here?"

"Perhaps we should ask Kevin's good friend, Dr. Charles Winchester," Madeline said nastily. "After all, he's a doctor, a man of science, and he certainly knew the victim. I saw the Winchesters arrive in the same carriage as the Hethertons, and it was quite evident that they all knew each other well."

Cecily glanced at Kevin. "Is that so?"

Kevin nodded, his eyes clouded. "Yes, it is. The Winchesters were well acquainted with the victims. I'm afraid Charles and his wife are most distressed about the deaths of their friends."

"Well, I shall quite understand if Emily does not feel well enough to perform her duties as a bridesmaid," Madeline murmured, sending a sly look in Cecily's direction.

"I'm certain that by the end of next week they will both have recovered enough to enjoy the wedding. Charles is my best man. I guarantee he will not let me down."

Again Cecily intervened. "Well, I'm sure since Sir Walter was so well-known in London, quite a few people would know where he planned to spend Christmas. That doesn't explain how the killer could count on the fact that we had Christmas crackers available. Why use ours? Why didn't he bring one of his own with him?"

"I have to agree, it is odd that he wouldn't bring his own cracker, rather than take a chance on having to steal one of yours."

"Unless it wasn't preplanned at all."

Once more Kevin blew a stream of smoke above his head. "You're suggesting that perhaps our devious murderer got the idea after seeing the crackers on the table?"

"Precisely." Cecily frowned. "He could have discovered that Sir Walter was staying here, decided to get rid of him for whatever reason, saw the crackers and decided to use them as a weapon."

"Which means he's almost certain to be staying here as one of your guests."

"Precisely." She stroked her forehead with her fingers.

"But then where would he get the chemicals that would make the cracker explode?"

"London, I would imagine. Though he would have to leave quite early in the morning and return by the evening train."

Madeline sat up straight and exchanged a meaningful glance with Cecily.

Alarmed, Cecily shook her head at her. Just because Dr. Charles Winchester had gone back to London for the day didn't make him a murderer. Accusing him of such was bound to anger Kevin.

Fortunately, the doctor was engrossed in crushing out his cigar in the ashtray on Cecily's desk to notice her apprehension. She sent a warning glance in Madeline's direction, and was relieved when her friend gave her a reluctant shrug of resignation.

"On the other hand," Kevin added, "if he were gone for the entire day, that would give him very little time to manufacture the exploding cracker."

Cecily gave Madeline another meaningful look, hoping that would be enough to convince her friend that Charles Winchester could not be considered a suspect. Madeline was far too inclined to jump to conclusions. "Perhaps the killer purchased the chemicals in Wellercombe. Would that be possible, do you think?"

Tucking the remainder of the cigar into his waistcoat pocket, Kevin murmured, "Well, yes, entirely possible, I suppose. Now that you mention it, there is a company in Wellercombe that supplies such chemicals. In fact, I have at least two of the ones I mentioned stored in my office."

"So anyone could have tampered with the cracker."

He shook his head. "Not just anyone, Cecily. As I said, he would need some scientific knowledge in order to know what chemicals to use. This was no amateur. Given that, it would be a simple matter of purchasing the chemicals and combining them either in his room, or somewhere close by."

"It would have been easy to steal the cracker. The tables in the ballroom were laid that morning. The crackers were sitting in plain sight all day."

"Precisely. The killer would wait for the Hethertons to leave their room for a fair amount of time. He could then slip in there, place the explosive inside the cracker and leave it lying there. From what Gerald tells me, the slightest friction when that cracker was pulled would be likely to cause an explosion strong enough to kill anyone standing close to it."

Cecily shuddered. "How utterly cold-blooded."

"Killers usually are." Kevin pulled a pocket watch from his waistcoat and glanced at it. "Good Lord, is that the time? I must get back to my surgery." He stood, looking pointedly at Madeline, who took her time rising to her feet.

"You will take care, Cecily?" She took hold of Cecily's hand in both of hers. "Let all this be until after Christmas. Or better yet, wait until Constable Northcott returns from London."

"Good advice." Kevin laid a hand briefly on her shoulder. "This is dangerous business, Cecily. Your tendency to involve yourself in such matters concerns me. I implore you to leave well alone, or at least report our suspicions to the constabulary. Let the inspector take care of it."

"I'll be careful. I give you my word."

He gazed at her a long time before nodding. "In any case, I assume we'll see you tonight at the carol service in the library?"

"I'm looking forward to it." Cecily ushered them out, then returned to her desk, where she sank down on her chair. Questions chased each other around in her head, all of them without answers. It was hard to believe that one of her guests had gone to all that trouble to kill Sir Walter.

Then again, as Kevin had said, choosing such an atrocious method of eliminating someone would certainly give the culprit plenty of time and space to create an alibi.

A shiver ran down her spine. Once more the Pennyfoot could be harboring a murderer.

"Gertie, take this tray of hors d'oeuvres into the library." Mrs. Chubb picked up the heavy tray from the kitchen table and held it out to her chief housemaid. "They'll be starting the carol singing soon."

Gertie grabbed the tray and headed for the door. This was her favorite night of the year. She loved to be in the library with everyone standing around the Christmas tree, all singing carols.

Miss Pengrath always made the room look so pretty, with the fir garlands over the fireplace and the decorations on the tree. There was a time when they used to light candles on the tree, but ever since it caught fire one year and nearly burned madam to death the candles remained unlit. Still, the tree always looked lovely.

Climbing the stairs, Gertie raised her chin and sniffed the air. The whole place smelled like Christmas, what with the fragrance of pine from the tree in the lobby, and the wonderful aroma of Michel's spice-filled and brandy-soaked Christmas puddings invading every corner of the lobby.

Smiling to herself, Gertie started down the hallway to the library. This was Christmas Eve, and her twins were beside themselves with excitement. Tomorrow they'd open their presents and then they'd have Christmas dinner in the kitchen later that day with all the staff and everyone would make a fuss of them. She still missed Dan, but at last she was finally beginning to feel the Christmas spirit.

She reached the corner just as the first strains of "God Rest Ye Merry, Gentlemen" drifted toward her. Quickening her step she hurried around the corner and ran smack into something big and solid.

The tray flew out of her hands, sending sausage rolls, stuffed eggs and Welsh rarebit squares smashing against the wall. Gertie stumbled backward, her foot slipping on the spilled food. Down she went, her bottom landing in the middle of all the horrible mess.

Blinking, she stared up at the human wall that had knocked her down. Clive stared back at her, his mouth hanging open in dismay.

Scrambling to her feet, Gertie glared at him. "You blithering idiot, look what you've bleeding done!" She twisted her head over her shoulder to examine the damage. "Look at me dress! It's me best one. Now I'll have to change into me second best."

Clive began stuttering. "Sorry. I'm sorry. I didn't see you. . . ."

"Don't just stand there, you twerp. Help me clean up this bloody mess." Close to tears, Gertie bent down to pick up the tray.

Clive bent over at the same time and whacked her head with his.

"Ouch!" Grabbing the tray, Gertie straightened. "Get out of me flipping way, you clumsy sod. Just go. I'll clean this up meself."

"I'm sorry. I . . ." For a long moment Clive stared at her, his face scarlet. Then, as she squatted down to start picking up the pieces, he shuffled off, muttering something she couldn't catch.

Gertie's hands shook as she scooped up sticky pieces of pastry and crumpled toast. This was all she needed. It would take her ages to get the mess cleaned up and then she'd have to change her blinking dress. What a dumb clot that Clive was. Not all there, that's what. From now on she'd take good care to stay out of his way.

"Absolutely divine gathering, Cecily dear. You always manage to put on such a lavish and elegant affair." The frail woman raised a graceful hand to straighten her hat. No small task since its wide brim was laden with artificial fruit and a rather anemic-looking robin perched on a sprig of holly.

She wore a deep purple gown of taffeta silk, with a black silk lace yolk and gleaming ebony buttons down the bodice. As always, she looked the essence of aristocracy, and no one but Cecily would have known that until Phoebe married her colonel, she was as poor as a street peddler.

"Thank you, Phoebe." Cecily smiled at her friend. "With all the excitement here yesterday I was worried we might have to cancel the carol singing ceremony."

"Oh, my dear, that would have been such a tragedy." Phoebe smoothed her black gloves over her elbows. "This celebration has been a tradition at the Pennyfoot Hotel for as long as I can remember. Though of course, it's not officially a hotel any more, is it. I keep forgetting it's a country club, although"—she gazed around with the air of someone seeing the place for the first time—"for the life of me I can't tell the difference."

She leaned closer and lowered her voice. "Such a dreadful thing to happen. At Christmastime, too. Those poor people. One never knows with gas lamps. Quite unpredictable. Not like the oil lamps we used when I was growing up. My Freddie is always saying how progress will be the end of us. How very true."

Cecily was inclined to disagree, but this wasn't the time to argue the point. "Where is the colonel? Did he not accompany you this evening?" She glanced around the room. The women, looking delightful in their silk and satin gowns, sat on the chairs and settees while the men, in white tie and black coattails, hovered over them.

Behind them, the polished paneled walls gleamed with the reflection of the leaping flames from the fireplace. Madeline had draped garlands of pine and holly, decorated with sprigs of mistletoe, all around the room, providing the perfect setting for her magnificent Christmas tree.

"Oh, you know Freddie." Phoebe waved a gloved hand in

the air. "He has to visit the bar before he can be sociable in a gathering. So many of your guests are so notable. I do believe he feels intimidated by them at times."

This came as quite a surprise to Cecily, who didn't think the intrepid colonel was intimidated by anyone.

"Take that gentleman over there." Phoebe nodded at a short, stout man talking earnestly to his neighbor, a man who towered over him and seemed bored by the whole conversation.

"Mr. Roland Crossley? Or are you referring to the taller gentleman? He's Dr. Charles Winchester. Dr. Prestwick's best man, in fact."

"Oh, really?" Phoebe peered in his direction. "I've met his wife, of course. I fitted her for her bridesmaid gown."

"That's right. Of course you did. You've met both Emily Winchester and Grace Danbury."

"The mousy woman with the nervous hands? I'm surprised Madeline picked such an unattractive woman for a bridesmaid. That Emily Winchester, however, is quite pretty, in an insipid sort of way."

"Would you like me to introduce you to her husband?"

Phoebe shook her head, making the robin bob up and down. For a startling moment, it looked as if it were alive. "Well, actually," she murmured, "I was referring to the other gentleman. The chubby one. Isn't he a member of parliament? Freddie seemed to recognize him as such when we passed him in the lobby."

"Mr. Roland Crossley is a member of the House of Commons, yes."

"So Freddie was right after all. I get confused. I thought the poor man who died in the explosion was the MP."

"He was." Cecily pulled in a deep breath. "He was the Speaker in the House of Lords."

"Goodness!" Phoebe drew back in dismay. "How utterly disastrous for you. The news must be all over the city of London by now."

"I'm sure it is."

"I'm surprised you haven't been invaded by a swarm of those irritating newspaper people."

That was highly likely, Cecily thought uneasily, if her suspicions were correct. The murder of such a prominent citizen was bound to bring the reporters down to the Pennyfoot. Inspector Cranshaw would not like that.

"Oh, there you are, old bean, what? What?"

The booming voice of Colonel Frederick Fortescue easily carried above the voices of the singers.

Noting several heads turned their way, Cecily nodded at the bewhiskered gentleman. "Colonel. How very nice to see you again." She glanced at Phoebe. "Now, if you will excuse me, Phoebe . . ."

"Dashed awkward, that parliament bloke popping off like that, what?" The colonel twirled the end of his luxurious white mustache with his fingers.

Awkward, Cecily thought grimly, wasn't exactly the word she would have used. "Most tragic, I assure you," she murmured. "We are all badly shaken by the incident."

"Heard his old lady bought it as well." The colonel's eyelids rapidly flapped up and down—a sure sign he was about to launch into one of his old war stories.

It was no secret that Colonel Fortescue had returned home from the Boer War suffering from a malady caused by the fighting he endured there. Most of the time he was merely irritating, but on occasion he was apt to imagine himself back on the front line, whereupon he would brandish an imaginary sword or rifle and attack whatever happened to get in his way.

Hoping fervently that this was not one of those times, Cecily smiled at him. "I'm sorry to run, Colonel, but I really must—"

"Oh, don't let me delay you, old bean. Mustn't keep the company waiting, what?"

Vastly relieved, Cecily was about to turn away when he

added, "Reminds me of the time my subaltern kept me waiting. Almost cost me my life, by Jove."

"Freddie, dear." Phoebe laid her fingers on the colonel's arm. "Not now. Cecily is busy."

He appeared not to hear her. Tucking his thumbs behind the lapels of his coat, he rocked back on his heels. "Ah, yes, there we were, stuck behind enemy lines, waiting for a chance to sneak back to our regiment . . ."

Cecily cast a desperate glance at Phoebe, who indicated with a toss of her head to escape.

Mouthing a silent "Thank you," Cecily slipped away.

The colonel's words followed her, loud and clear. "Blasted fool had to take a whiz. Couldn't have blasted picked a worse time."

Wincing, Cecily slipped through a group of singers and out the door.

# CHAPTER

## 7

Out in the hallway, the first thing Cecily saw was Gertie, on her hands and knees, surrounded by what appeared to be the remains of someone's supper. "What happened?" She hurried forward, dismayed by the horrible mess all over the Axminster carpet.

Gertie looked up, her eyes bright with unshed tears. "Sorry, m'm. I bumped into Clive. I didn't see him as I came around the corner and all of a sudden there he was and down I went and everything spilled all over everywhere and me dress is a mess—"

"What's all this wailing about?"

The deep voice made them both jump.

Looking up at her husband's outraged face, Cecily said quickly, "We've had a bit of an accident, that's all. We'll have it cleaned up in no time." She gave him an imploring smile. "Would you be a dear and go in there and find the colonel? I'm afraid he's embarking on one of his stories and he just might attack the Christmas tree."

"Oh, good Lord." Shaking his head, Baxter strode down the hallway to the library.

Gertie looked up. "Thank you, m'm."

"Not at all." Cecily lifted the hem of her gown and stepped over the gooey litter on the floor. "I'll go down to the kitchen and tell Mrs. Chubb to send up some help."

"I can manage, m'm." Gertie started scooping up more scraps onto the tray. "Just give me a minute or two."

"You'll need to change your frock. The other maids can clean this up for you." Leaving her, Cecily hurried down the hallway.

As she emerged into the lobby, she caught sight of Grace Danbury, who was crossing the floor on her way to the stairs. Taken aback to see her still in day clothes, Cecily called out to her. "Miss Danbury, the carol singing has already started in the library!"

The news no doubt came as little surprise, since the sound of robust voices slightly out of tune floated down the corridor. Feeling somewhat awkward, she added, "I do hope you will be joining us."

Grace shook her head. "Oh, I absolutely couldn't! I have no voice for singing, Mrs. Baxter. Absolutely none. I should only manage to irritate everyone, I'm afraid."

"Oh, you don't have to sing. We have plenty of spirits and good food——" She broke off, remembering the mess on the floor. "Oh, good heavens. I must fly. But do join us. I'm sure you will enjoy it." Noting that Grace was rubbing her hands, she added, "It's a good deal warmer in there than out here in the lobby."

Grace rubbed her arms. "I am rather cold. Perhaps I will come down later."

"Oh, good." With a wave of her hand Cecily sped toward the kitchen steps. Glancing back over her shoulder, she was just in time to see Grace disappearing around the bend in the stairs.

Strange woman, she thought, as she ran down the steps. Not at all the kind of woman she would have thought Madeline would befriend. Then again, they did share a love of biology and Madeline had always been protective of the weak. She really seemed to care for the naive Miss Danbury.

Reaching the kitchen door she put Grace Danbury out of her mind. She needed to get that mess cleaned up before people started leaving the library, or she'd have crushed stuffed eggs all over the lobby, too.

A few minutes later on her way back to the library, she was pleased to see that Gertie had managed to clean up most of the chaos. "Mrs. Chubb is sending up two of the maids with mops and buckets," she told the perspiring young woman. "You can leave this and go to change your dress. By that time the evening will be half over, so if you like you may spend the rest of Christmas Eve with the twins."

Gertie beamed her gratitude. "They'll be so happy to see me, m'm. Thank you ever so much."

"Entirely my pleasure." Cecily smiled back at her. "Do give my godchildren an extra hug from me, and tell them we will look forward to seeing them tomorrow. I've been too busy to spend time with them this week, so it will be very nice to enjoy their company."

Gertie got to her feet and brushed the back of her hand across her forehead. "You might change your mind, m'm, when you see them. They're so bloody excited they can't sit still for a moment."

Cecily laughed. "I'm sure they'll find plenty to occupy them after Father Christmas has paid them a visit."

"Yes, m'm. I certainly hope so."

Something in Gertie's expression made Cecily pause. "Is something wrong?"

"No, m'm, it's just . . ."

Worried now, Cecily insisted. "Just what, Gertie? Please tell me."

"Well, it's this snowman, m'm."

Cecily waited, but her housemaid seemed to be having a problem getting the words out. "Snowman?" she prompted at last.

"Yes, m'm. The one out by the rockery. I think."

"I don't think I've seen a snowman out there. Did the twins build it?"

"I think so, m'm. At least, I saw them talking to it. I haven't had time to ask them but I will tonight."

Cecily nodded. "Well, don't worry, Gertie. I don't mind if the twins build a snowman on the grounds. It will actually add to the Christmas atmosphere, don't you think?"

"Yes, m'm, but . . ." Once more Gertie's voice trailed off.

"What is it, Gertie?"

"I know this sounds daft, but . . ." Gertie paused again then finished in a rush, ". . . it keeps moving, m'm."

"Moving?"

"Yes, m'm."

"I don't think I understand."

"Nor do I, m'm. I saw it first by the bowling greens, and then Pansy says as how it were over by the tennis courts and then this morning it were by the rockery and now it's disappeared altogether. I can't see it anywhere."

Cecily raised her eyebrows. "You must be seeing different snowmen."

"No, m'm. It's the same one. I know it is. It's moving about."

Cecily frowned. "Someone is playing a joke on you, I think."

Gertie looked unconvinced. "Yes, m'm. I reckon you're right about that. Right then. I'll get off now, thank you very much."

"Enjoy your evening." She watched the housemaid disappear around the corner, then made her way to the library. Gertie's behavior worried her. Perhaps they were working that young woman too hard. It had to be difficult raising two young children on her own as well as working so much of the time.

True, she had a competent nanny in Daisy, who was once a maid at the Pennyfoot before taking over the duty of caring for Gertie's twins. Still, a mother needed to spend time with her little ones. She would have to see that Gertie had a little more time off, once the Christmas season was over.

Arriving at the library door she realized the singing had ceased. No doubt the musicians, a string quartet provided by Phoebe, were taking a break. Phoebe had orchestrated various events at the Pennyfoot for years and was, in fact, in charge of the arrangements for Madeline's wedding.

Cecily had been astonished that Madeline had allowed her such a responsible task. Then again, Madeline's tongue was often sharper than her convictions. Although she pretended that Phoebe annoyed and irritated her no end, underneath all that animosity she harbored a genuine affection for the colonel's wife.

Thinking of the colonel reminded Cecily that she had left him in a less than stable mood. Glancing around, she was relieved to see the gentleman snoozing in a corner armchair. No doubt the several brandies he most likely had consumed had taken effect.

Phoebe was seated at his side, talking to one of the lady guests. Judging by the way she was inscribing arcs in the air with her hands, she seemed to be thoroughly enjoying the conversation.

Over by the window, Baxter stood talking to Emily and Charles Winchester, and Cecily hurried over to join them. The doctor turned as she approached, inclining his head in a slight bow. "Delightful evening, Mrs. Baxter. Most enjoyable. The carol singing is quite lovely."

"I'm so glad you are having a good time, Dr. Winchester." Cecily smiled at Emily. "How are you this evening, Mrs. Winchester?"

"I think we can dispense with the formalities," Charles said, capturing her attention again. "If we may call you Cecily?"

"Please do." She looked back at him. He was a handsome man in a dark sort of way. Though his eyes were the lightest of blue. They reminded her somewhat of her husband's, which were gray, but could be just as sharp and penetrating at times.

Emily kept her face turned down, and Cecily suspected she had been shedding tears, judging by the puffiness around her eyes.

Immediately sympathetic, she laid a hand on the woman's arm and felt it trembling beneath her fingers. "My dear," she said softly. "I'm so sorry about your friends. You have suffered such a loss. I sincerely hope this won't make your Christmas here unbearable."

"Not at all," Charles said briskly. "It is sad and unfortunate, and all that, but life must go on." He grasped his wife's arm and gave it a little shake. "Isn't that right, my precious?"

Emily nodded, but still didn't look up. "I feel rather weary," she said, her voice barely above a whisper. "I think I'd like to retire for the evening."

"Is there something I can get for you?" Cecily moved aside to let her pass. "A nightcap, perhaps? Some warm milk with a pot of brandy?"

"Thank you, but no. I shall go to bed and try to sleep." She looked up at her husband, but he avoided her gaze.

"You go on ahead, my love," he said, giving her a slight push. "I'll be up in a little while."

She nodded, whispered "Good night," and threaded her way through the crowd to the door.

"Will she be all right?" Cecily watched her leave. "She seems very fragile."

"She's upset, of course," Charles said, patting the pocket of his waistcoat. "The Hethertons were close acquaintances and to die in that manner was utterly shocking."

"Oh, good Lord." Baxter nodded over to the corner, where the colonel was struggling to get out of his seat. "I'd better get over there and escort that gentleman to the door, before he mistakes us all for an army of marauders."

Left alone with the doctor, Cecily said carefully, "I understand you knew the victims quite well."

The doctor's mouth seemed to tighten a little. "Yes, fairly well, I suppose. My wife and Lady Clara were quite close friends."

"I'm sorry." Cecily paused. "I imagine Sir Walter will be sorely missed in London."

Charles grunted. "I don't know about that. I understand he wasn't too popular, especially with some members of Commons. Take that chap over there." He nodded at a group of people over by the fireplace. "That Crossley chap. Doesn't seem too broken-hearted, does he."

Watching Roland Crossley throw back his head with a loud guffaw, Cecily had to agree. "I suppose there will always be a certain amount of animosity between some members of the House of Commons and the House of Lords."

"Too right." Charles's steely gaze cut across the room. "I heard Crossley sounding off the first night we arrived. He'd just heard that Hetherton was staying here, and he made it very clear he wasn't happy about it."

"Did he say why?"

Charles switched his gaze back to her, giving her a slight chill, for some reason.

Behind that cold mask she could sense intense emotions being held in check. Having spent a good amount of her life trying to read people's thoughts, she felt quite certain that Charles Winchester was hiding something that caused him a great deal of turmoil. She suspected his torment had something to do with his wife. It would be a shame to see the marriage of such an apparently well-suited couple in jeopardy.

"He said something about Hetherton striking down two bills that Crossley had introduced." Charles frowned. "A land act for one, from what I remember, and one concerning payment for members. Actually, Crossley's right on that score. An MP should be paid for the work he does."

Cecily was inclined to agree. "So Mr. Crossley was upset at Sir Walter?"

"Rightly so. Hetherton was a pompous ass, completely biased when it came to bills from the Commons. Looked down on the lot of them, and wouldn't let anything pass unless it was in his own interest. From what I understand, Crossley is working on another bill to take away the rights from the House of Lords to strike down any bills. If it passes, all they would be able to do is delay them for a year at the most."

Cecily raised her eyebrows. "That's quite an ambitious bill."

Charles smiled, though she could see no humor in his cold gaze. "One that has a much better chance of passing now that Hetherton is out of the picture."

Cecily was about to speak when she was interrupted by the quartet launching into a spirited version of "The Holly and the Ivy." As voices all around her raised in chorus, she excused herself and went in search of Baxter.

She found him in the bar, where he was attempting to persuade Colonel Fortescue to refrain from drinking the large brandy he had in front of him.

Pausing in the doorway, Cecily beckoned to her husband.

After leaning across the bar to give instructions to the barman, he joined her at the door. "Not another calamity, I hope?"

"Not as far as I know." She pulled his sleeve to draw him out into the corridor. "I need to talk to you. Right away. In my office."

He looked about to protest, but she turned before he could give her an argument and headed down the hallway. After a moment's hesitation, he followed her.

Once inside her office she closed the door and sat down behind her desk.

"This doesn't have anything to do with the Hethertons, does it?" Baxter demanded.

Cecily sighed. Her husband knew her too well. "I haven't

said anything to you earlier, because I knew what you would say," she began. "But now I feel I must speak up, and you should know what I have found out."

Groaning, Baxter sunk onto a chair. "All right, I'll listen. But don't expect me to agree with anything you might suggest."

She pulled a face at him. "Really, Bax, you can be quite tiresome at times."

"No doubt, but it's always for good reason. You have a vexing habit of causing me concern for your safety. I have a nasty feeling that this is one of those times."

"Piffle. You haven't even heard one word and already you are jumping to conclusions."

"Can you blame me?"

Again she puffed out a sigh. "Just listen to what I have to say and then you can pass judgement." She then proceeded to tell him about the cracker wrappings Samuel had found, Kevin's discourse on how to load a cracker with a lethal substance, and her conversation with Dr. Winchester. When she had finished, she sat back and waited for his reaction.

He didn't speak for several long seconds, while the only sound in the room was the ticking of her clock and the faint chorus of "We Three Kings."

Finally he stirred, and gave her a grave look. "I'm not sure what to make of all this, Cecily, but one thing I do know. If what you suspect is true, we could once more have a dangerous killer within these walls. I must insist, however, that you do nothing until P.C. Northcott returns."

"But he won't be back until after New Year's Day."

"There is an alternative." He paused, as if knowing how she would react. "You could inform Inspector Cranshaw of your suspicions and let him deal with it."

"No!" She stood up. "I won't have that man poking around here unless it's absolutely unavoidable. You know how he feels about the Pennyfoot. He's always looking for an excuse to shut us down. I wouldn't be surprised if he accepted Sam Northcott's conclusion that the explosion was caused by a gas leak, just so he can declare us unsafe to continue business."

"Nonsense." Baxter had risen with her, and he headed for the door. "I admit, the man doesn't bother to hide his disapproval of the Pennyfoot, but he is a policeman, and as such is bound to follow up on any suspicious circumstances."

"Well, he won't get the chance on this one. Not if I can help it."

"You don't even have a viable suspect at this point."

"I have someone with a motive."

"Just because Roland Crossley stands to gain something by Sir Walter's death doesn't necessarily mean that he killed the man."

"He certainly had a good reason. Who else had reason to want him dead?"

"I don't know. But from what I've heard, Sir Walter wasn't exactly a cherished member of society. I'm quite sure there must be plenty of people who would like to see him removed from office."

"All of whom are staying at the Pennyfoot, I presume."

Baxter glared at her for several moments. "All right, so what do you suggest I do? Even if you are right, and I don't see how you can possibly ascertain that at this stage, we can't detain the man. Even the inspector couldn't do that without some kind of proof."

"Exactly. Which is why we must find the proof."

"You know how I feel about you delving into matters like this on your own. You certainly know how the constabulary feels about you interfering in its business. Especially Inspector Cranshaw. Need I say more?"

"I'll be careful."

He rolled his eyes at the ceiling. "How many times have I heard you say that?"

"I give you my word I will be careful."

All at once it seemed as if all the air seeped out of him. His shoulders slumped, and the look he gave her was full of appeal. "I know you well enough to know that nothing I can say will dissuade you, so I will say only this. Can we at least have Christmas Day before you start causing all sorts of havoc, and please, if you value my sanity, do not do anything reckless without coming to me for help."

As usual, it had been a hard-won battle, and in her victory she would have promised him anything. "I wouldn't dream of it, Bax, dear."

He muttered a fierce, "Hrrmmph!" then pushed open the door and left.

Sinking onto her chair, Cecily folded her hands on the desk and stared at them as she went over her conversations with the two doctors.

Charles had mentioned that Roland Crossley was surprised to learn that Sir Walter was staying at the Pennyfoot. So if he were the killer, it would seem that she was correct in assuming that using the Christmas cracker as a weapon was an impromptu decision.

That being the case, Mr. Crossley would need time to purchase the chemicals and combine them into the deadly compound. His wife would surely know if he had been missing for a certain amount of time. She must have a word with her.

Opening the heavy ledger on her desk, she ran her finger down the page until it almost reached the bottom. There it was. Sarah Crossley. Sarah. That was her name.

Cecily closed the ledger with a snap, and stood up. There was still time. She had promised Baxter Christmas Day, but it was not yet Christmas and judging by the voices wafting down the hallway, several people were still in the library. She might just have a chance to have that conversation with the MP's wife before they retired for the night.

Gathering up the hem of her gown, she skirted her desk and hurried to the door.

# CHAPTER
## 8

"If I've told you once I've told you a hundred times." Gertie folded her arms and stared at each of her twins in turn. "Father Christmas won't come unless you are both sound asleep. So if you want to find toys in your pillowcases tomorrow, you'd better get into bed this minute and go to sleep."

James got up from the floor, leaving crayons scattered all over the carpet. The book he'd been coloring had a page torn in half, and the remnant lay crumpled up at his feet. "I want to see the reindeer!"

Lillian jumped up, spilling her malted milk down her apron. "Me, too! Me, too!"

Gertie sat on the edge of Lillian's bed and folded her arms. "All right, then, you can see the reindeer. But then, like I said, you'll be awake and Father Christmas won't leave you any toys."

The twins looked at each other, obviously struggling with

this difficult choice. Finally James mumbled, "All right. I'll go to bed."

"Me, too." Lillian climbed up on the bed and snuggled into Gertie's arm. "Tell us a story, please Mama?"

"Yeah!" James bounced up beside her. "Tell us about the snowman!"

Taken off guard, Gertie stared at him. She'd put off asking them about the snowman. It all seemed so ridiculous when she thought about it, and it had occurred to her that maybe she was imagining things. Or maybe madam was right and someone was playing a joke on her. If so, she'd have their bloody guts for garters.

"Yes, Mama." Lillian leaned in closer. "Tell us a story about a snowman."

"Like the one outside," James added.

Deciding that she needed to settle this once and for all, Gertie smiled at him. "You mean the one you built?"

The twins looked at each other. "We didn't build it, Mama," Lillian said earnestly. "It was already there when we went out to play."

"It was? Who built it, then?" Gertie looked hopefully at her son.

James shrugged. "Dunno."

"It likes to go for walks," Lillian said.

Gertie felt sick. "Snowmen don't walk about," she said sharply. "They can't move."

"This one can." Jamie lifted his chin. "It talks as well. So there."

Thoroughly shaken now, Gertie frowned at him. "Don't you talk to your mother in that tone of voice." She looked down at her daughter. "Tell me the truth, Lillian. The snowman can't talk, can he."

Lillian wrinkled her forehead. "The one outside can talk and whistle," she said. "Like this." She pursed her lips, but only managed to blow out air.

"Like this," James said. He pulled in a breath, then whistled a few notes.

Gertie went cold. James had been out of tune, but she recognized the refrain instantly. She should—she'd heard that melody a million times. It had been whistled up and down the hallways of the Pennyfoot years ago . . . by the man who had fathered her twins. Ian Rossiter.

Cecily was pleased to see that the Crossleys were still in the library, though the room had emptied out quite a bit. There was no sign of Phoebe or her colonel, and Cecily assumed they had left for home. It was only then that she realized Madeline and Kevin had not attended the gathering.

That worried her a great deal. Madeline hadn't missed a Christmas Eve at the Pennyfoot in all the years Cecily had known her. It was not like her friends to simply fail to appear without some word of explanation.

Concerned that something might have happened to them on their way to the Pennyfoot, Cecily toyed with the idea of asking Samuel to trace their journey from Madeline's house. Then she remembered she had given him the rest of the evening off to give his itching hands a chance to respond to the medicine Kevin had prescribed.

The footmen had already been dismissed for the day, and only the maids remained to clean up the library once all the guests had departed.

Deciding she would have to wait until the morning for news of her friends, Cecily made her way across the room to where Sarah Crossley sat talking to a rather pinched-face woman.

Having momentarily forgotten the other woman's name, Cecily smiled at both ladies, saying, "I do hope you both enjoyed the ceremony?"

Sarah Crossley's companion sniffed constantly into a delicate lace handkerchief, and failed to answer. Sarah, however, answered for them both. "Absolutely delightful, Mrs. Baxter! As always. I do love to hear the singing of carols. It makes for such a festive evening."

"Yes, indeed." Cecily addressed the other woman. "Are you ailing? I can have my housekeeper make up a hot toddy for you if you like. It does wonders for a cold."

"Oh, no, thank you, Mrs. Baxter." The woman rose, her cheeks warming. "It's not a cold. For some strange reason, whenever I'm close to a Christmas tree, my eyes start watering and my nose won't stop running. Do forgive me. I think I will retire to my room."

It was too bad Madeline wasn't there, Cecily thought, as she watched the woman leave. Her friend would have had an instant remedy for the poor soul.

"I think I will depart as well." Sarah Crossley struggled out of her chair. Like her husband, she was a rather robust woman, and had difficulty getting to her feet. "Roland retired to the bar some time ago. I hope he hasn't consumed too much of your excellent spirits. It tends to make him snore so and then I can't sleep a wink."

Cecily closed her mind to the vision of Sarah lying next to her snoring husband. "It must be difficult for you to spend much time with Mr. Crossley," she said, barring the woman's path to the door. "His work must keep him well occupied."

"Quite so." Sarah looked over at the door in a rather pointed way.

Ignoring her, Cecily blithely continued, "So nice that the two of you can get away from the city at this time of the year. You must really enjoy having so much precious time to spend together."

"Well, I don't know about that." Sarah was beginning to look put out. "The very day after we arrived he spent the entire day hunting. He's planning on going again on Boxing Day. I understand it's a tradition at the Pennyfoot."

"Yes, it is." Cecily beamed at her. "The men seem to enjoy

it, and the woman usually gather together in the library to play a few hands of cribbage. I'm sure they would be delighted if you would join them."

"Thank you, Mrs. Baxter. I think I might do that." Sarah edged sideways in an effort to pass by her.

Sliding in front of her again, Cecily said brightly, "Someone told me your husband had a scientific background. Is that right?"

Sarah seemed taken aback by the comment. "Well, yes, he does, actually. Before he got into politics he was a technical engineer. As a matter of fact, he helped design the first motor cars. Rather crude by today's standards, but at the time he was considered quite brilliant."

It had been a rather clumsy attempt to get the information she needed, but much to Cecily's surprise and gratification, it had actually worked. Until that moment, she hadn't had a clue whether or not Roland Crossley had any kind of scientific background.

Flushed with triumph, she gushed, "I'm so impressed. How utterly fascinating. He must have had a formidable education for such an important vocation."

Sarah seemed to have forgotten her desire to leave. Obviously pleased by Cecily's interest in her husband's achievements, she was more than ready to oblige with the details.

"Oh, indeed. His father was quite wealthy, you know. Made his money in America. He was helping to build the railroad when he found gold. He returned home at once and bought a very nice piece of land in the Cotswolds. That's where Roland grew up. After leaving boarding school he attended King's. One of the few colleges offering chemistry and science at the time."

"I hear it's an excellent college."

"So it is. I often think Roland would never have attempted politics if it hadn't been for the education he received there."

"He must be extremely upset by the death of Sir Walter Hetherton. I imagine they were colleagues?"

Sarah's expression changed to one of wariness. "My husband didn't much care for the gentleman. Nevertheless, he is saddened by the death. No one likes to see a colleague struck down in such an unfortunate accident."

"It was most distressing for all of us." Cecily longed to tell the woman that it was not the fault of her gas lamp, but held her tongue. As long as the killer was unaware that foul play was suspected, he would remain off guard, which could help in her enquiries.

"I really must retire now," Sarah said firmly, and rather rudely pushed Cecily to one side so she could make her way to the door.

Watching her leave, Cecily wondered how soon it would be before she could search the Crossley's room. According to Madeline, in whose infallible talents she had no doubt, one cracker was still missing. Once she found its hiding place, she could very well have the proof she needed.

Christmas Day dawned cold and clear, with the sun gleaming on freshly fallen snow. The sloping lawns looked like icing on a Christmas cake, smooth and glistening. Cecily stopped to admire the sight from the dining room windows before making her way to her office, where she immediately rung Kevin's office.

She really hadn't expected him to be there, but he answered her at once, his voice sounding quite unlike his usual cheerful tone.

Alarmed, she said quickly, "Cecily here. Is anything wrong?"

He sounded wary when he answered. "What precisely do you mean by wrong? Happy Christmas, by the way."

"Oh, Kevin, I'm sorry. Happy Christmas to you, too. I was just concerned. You sounded a little despondent, and you and Madeline didn't come to the carol singing last night and now you are in your office on Christmas morning. . . ."

"Nothing's wrong, Cecily. At least, nothing that can't eventually be put right, I trust."

Fearing the worst, Cecily spoke with care. "Has it to do with Madeline?"

There was a long pause, then he answered gruffly, "Your friend can, at times, be quite intolerable."

"Oh, dear, I was afraid of that." She hesitated, then added, "It's only wedding nerves, Kevin. You are both sensitive people who are marrying late in life. It's only natural you would both have misgivings. Just remember how much you adore Madeline. Is it worth losing all that because of a little disagreement?"

"It's not a little disagreement, Cecily. We disagree on just about everything. So much so that last night Madeline told me she'd changed her mind about marrying me."

Cecily sighed. "I love you both dearly, and I will not allow you to destroy a wonderful life together before its even begun. I must insist you share Christmas dinner with us this afternoon, as we planned. We are having it served in our suite so it will be nice and private. Perhaps we can sort out what it is that's worrying Madeline so."

"I doubt if she'll listen to anyone, much less come with me to have dinner with you."

"Ask her to do it for me. Tell her it's vitally important to me that she come."

"You think she'll believe that?"

"It's the truth, Kevin. I really need her to come this afternoon."

After another long pause he said heavily, "Very well. I'll convey your message to her. But don't put the blame on me if she refuses to come."

Cecily hung up, a frown furrowing her brow. Madeline had taken so long to agree to marry Kevin. During that time she'd had many doubts and had, in fact, parted company with him on occasion. Yet always she had gone back to him, and Cecily had no doubt that her friend was very much in love with the handsome doctor.

Then again, Madeline was supremely independent, and it would take a strong, wise and gentle man to keep her happy and contented. Cecily had no doubt that Kevin was that man, and she was quite sure that Madeline also knew it.

Somehow she had to get her dear friend through the next week and safely married. After that, it would be up to them both to settle their differences.

Knowing Madeline, though, Cecily was quite sure that once married, she would do everything in her power to make a success of it. All Cecily had to do was get her to the altar.

"It's coincidence, that's all." Mrs. Chubb banged her rolling pin on the board to shake off the excess flour. "I've heard that tune your Ian used to whistle a hundred times. So has Michel. Haven't you, Michel?"

Gertie switched her gaze to the chef, who had his head in the oven basting the sizzling roast beef. "Not since he left," he said over his shoulder. "Why are these Yorkshire puddings so flat, Gertie? You did not beat them enough, *non*?"

"I beat them until my bleeding wrist fell off." Gertie glared at his back. "If you keep opening the bloody oven door of course they're going to go flat."

Michel straightened and scowled at her. "Are you telling me how to cook my puddings? You know better than Michel, the famous French chef, how to cook ze Yorkshire puddings?"

"French chef, my blinking arse. You're about as French as that beef in the oven." Gertie tossed her head. "Anyhow, Yorkshire puddings are English, so what's that flipping got to do with French cooking?"

"Quiet, you two." Mrs. Chubb banged her rolling pin louder. "It's Christmas Day. Can't you get along for at least one day in the year?"

Turning away, Gertie muttered, "All right, all right. Are them potatoes done? I have to get them mashed. They've almost finished the fish course in the dining room."

Mrs. Chubb peered at her. "Don't let them twins upset you, Gertie. They're excited about Christmas, that's all. Did they like all their toys?"

Still unsettled by the memory of James whistling the familiar tune, Gertie nodded. "Got me up before dawn this morning, they did. At least Daisy will have an easy day with them today. They'll keep themselves amused all day with all their new things, I reckon."

"I'm looking forward to seeing the twins at the staff dinner tonight." Mrs. Chubb smiled.

"Madam said she'd stop by and see them this afternoon." Gertie pulled a large, steaming pot off the stove and carried it to the sink. "They'll like that. They don't see too much of her anymore." Tipping up the pot, she held the lid against it and allowed the hot water to pour through the gap.

"She keeps busy, that's for sure." Mrs. Chubb started rolling out pastry dough. "What about Mr. Baxter? Is he visiting the twins as well?"

"I hope so." Gertie cut butter into the strained potatoes, then picked up the masher. She was anxious now to start serving. So far Pansy had done all the serving, but it took two of them to serve the main course. Once that was done she could relax a bit, and maybe even get off for a while so she could spend some time with the twins.

"I'm ready to carve," Michel announced. He picked up the carving knife and ran his finger down the blade. "Where are those maids with the dirty dishes?"

Just as he spoke the door flew open and one by one the three maids rushed in with trays full of dishes. Pansy brought up the rear, panting a little as she carried the heavy tray over to the sink.

"Tables are cleared," she announced, sounding breathless. "They're ready for the main course."

The next few minutes were taken up with a flurry of activity as Gertie helped the maids drain vegetables and pile them into the individual serving dishes. Then, with a nod at Pansy, she whipped off her overall and headed for the door.

The maids were already stacking the warm plates and hot dishes into the dumbwaiter, and Gertie needed to be in the hallway outside the dining room before the lift got up there so she could grab the food before it got cold.

With Pansy hot on her heels she ran up the stairs, across the lobby and down the hallway. Pulling open the door, she grabbed a couple of serving dishes and then sailed into the dining room to deposit them on the tables.

Back and forth she and Pansy went, until the last load came up on the waiter. Having placed a large plate of sliced beef in the center of the last table, Gertie reached for a vegetable dish that had already been emptied.

Straightening, she turned to leave. Her glance fell on the closest window, and out of the corner of her eye she saw something move.

Frozen in shock, she stared at the white face pressed close to the glass. A glassy face made of snow, with two staring black eyes and a carrot for a nose.

With a shrill shriek she dropped the dish, unheeding as it crashed to the floor while her gaze locked on the face of the snowman.

# CHAPTER
## ❀ 9 ❀

Cecily heard Gertie's scream from out in the hallway, and immediately rushed into the dining room to find her chief housemaid sprawled on the floor in a dead faint.

Fortunately, she had just greeted Kevin and a rather morose Madeline, and the doctor was right behind her as she leaned over Gertie.

Some of the guests also crowded around to see what had happened, and Kevin ushered them back to their seats before attending to his patient.

After a quick examination, he picked the housemaid up in his arms and carried her past the tables to the hallway outside.

Cecily was impressed, since Gertie was no lightweight, and although the doctor grunted as he passed through the doorway, he seemed to have no trouble carrying the sturdy young woman to the library.

Someone must have summoned the housekeeper, as she

appeared at the door just as Kevin laid Gertie on the davenport. "Oh my, oh my," she kept saying over and over.

"Don't worry." Kevin opened his bag and gave her a small bottle. "She's fainted, that's all. Try waving this under her nose. If she hasn't come around in a few minutes then come and find me."

"I will, doctor, thank you." With a worried frown Mrs. Chubb took the bottle from him and hurried over to where Gertie still lay with her eyes closed.

Cecily followed him out into the hallway. "Will she be all right?"

"She's as strong as an ox. A little faint won't hurt her. I'm just curious to know what caused it."

"Pansy was in the dining room at the same time. I shall ask her if she knows what happened."

Kevin nodded. "Good. Meanwhile I'd better find Madeline before she changes her mind about having dinner here and decides to leave."

Cecily watched him stride away, dismayed that apparently he had not resolved the problem with Madeline. If things didn't improve between them fairly soon, the wedding could indeed be called off. And that would be disastrous for both of them.

"Gertie? Open your eyes, there's a luv." The sound of Mrs. Chubb's voice was accompanied by a sharp, bitter smell that made Gertie's nose run. Slowly she forced her eyes open and saw the housekeeper's worried face staring down at her.

"She's coming around," Mrs. Chubb said, as another figure moved into Gertie's vision.

"Oh, thank goodness," Pansy said, sounding scared.

Gertie sat up, surprised to see she was in the library on madam's best brocade davenport. "What happened?"

"You fainted." Mrs. Chubb shook her head. "I had no idea you were so tired. Why didn't you tell me?"

"I'm not tired." Gertie looked at Pansy. "Did you see it? Right in the window it was, staring at me with those bloody black eyes."

Pansy looked confused. "I didn't see nothing."

"You must have bloody seen it!"

"I didn't. Really I didn't."

Gertie struggled to get up but the housekeeper laid a hand on her arm. "Sit there for a minute or two until you get your head back on right."

"It was the snowman." Gertie clutched Mrs. Chubb's arm. "I saw it again. It was right there in the window staring at me. Its face was pressed right up to the glass." She shuddered. "Bloody horrible, it was. Like looking at a ghost."

Seeing the disbelief on both their faces, she felt a moment of panic. "I'm not imagining things, honest. It was really there. I really saw it."

"There, there." Mrs. Chubb patted her arm. "Calm down, there's a good girl. Let's get you back to the kitchen and I'll have Michel pour you a drop of his good brandy. That'll make you feel better."

"I'm not going to feel better until I know who's trying to scare the bloody daylights out of me."

Mrs. Chubb looked even more worried. "Well, all I can say is that if there really was a snowman out there, whoever's moving that thing around is going to a lot of trouble."

"Someone's trying to frighten me, that's for sure." Gertie swung her legs over the side of the davenport and planted her feet on the carpet. "Just wait until I get hold of the bugger. I'll bloody tear him apart with me bare hands, so help me I will."

"Pansy, get on down to the kitchen and have them start serving the plum pudding and mince pies. Gertie and me will be down in a minute or two."

"Yes, Mrs. Chubb." After another scared glance in Gertie's direction, Pansy fled from the room.

"I'd better get cracking, too." Gertie got unsteadily to her feet. "Pansy can't do all that on her own."

"It's not like you to faint." Mrs. Chubb peered closer into her face. "Are you sure you're all right, Gertie? You're not hiding something from me, are you?"

Touched by her concern, Gertie gave her a shaky smile. "I'm as fit as a bleeding spring lamb, so don't you go fretting over me. I'm not Ross, you know. I'm not going to keel over the way he did."

"I certainly hope not."

"I'd just like to know who's trying to scare me to death, that's all."

"It may not be you he's trying to scare."

Gertie stared at her. "Watcha mean?"

"It could be someone trying to scare the guests. To make trouble for the Pennyfoot. What with that lamp blowing up and all. There's all these hotels going up along the coast now. I wonder if it's someone trying to get rid of the competition. Remember when something like that happened before?"

"Yeah." Gertie nodded. "It could be that, all right." She tried not to think about the tune James had whistled. "We should have a word with madam about it."

"I will do that." Mrs. Chubb took her arm. "Do you feel well enough to come back downstairs now?"

"Course I do." Unwilling to admit her knees felt shaky, Gertie allowed the housekeeper to lead her down the hallway.

She wanted to think that the roaming snowman was the work of a vindictive competitor. But somehow she kept hearing that same tune echoing inside her head, and she couldn't help wondering if her ex-boyfriend had somehow died, and the snowman was really his ghost—coming back to make her life miserable again.

Thinking about boyfriends reminded her of Dan. She didn't want to think about Dan right now, really she didn't. Yet there he was, right there in her mind, smiling at her with those crinkly eyes of his that always made her feel warm inside.

A wave of pain hit her, so deep she had to fold her arms across her stomach.

Mrs. Chubb paused, grabbing her arm. "Gertie, are you all right? Shall I fetch the doctor again?"

"No, no, I'm all right." She shook her head fiercely, in an effort to banish Dan from her mind. "It's just indigestion, that's all. All the excitement and everything. It's gone away now, honest it has."

Mrs. Chubb peered anxiously at her, then, apparently satisfied, let go of her.

Gertie let out her breath. She'd said the first thing that came to mind and Chubby had swallowed it. Which was good, for how could she have explained that the pain she felt was all in her head, and all because she was never going to see Dan's lovely face again?

"I asked everyone in the ballroom," Cecily said, as she handed a dish of mashed potatoes to Madeline. "No one seems to know what happened to make Gertie faint."

"It could just be exhaustion." Kevin reached for his glass and took a sip of the excellent claret. "Though Mrs. Chubb tells me that when Gertie recovered she was mumbling something about a snowman."

Cecily felt a twinge of misgiving. "She mentioned something about a snowman to me earlier. She seemed to think it was moving about. I told her someone was playing a joke on her, but now I wonder . . ."

Kevin gave her a sharp glance. "Wonder what?"

"I wonder if she's having some kind of hallucinations."

Kevin frowned. "It's possible. If so, we shall have to find out the cause. Tell her to come and see me at my surgery on her next afternoon off."

"I'll do that." Cecily frowned. "Though, come to think of

it, she did mention that Pansy had seen the snowman, too. I'll have another word with that young lady later. When I spoke to her earlier, she had no idea what had caused Gertie to faint. I even questioned some of the guests, but they all said the same thing. They saw nothing that would have upset her so."

"Well, let me know if Pansy tells you anything useful." Kevin glanced at Madeline, who hadn't said a word since she'd sat down. Which obviously bothered Baxter, as he kept sending furtive glances to her end of the table.

"Madeline!" Cecily said brightly. "You haven't taken any Brussels sprouts. I know they are your favorite vegetable."

Madeline turned her unhappy face toward Cecily. "Oh, I didn't see them."

"Here you are, my love." Kevin handed her the dish, and she took it from him without meeting his gaze.

Seriously troubled now, Cecily promised herself she'd have a word with her friend as soon as they were alone. In an effort to take the doctor's attention away from his dejected betrothed, she asked, "Have the relatives of the Hethertons arrived yet to claim the bodies?"

"As a matter of fact, that's why I was in the surgery when you rang this morning." Kevin dragged his gaze away from Madeline. "I met the Hetherton's son to make arrangements. He's taking the deceased back to London by train the day after tomorrow."

Cecily sighed. "He must be devastated. Such a tragedy, and such a particularly awful time for it to happen."

"I don't think I told you." Kevin reached for a buttered roll. "The actual explosion didn't kill Sir Walter. Not directly, anyway. He died from a heart attack."

"Oh, my goodness." Cecily laid a hand at her throat. "What about Lady Clara?"

"She definitely was killed by the explosion." Kevin tore off a piece of the roll with his teeth. "Her lungs were scorched by the force of it and—"

"I say, old chap." Baxter's voice cut off the doctor's. "Do you think we could postpone the lurid details until after we have finished the meal?"

Cecily winced as her husband's steely gaze sliced across her face. "I'm so sorry, darling. I wasn't thinking. Let's talk about something brighter, shall we? Such as the wedding?" She looked hopefully at Madeline, and received a reproachful frown from her friend.

"I prefer not to discuss that right now," Madeline muttered. "Please pass the gravy."

Kevin grabbed the gravy boat and handed it to her, while Cecily let out a heavy sigh. Someone had better do something soon to solve matters, or she was very much afraid that Madeline would remain alone the rest of her life.

The following morning Cecily was dismayed when she woke up to see snow falling thick and fast past her window. She stood for a while overlooking the lawns, watching the lacy flakes fall silently onto the laden branches of the oak trees. This would cause problems for the Boxing Day hunt, no doubt.

She always felt sorry for the birds when it snowed, wondering how they would find food when everything was buried beneath a frozen mantle. She would have to ask Mrs. Chubb to scatter crumbs out for them.

Uttering a sigh, she had to acknowledge that her melancholy had nothing to do with the inconvenienced hunters or the hungry birds. It seemed that this Christmas had been plagued with more problems than ever.

First and foremost, there was the question of who had given that lethal cracker to the Hethertons. Equally disturbing was the matter of the other missing cracker and the questions it raised. Why had the killer taken two crackers, and what did he intend to do with the second one?

She must find a way to search the Crossley's room that very

morning, since he seemed such a likely suspect. Then, if she found the second cracker there, she could present the inspector with a fait accompli and he would be forced to close the case as quickly as possible, thereby avoiding a lengthy and unpleasant investigation.

Her chief housemaid's apparent mental problems also greatly disturbed her. Quickly she scanned the horizon but could see no sign of the infamous migrating snowman.

Gertie was usually supremely confident and capable, and was the last person Cecily would have expected to have any kind of emotional upset. She would have to get to the bottom of that. A word with Pansy seemed in order, and as soon as possible.

Then there was the problem between Kevin and Madeline. She had been unable to corner her friend alone last night, and the two of them had left still with that air of discord separating them. Cecily hated to see that, and she intended to waste no time tackling Madeline on the subject.

All in all, a depressing day lay ahead of her.

She was about to turn away from the window when two strong arms closed around her. "Why so pensive, my love? You are not still worrying about Gertie, are you?"

"That, and a few other things." She turned in Baxter's arms and smiled up at him. "The men will be leaving for the hunt very soon. I hope the snow won't make things difficult for them. By the way, I understand Roland Crossley went hunting the day before the explosion."

Baxter's eyes grew wary. "And what, pray, is that supposed to mean?"

She gave him an innocent look. "I was just making a comment, dearest."

He still looked suspicious. "Come now, Cecily. I know you're up to something."

She sighed. "Very well. Kevin said that whoever killed the Hethertons would have had to purchase the chemicals, probably in Wellercombe."

Baxter's frown deepened. "How so? Why couldn't the killer have brought the chemicals with him?"

"We think there's a good possibility that the killer didn't get the idea of doctoring the crackers until after he arrived here. Otherwise he would have brought his own and not used one of ours."

"Well, that's logical, I suppose."

"And since Roland Crossley had a better chance of passing his important and ambitious bill without Hetherton to strike it down, and also the fact that he does have some scientific background—"

"How the devil did you find that out?"

"I talked to his wife. What's more, Roland's father discovered gold while working on the railroad in America. He could well be an expert in explosives and have handed that knowledge down to his son."

Baxter rolled his eyes at the ceiling. "Cecily, you are incorrigible."

"And incredibly resourceful."

"That, too."

"Anyway, Mr. Crossley was supposed to be out hunting the day before the explosion. But what if he went into Wellercombe instead? What if he didn't go hunting at all, but went to purchase the chemicals he needed to put in the cracker?"

Baxter rubbed his chin. "I suppose it's possible. But how are you going to prove it? He's bound to lie if you simply ask him."

"Which is why I need you to talk to the gamekeeper and find out if Mr. Crossley was with the hunting party that day. Discreetly, of course. We don't want him to find out we are spying on him. Heaven knows what he might do."

"Which is precisely why we should report all of this to the inspector."

"When I find the proof, I promise." Cecily grabbed his sleeve. "Please, Bax. Just do what I ask and talk to the gamekeeper."

Baxter's scowl gradually faded into resignation. "Very well. But I warn you, if there are any repercussions at all, we will go straight to the inspector."

"Of course, dear." She gave him her brightest smile. "I'd suggest going into Wellercombe to talk to the company that sells chemicals, but with this being Christmas week, they won't be open until after New Year's Day. At least we'll know if Mr. Crossley was lying about his hunting trip."

"Very well. Meanwhile, I suggest you have a long talk with Gertie." He let her go and walked over to the door. "That young woman needs some common sense talked into her. Walking snowmen, indeed."

Cecily waited for a few minutes after the door had closed behind him, then gathered up her skirts and stepped out into the hallway. By now Roland would be out hunting, and with any luck, Sarah Crossley would be in the library immersed in a game of cribbage.

Taking the ring of house keys from their hiding place in the hall cupboard, Cecily trod quietly along the soft carpeting to the Crossley's door.

Just to be sure, she tapped lightly on the cherry wood paneling. Another door opened farther down the hallway, and Cecily quickly turned and began walking toward the stairs.

She passed the couple, nodding and smiling as they exchanged greetings. Passing by the top of the stairs, she kept walking toward the steps leading up to the roof garden. As she reached them, she glanced over her shoulder, and was greatly relieved to see the couple had disappeared. Had they not, she would have had to continue on her way. Standing on the roof in the bitter cold was not an appealing prospect.

Retracing her steps, she arrived back at the Crossley's door and quickly fitted the key into the lock. The door swung inward and she slipped inside, carefully closing it behind her.

The room looked neat and tidy. The morning maids had obviously done their work well. Cecily tiptoed across the thick carpet. Experience had taught her that if any of her guests had something to hide, they usually hid it in the wardrobe.

Opening the door, she peered inside. At first glance she could see nothing but clothes, and after moving a muff, hat box and parasol aside, she was assured that the missing cracker was not inside the wardrobe.

A search of the chest of drawers and every drawer in the dresser produced no cracker, nor was it hidden under the bed or in the commode. The trunk in the corner was also empty, as was the coal box next to the fireplace.

Frustrated, Cecily looked around. There was just no other place she could think to look. If Roland Crossley had another cracker in his possession, she was reasonably certain it was not in this room.

Just as she was about to leave, she heard voices in the hallway. A man's voice, and the unmistakable shrill tones of Sarah Crossley.

Cecily didn't stop to think. She dived for the wardrobe, climbed inside and scrunched up into the corner. There was no way she could hide from view, and all she could hope for was that the MP's wife would not need to open the wardrobe door.

She also prayed that Sarah Crossley would not stay for long in the room, since already her legs were cramping from the uncomfortable position she was forced to maintain. Baxter could well be right. Perhaps she *was* getting too old for this kind of behavior.

The inside of the wardrobe smelled of body odor and stale lavender water. Trying her best not to breathe too deeply, Cecily waited. She heard Sarah enter, and the floorboards creaked as the heavy woman crossed the room.

The sound of drawers opening and shutting gave Cecily some concern. She hoped fervently that she had left no sign of her hurried search through the Crossley's unmentionables.

As the seconds ticked by, the pins and needles attacking

her legs intensified until she simply had to stretch them out or she would go quite mad. Just as she could bear the pain no longer, Sarah muttered something aloud, slammed a drawer shut then stomped across the room.

Cecily heard the door close, and made herself wait an excruciating moment or two before slowly opening the door. Sagging in relief she saw the room was empty and thrust out her quivering legs.

Her feet landed on the floor, but she might just as well have sunk into cotton wool, since all feeling in her legs had disappeared. Her bottom hit the floor with a resounding thud.

Staring at the door, Cecily prayed that Sarah had moved far enough away not to have heard the floorboards groan in protest. For if that lady had heard something and returned to investigate, Cecily was incapable of getting to her feet, much less climbing back into the wardrobe.

# CHAPTER

## ❀ 10 ❀

After a lengthy wait fraught with anxiety, Cecily could finally relax in the knowledge that Sarah had most likely returned to the library.

It was several minutes before she regained enough strength in her legs to stand and hobble to the door. Stamping hard on her feet, she managed to alleviate the tingling enough to walk down the hallway in a relatively normal manner, though she had to cling to the bannisters on her way down the stairs.

She reached the bottom just in time to catch sight of Samuel leaving the reception desk. She called out to him, and then drew back in the corner behind the Christmas tree as he hurried toward her.

Breathing deeply to catch her breath, she leaned her back against the wall. She stretched her ankles, hoping to rid herself entirely of the annoying tingling in her toes.

The fragrant smell of pine went a long way toward chasing away the memory of that stuffy wardrobe. Thank heavens Sarah Crossley hadn't looked in there; that would have been quite a predicament.

Samuel appeared at that moment, poking his head around the Christmas tree. "You wanted me, m'm?"

"Yes, Samuel. I need to ask you about the day you took Mr. Crossley to the hunt."

Samuel looked confused. "We took all the gentlemen this morning."

Cecily shook her head. "No, I'm talking about the one a few days ago."

"Oh, that one. No, m'm. The gentleman took his own motor car that day. Said he needed some fresh air and wanted to drive his car to the hunt."

Cecily sighed. She would have to wait for Baxter's report after all.

"It was just as well, anyhow. I had a right busy time of it that day." Samuel pulled his cap from his pocket. "I was taking guests to the hunt, and I had to take Miss Danbury to the station, then when I came back Dr. Winchester needed to go to the station. Then that afternoon I brought back the hunters, and then I had to go back to the station to fetch Dr. Winchester and Miss Danbury. I was running my tail off all day."

Cecily frowned. "You need to get one of the stable lads to help you, Samuel. You shouldn't have to do all that on your own."

"Oh, I wouldn't trust those twerps with the carriage, m'm. They'd put it in the hedge, or run the horses into a motor car. Not too sharp, that lot."

"Well, we'll have to find someone who can handle the horses when we get this busy." Spotting Sarah Crossley heading toward her, she added hastily, "I won't keep you now, Samuel. I'll have a word with Baxter about finding another coachman."

"Yes, m'm. Thank you, m'm." Samuel took off across the lobby, pulling his cap on his head as he went.

Cecily had hoped to avoid the MP's wife, and couldn't imagine how the woman had managed to spot her in the corner. Sarah was already within calling distance, and there didn't seem any way to leave without seeming rude.

"There you are, Mrs. Baxter." Sarah halted in front of her, her ample bosom heaving with the effort to regain her breath. "I wonder if I might trouble you for a moment?"

Worried now, Cecily did her best to smile. "Is something wrong, Mrs. Crossley?"

"Wrong? Oh, no. At least, I certainly hope not." Sarah patted her hair. "No, it's just that I seem to have left home without my hairpins. I was wondering if I might steal some from you."

Relieved that her intrusion into the woman's personal belongings had not been discovered after all, Cecily was only too happy to oblige. "Why, of course! Please, come with me upstairs and I'll give you all you need."

"So good of you." The MP's wife trotted up the stairs, panting and heaving with the exertion. She paused at the top, grasping her throat. "My, those stairs are exhausting. I don't know how you run up and down them as easily as you do."

Reflecting that she had a lot less weight to carry up them, Cecily murmured. "I'm used to them." She led the way down the hallway to her suite and opened the door. "Do come in. I shan't be but a moment."

"Thank you. Awfully good of you." Sarah walked into the room and gazed around. "My, this is certainly a handsome room." Her gaze wandered over to the door leading to the water closet. "Oh, my, don't tell me—is that a personal lavatory? How positively decadent!"

Cecily smiled. "My cousin had it installed when he was supervising the country club. Officially we are still a country club, I suppose, though since Baxter and I returned here the Pennyfoot has been run more or less as it was when it was a hotel."

"Except that now you have a license for gambling."

She looked somewhat disapproving, and Cecily hastened to change the subject. "Ah, here are the pins." She opened the tin and poured some into her hand. "How many do you need?"

"Oh, that will be more than enough. Thank you so much." Sarah took the pins and tucked them into the pocket of her cotton frock. "I must have left my pins at Roland's father's house. We went to visit him before we came here. The poor man is dying I'm afraid. He looked quite poorly when we left."

"Oh, I'm so sorry. That must be a great worry for your husband."

"Oh, it is, indeed." Sarah sat down on an armchair, appearing to be in no hurry to leave. "Roland is particularly bitter, since he has worked so hard to keep that land in good order. Now it seems that the land actually belongs to the crown and he won't be able to claim it upon his father's death. He'll lose all rights to it and the family home."

"Oh, how disappointing for him."

Sarah leaned forward and flapped her hand. "Utterly devastating, my dear. Roland tried to introduce a bill amending all that, but of course it was struck down in the House of Lords."

"Which is why Mr. Crossley wants so much to curtail the powers of the House of Lords."

Sarah nodded. "Exactly." She looked thoughtful. "Of course, now that Sir Walter is no longer with us, my husband might just be successful this time."

*Exactly*, Cecily thought darkly. "I'm sorry, Mrs. Crossley. I don't mean to be rude, but I have some errands to attend to and—"

"Oh, of course, my dear." The other woman rose awkwardly to her feet. "Don't let me detain you a minute longer. And thank you so much for the hairpins."

"Not at all." Cecily accompanied her to the door. "I trust you will be joining the cribbage players?"

"Oh, I already have. Such fun. I'm going back to the library right now and try my hand again. Good day, Mrs. Baxter." With a flurry of rustling silk, she swept from the room.

Cecily shut the door and pulled in a deep breath. It seemed that Roland Crossley had more reason than she'd imagined to get rid of Sir Walter. The more she heard, the more convinced she was that the MP was guilty of murdering the Hethertons. Now she would have to leave it to Baxter to find out what he could from the gamekeeper.

"Gertie, be a luv and fill the coal scuttles for me." Mrs. Chubb rubbed her hands together. "It's getting cold in this kitchen and we need to heat up the ovens before Michel gets back here or there'll be a pretty penny to pay."

Gertie carefully poured salt into a silver saltcellar. "I'm busy. Why can't one of the maids do it?"

"Because they're all busy getting their chores done so they can be finished in time for the Boxing Day ceremony in the ballroom. They can't wait to get their Christmas bonus."

"Well, I'm busy, too." Gertie reached for another saltcellar. "I've got to get these done and back on the dining room tables."

"You have plenty of time to do that. I need the coal now, or do you expect me to go out there myself?"

Gertie sighed and laid down the tin of salt. "All right, I'll go. But don't make a habit of asking me to do the maids' jobs."

Mrs. Chubb gave her a sharp glance. "Still feeling liverish, are we? Maybe you need a dose of cod liver oil."

"What I need is a bleeding holiday." Gertie grabbed the handle of a coal scuttle in each hand and marched to the back door. "All I do is work, work, work. I never see me twins anymore, and I can't remember the last time I went out. Not even for a walk."

The ache came back, deep in her chest. That was a lie. She

remembered the last time only too well. Dan had taken her and the kids on a picnic. It was late in August, a warm, sultry day with just a hint of the thunderstorm to come.

They'd sat on a blanket at the edge of the woods overlooking the downs. Dan had been laughing at the twins trying to turn cartwheels when he'd suddenly turned to her and blurted out that he was moving back to London. He said he was a city boy and couldn't get used to the quiet, boring country life.

Before she really had time to take it in, he asked her to move back there with him. Her and the twins.

James and Lillian came tumbling back to them before she had time to answer him, but for the rest of that afternoon she couldn't think about anything else. At first she was tempted—oh, so tempted—but then the more she thought about it, the more she realized what a mistake it would be.

She told him that night, with lightning flashing and the rumble of thunder drowning out her words. It was the last time she'd seen him.

"You're just feeling the after-Christmas blues."

Mrs. Chubb's voice jolted her out of her memories. "Yeah," she mumbled. "That's what it is, all right. The after-Christmas blues."

The housekeeper opened a cupboard door and peered inside. "It looks like I'll have to order some more serviette rings. I'd like to know what happens to them. This is the third time this year I've had to order more."

Gertie was only half listening as she opened the back door. The bite of the cold winter wind stung her cheeks as she stepped outside. Crunching across the snow, she shivered, cursing herself for forgetting the warm shawl she kept by the door.

The door of the coal shed got stuck when she pulled it open, and she had to kick the icy snow out of the way so she could get inside.

How she hated being in the coal shed. The cold seemed

to bite into her bones, and the windows were so thick with dust she could barely see in the shadowy darkness. The smell of the black coal seemed to fill her nose and throat until she could hardly breathe.

Quickly she shoveled the chunks of gleaming black rock into each scuttle then pushed the door open wide so she could carry them through. As she did so she saw the bulky figure of the maintenance man across the yard.

He stood by the door to the wine cellar, a broom in his hands, and he was watching her.

Her nerves jumped, and she quickly looked away. Hauling the coal scuttles off the ground, she kicked the door of the shed shut with her foot and hurried across the yard to the kitchen door.

Out of the corner of her eye she saw Clive start toward her. Panicking now, she bolted for the door, the scuttles swinging in her hands and bits of coal flying out everywhere. She reached the door and dropped one of the scuttles on the ground, then scrabbled to get the door open and step inside.

Leaning out again, she grabbed the handle of the scuttle to pull it inside. Clive stood in the middle of the yard, not moving at all, just staring at her.

Swearing under her breath, she slammed the door shut. When she turned around, Mrs. Chubb was staring at her, too.

"What's the bleeding matter with everybody," Gertie snapped, dumping the coal scuttles in front of the stove. "Why is everyone staring at me? Have I got flipping horns growing out of me bloody head or something?"

"I was just wondering why you were in such a big hurry." Mrs. Chubb wiped her hands on her apron. "You came in that door as if a herd of bulls was after you."

"It's that bloody Clive. Gives me the bleeding willies, he does. Kept staring at me out there, then he started coming over to me. I had to get out of his way in a hurry."

Mrs. Chubb shook her head. "He probably just wanted to help you carry the coal in. I don't know why you get so jumpy around him. He's harmless enough. Actually I think he's a really nice man."

"Then you can play hide-and-seek with him and maybe he'll leave me alone. Every time I turn around he's out there staring at me."

"Offer your grateful thanks that someone wants to stare at you," Michel said from the doorway. "Why does my kitchen feel like ze north pole?"

"We were just about to stoke up the ovens." Mrs. Chubb gave Gertie a meaningful look. "Weren't we, Gertie."

Scowling, Gertie opened an oven door and shoveled coal inside. "All I can say," she muttered, "is that my Christmas bonus had better be a bleeding good one."

On her way to the Boxing Day ceremony that afternoon, Cecily bumped into Grace Danbury, who was apparently on her way out since she wore a heavy coat and a scarf tying down her hat. "You don't care for cribbage?" Cecily asked her, as the woman paused at the door.

"I'm afraid I don't know the game." Grace tucked a hand inside her coat. The thin silky gloves she wore obviously offered little warmth. "I thought I'd go outside for a breath of fresh air."

"It's really chilly out there." Cecily hesitated. "Would you care to borrow a muff?"

"No, thank you. Actually I have one in my room. I bought it the other day in Wellercombe. I don't like wearing it, though. I find it rather constricting."

Cecily smiled. "Your visit to Wellercombe must have been quite productive."

Grace tightened the scarf under her chin. "I did find a few bargains, yes. It was well worth the effort."

"How nice. You should have brought your friend back to the Pennyfoot with you. We would have been happy to provide her with a meal as your guest."

Grace looked uncomfortable. "My friend had to return to London for the evening. I appreciate the thought, though."

"Well, perhaps another time."

The other woman nodded and slipped out of the door.

Shaking her head, Cecily made her way to the ballroom. Some women would brave the most bitter cold out of sheer pride.

When she entered the ballroom her entire staff had assembled. This was one of her favorite moments of the holiday season—handing out the Christmas bonuses on Boxing Day. It was a tradition that she truly enjoyed—an opportunity to thank her hard-working staff for their loyalty to her, and for holding true to the Pennyfoot Country Club's stellar reputation.

One by one they came forward—the footmen, the maids, the gardeners, Pansy and Gertie, Michel and Mrs. Chubb, Clive and Samuel. As she handed each a box of nuts and fruit with pound notes tucked inside, she thanked them all for their service and expressed the hope that they would continue to work in the cherished establishment.

As always, she felt a deep sense of satisfaction by the time the ceremony ended. Convinced she had the very best staff in the world, she counted herself fortunate to be so blessed.

She had barely returned to her suite when Pansy tapped on her door, announcing that Phoebe had arrived for the final gown fitting.

Cecily had completely forgotten that Phoebe had scheduled the meeting, as apparently had Grace Danbury, unless she had returned from her walk. "See if you can find both Miss Danbury and Mrs. Winchester and ask them to come to my suite as quickly as possible," she told Pansy. "And ask Mrs. Fortescue to come up as well."

"Very well, m'm." Pansy dropped a half curtsey and fled down the corridor.

"I suppose this means I have to go downstairs." Baxter,

who had been sitting in the window, folded his newspaper and got lazily to his feet.

"Unless you want to be witness to several ladies disrobing in front of you," Cecily said with a smile.

Baxter shuddered. "I shall take refuge downstairs in your office until this sideshow is over. The idea of Phoebe twittering around while the rest of you shed your clothes is just too horrifying for words."

Cecily raised her eyebrows. "Are you saying you are horrified by the thought of me shedding my clothes?"

"Not at all, my dear." He walked toward her and dropped a kiss on her forehead. "In fact, should you be so inclined, I should be more than pleased to give you a helping hand."

She grinned at him. "I shall keep that in mind."

"Please, do." With a lascivious wink, he strode across the room and left.

Moments later, a tap on the door heralded Phoebe's arrival. She rushed into the room, her arms full of glistening lilac silk, and dumped her load onto Cecily's settee. "Goodness," she said, puffing between her words, "the snow is quite deep outside. Several times I heard the horse's hooves slip and slide. I quite thought the carriage would end up in the ocean. The Esplanade is absolutely treacherous for travel."

"I'm so sorry, Phoebe." Cecily reached for the bell rope and gave it a tug. "I shall have hot chocolate and brandy sent up immediately. You must be frozen."

"Not as much as that Danbury woman. I saw her prancing along the Esplanade moments ago. She does know she's supposed to be here for a fitting, I trust?"

"I'm sure she'll be here any minute."

"She really is a dowdy little thing. Not a scrap of elegance. I can't imagine her wearing one of these." She picked up a slip of material and let it slide through her fingers. "No wonder she and Madeline get along so well."

Another tap on the door interrupted her. Cecily was

relieved to see Emily Winchester standing out in the hallway and beckoned her into the room. "Miss Danbury is not here yet," she said, "but I'm sure by the time Phoebe has finished with the two of us she will have arrived."

"If not," Phoebe said tartly, "she will have to make do with the way the gown is now."

"I'm sure it will be perfect," Cecily assured her.

For the next hour she endured Phoebe's chatter while she flitted about the room, pinning here, tucking there until Cecily was thoroughly tired of the whole procedure. When Phoebe insisted on lowering a lace frill for the umpteenth time, Cecily put her foot down. Literally.

"I'm really tired, Phoebe, dear," she said, as she sank onto her favorite armchair. "I really can't imagine how you can make these gowns any more perfect than they already are. Don't you agree, Emily?"

The doctor's wife eagerly nodded. "Oh, indeed. The gowns are lovely and fit us both to perfection."

"Very well." Sighing, Phoebe straightened from the hem of Cecily's gown. "I suppose they will have to do. And Miss Danbury still isn't here. While you are changing out of those gowns I will run downstairs and see if she is anywhere in the hotel. No doubt she has forgotten about the fitting."

Cecily and Emily exchanged guilty glances.

"That's a very good idea, Phoebe." Cecily wearily rose to her feet. "You might find Miss Danbury in the library, now that the cribbage party is over. The men should be returning from the hunt anytime now."

"Then I shan't be long. If I don't find the dratted woman right away then I'll come back here for the gowns. My dear Freddie will be wondering what has taken me so long."

She bustled out the door, and Cecily let out a sigh. "Such a dear woman, and a talented seamstress. If only she wasn't so fussy."

Emily smiled. "I must confess, I did forget about the fitting until your maid reminded me."

"Yes, well, so did I, so it really doesn't surprise me at all that Miss Danbury forgot."

Emily began unfastening the tiny pearl buttons on her bodice. "I'm glad we have this opportunity alone together, Mrs. Baxter."

Cecily held up her hand. "I thought we'd agreed on Christian names."

"Oh, yes, I'm sorry. Cecily, then."

The woman seemed nervous, and Cecily peered at her as she stepped out of her gown. "Is something the matter?"

"I really don't know."

Emily appeared about to cry, and concerned now, Cecily took the gown from her and laid it on the settee. "If there's any way I can help?"

"I don't think anyone can help." She reached for her skirt. "I'm so very worried, and I really don't know what to do."

"What are you worrying about?"

"My husband." She looked up, her blue eyes swimming with tears. "I shouldn't be telling you this, but I'm at my wits end with worry and I have no one else to whom I can turn."

Anxious to help, Cecily laid a hand on the woman's fragile arm. "Why don't you simply tell me what's wrong, and perhaps we can do something about it together."

"I don't think so." Emily swallowed, then blurted out the shocking words. "I'm very much afraid that Charles might have murdered the Hethertons."

# CHAPTER

## ❁ 11 ❁

Cecily waited a full five seconds before drawing a breath. "I'm sorry," she said at last. "I don't think I understand what you're saying."

Emily gulped on a sob. "I think my husband might be responsible for the deaths of Sir Walter and . . ." she paused, struggling for composure, ". . . and Lady Clara."

"Great heavens." Cecily sat down rather heavily on the armchair. "Whatever makes you think such a thing?"

Tears ran freely down the other woman's face as she sank onto the settee, crushing the fine silk gowns beneath her. "I'm afraid I've been extremely stupid. Sir Walter and I . . . well, we . . . ah . . . met on occasion . . . without my husband's knowledge."

Cecily let her breath out in a rush. "I see."

"I believe Charles suspected as much. He had become rather cold toward Sir Walter, and he showed no grief upon hearing of the deaths."

"You could well be mistaken. I'm of the opinion that your husband tends to hide his emotions."

Emily pulled a handkerchief from her pocket and dabbed at her nose. "You are most observant, Cecily."

"I have dealt with a good many people over the years. One learns to sum them up quickly. It helps me in my position."

"Yes, I'm sure it does."

"As for your husband, he doesn't strike me as the vindictive sort."

Emily's shoulders lifted slightly. "I would like to agree with you, but in truth, I hardly know what my husband is capable of doing. I only know that he is somewhat possessive, and could well have removed a perceived threat to his marriage."

Cecily leaned forward. "I'm curious to know why you believe the Hethertons were murdered."

Emily mopped her cheeks with the handkerchief. "I happened to overhear Kevin discussing the matter with Charles. It was in the strictest confidence, of course. They had no idea I was there. Kevin said something about an exploding Christmas cracker, and that the killer would have had to have scientific knowledge."

*So much for Kevin's promise to be discreet*, Cecily thought darkly. "That's true, but—"

"Cecily." She slid a worried glance across Cecily's face. "Charles was away the whole day before the explosion. He said he was going to London to see a patient, but I thought I saw him in the lobby that afternoon. At least three hours before he supposedly returned on the evening train. If so, he lied to me about going to London. Why would he do that, unless he had something to hide?"

Thoroughly taken aback, Cecily took a moment to answer her. "But you aren't sure it was Charles you saw," she said at last.

"No, I couldn't be certain it was Charles. I was at the top of the stairs and by the time I reached the lobby he'd left. I suppose it could have been someone else, but even so, I can't help feeling it was my husband I saw. . . ." Her voice trailed off into miserable silence.

A loud rap on the door startled Cecily, and she rose to her feet. "I would try not to worry," she said, attempting to sound reassuring. "You were most likely mistaken. I'm sure your husband had nothing to do with the deaths of the Hethertons, and I would greatly appreciate it if you would refrain from repeating what you overheard to anyone else. We don't want to start a panic."

Another loud rap brought Emily to her feet. "Of course," she said hurriedly. "I shan't say a word."

Nodding her approval, Cecily called out, "Do come in!"

The door opened and Phoebe bustled in, followed by a worried looking Grace.

"I found Miss Danbury," Phoebe declared. "She had completely forgotten about the fitting, of course. Can you imagine?"

"I'm so dreadfully sorry. I can't imagine how that happened. I quite thought, since we had already tried the gowns on, that the fittings were over." She picked up one of the gowns and let its silky folds slip through her fingers.

"The lace frills have to be placed just right." Phoebe snatched the gown from her. "I have to see it on you to determine where they go."

"Lace frills?" Her look of dismay was quite comical. "I thought they had long gone out of mode."

Phoebe bristled. "It is no wonder that you and Madeline are such close friends. You both have a most unfortunate lack of fashion sense."

Grace tossed her head. "That's a matter of opinion."

Surprised to see an assertive side to Grace, Cecily quickly intervened. "If you will excuse us, Emily and I will leave you to finish the fitting, Phoebe. "If you wish to see me before you leave, I will be in the library."

Phoebe started to protest, but Cecily took hold of Emily's

arm and hustled her out of the room, before either woman noticed her teary face.

Outside in the hallway, Emily whispered, "Thank you, Cecily, for your understanding. I will try not to worry about what Charles might or might not have done. I must confess, however, I will breathe easier once you discover the identity of the true culprit."

Cecily watched her until she had disappeared into her room, then made her way to the stairs. Much as she sympathized with the woman, she couldn't help wondering if perhaps there was someone else after all who had reason to want Sir Walter out of the way.

Dr. Charles Winchester had certainly gone to a lot of trouble to convince his wife he was going to London. Samuel had actually taken him to the station that morning and fetched him back from there that evening. Yet apparently he had made his way back to the Pennyfoot for the day.

To concoct a lethal weapon out of a Christmas cracker? Could the doctor have been so consumed with jealousy that he took the lives of people he'd considered his friends? It was hard to believe, yet Cecily knew only too well how sane men, or women for that matter, could commit unimaginable crimes when caught up in passions of the heart.

Perhaps she should search the Winchesters' room for the missing cracker, much as she deplored the idea. One narrow escape was enough. She had little information to work with, however, if she was to learn the identity of the man who had possibly murdered two of her guests. Finding that cracker seemed the only option.

Sighing, she started down the stairs. Halfway down she saw Baxter crossing the lobby. He caught sight of her, and paused at the foot of the stairs until she reached him. She could tell at once by his expression that he had something important to tell her.

At that moment the front doors opened and a group of

men, headed by Roland Crossley, entered the lobby amid boisterous comments and loud laughter.

"They've returned early," Baxter muttered. "They must have had a good day."

"They are most likely hungry and ready for supper." Cecily nodded at Roland Crossley as he came toward her, his riding crop still in his hand.

"Mrs. Baxter!" Crossley's strident tones rang out above the jovial chatter of the huntsmen. "Jolly good hunt today, I must say."

"As good as the one a few days ago?" Baxter murmured.

Cecily gave him a sharp look, then turned back to Crossley, just in time to see a fleeting wariness flash across his colorless eyes.

"Quite, quite." Crossley took out a large handkerchief from his waistcoat pocket and mopped his forehead. "Well, I should be getting upstairs to the little lady. Can't keep her waiting for supper, can we." Nodding at Cecily, he tucked his handkerchief back inside his waistcoat pocket, then slapped his thigh with his riding crop and galloped clumsily up the stairs.

"We need some privacy," Baxter said, as a small group of women entered from the hallway. He took hold of Cecily's arm and guided her through the crowd and out into the hallway.

Once inside her office he closed the door and waited for her to sit down. "I talked to the gamekeeper," he said abruptly. "Roland Crossley didn't go hunting before today."

Cecily drew a sharp breath. "I guessed as much. Now what do we do?"

Baxter took a seat opposite her. "I don't see that we can do anything. Just because Crossley lied about his whereabouts doesn't prove he is our killer. There could be a dozen reasons why he didn't want his wife to know where he went."

Emily Winchester's tearful confession popped into Cecily's mind. "Well, we have another possible suspect." She gave him a brief summary of her conversation with Emily. "If she did see her husband in the lobby that afternoon, then Roland Crossley wasn't the only one lying about his where-abouts."

Baxter leaned back in his chair with a weary sigh. "We don't know that for certain. Winchester's wife isn't sure she saw him in the lobby. It could have been someone resembling him in some way."

"True. Then again, a wife doesn't usually mistake some-one else for her husband."

"Well, short of actually asking Crossley and Winchester where they were, I can't think of any way we can know for cer-tain where either of them went that day, or for that matter, what they were doing." Baxter leaned forward, his gaze hard on Cecily's face. "Take my advice. Either wait for Northcott to get back from London or report what we know to the in-spector and let him deal with it as he sees fit."

"Even if I did report it to the inspector, it would be a while before he found the time to come here to investigate. We are low on his priority list. Meanwhile, our killer could be running around the Pennyfoot with another lethal cracker waiting to explode."

Baxter shook his head. "Unlikely. It's more likely that he took two crackers in case the first one didn't do the job. If Hetherton was murdered, and we still don't know that for an absolute certainty—"

"What other reason could there possibly be for a cracker to explode with enough force to kill someone?"

"Very well. I have to admit it's a probability that some-one wanted Hetherton dead. So let's assume that he was murdered. Since the killer has achieved his purpose, he has no reason to strike again." He gave Cecily a dark look. "Un-less, that is, he discovers that someone is closing in on him."

"Which we are not." She lifted her hands and let them drop. "We have two suspects and no way of finding out if ei-ther of them is a killer." Except she hadn't yet searched the

Winchesters' room. That was something she'd keep to herself for the time being.

"Quite. Which is why I'm in favor of letting the authorities take care of the matter. As long as we can be reasonably sure that no one else is in danger, it seems prudent to leave the matter alone until we can hand it over to the constabulary."

"By which time the killer will have returned home."

"And it will no longer be our problem."

Cecily gave him a long look.

Baxter puffed out his breath. "Yes, I know how you feel about allowing a criminal to go free, but I'm sure the constabulary will catch up with him eventually."

"You mean *our* constabulary?"

He brushed a hand irritably across his forehead. "Well, granted, they are not the most competent—"

"Hah!" Again her gaze clashed with his. "Someone murdered two of our guests in cold blood. It was despicable enough that he took a man's life, for whatever reason, but to deliberately allow an innocent woman to die as well was inhuman. Are you really willing to allow a monster like that to go free?"

"No, of course not, but—"

"Then we shall have to do everything in our power to apprehend this vile creature, and as soon as possible."

Baxter closed his eyes. "I was afraid you'd say that." He opened his eyes again. "I'm terrified to ask, but what plan do you have in mind?"

"Nothing yet." She still planned on searching the Winchesters' room, but saw no need to worry her husband on that subject just yet.

"You will discuss with me before embarking on anything that could remotely present a risk?"

She smiled. "Of course."

Sighing heavily, he rose to his feet. "I suppose I shall have to be satisfied with that."

"Oh, before you go, there's something I keep forgetting to mention. We need to hire another coachman. Samuel has far too much to do, what with taking care of the horses and the motor cars. He really doesn't have the time to transport people back and forth to the railway station as well."

"Very well, I'll see to it." He walked to the door. "Now can we retire for the evening? I'm quite famished."

"I'll have supper sent up to the suite." She followed him out into the hallway, her mind already busily working out the best time to search the Winchesters' room.

All she could hope was that the doctor was not the killer, for if he was, and she had him arrested, that would leave Kevin without a best man and Madeline with one less bridesmaid.

As it was, she had little time to find the Hethertons' killer. New Year's Eve and the wedding was less than a week away, and the day after that, New Year's Day, her guests would be departing for their homes.

Since Madeline had no family and few friends, she had graciously agreed to allow the Pennyfoot guests to attend the wedding and reception, thus saving the staff from having to arrange two separate suppers that evening.

It had promised to be a fitting finale to the holiday celebrations, but now not only were two of the main participants in doubt, Madeleine herself seemed to be having reservations about marrying Kevin.

Cecily frowned as she preceded her husband up the stairs. She must have a word with Madeline about that, just as soon as possible.


Gertie turned over in her bed, batting away the annoying pressure on her shoulder that disturbed her sleep. The pressure returned, more urgent, more demanding. Muttering a curse, Gertie opened her eyes.

At first, she could see nothing but blackness, but as her

eyes adjusted to the dark she could see a shape leaning over her. Already disturbed by nightmares, she opened her mouth to scream. A cold hand descended, smothering the sound before it could escape.

"Shhshh! You'll wake everyone up."

Gertie blinked, then shoved the hand away from her mouth. "Pansy? What the bloody hell are you doing? Are you blinking bonkers?"

"Shhshh." Pansy leaned closer. "It's out there. I saw it moving."

Gertie sat up. "What's out there?' she demanded, even though she had a horrible idea she already knew.

"The snowman. It's walking about out there."

"You're bloody dreaming."

"I'm not. Honest, I'm not. I seen it, Gertie. With me own two eyes I seen it walking about."

"Mummy?"

Gertie swore under her breath as the soft voice spoke from across the room. "It's all right, Lillian. Go back to sleep. I've just got to go to the lavatory. I'll be coming back right away."

Lillian mumbled something and then was quiet.

Gertie waited for a moment then slipped out of bed. Reaching for her dressing gown at the foot of the bed, she whispered, "Wait for me outside."

Pansy slipped away from her, opened the door and shut it quietly behind her.

Gertie felt around with her foot until she found her slippers and tugged them on. Then treading as quietly as she could across the cold, hard floor, she reached the door and opened it.

Pansy stood shivering outside, clutching her dressing gown around her throat. "I wanted you to see him, too," she whispered. "No one would believe me if I told them, but if you see him, too . . ."

"Where is he?" The last thing on earth Gertie wanted to do right then was go looking for a snowman that apparently came to life whenever it felt like it.

Pansy, however, was already creeping down the hallway toward the kitchen stairs. "It was walking across the back yard," she said, in a hoarse whisper. "The moon's out. I saw it plain as day."

"How could you see anything in the back yard from your room?"

"I went into the pantry to get something to eat. I was hungry."

"You're not supposed to do that."

"I know."

Gertie swallowed. Her throat hurt from trying to whisper loud enough for Pansy to hear her. She kept quiet until they were both inside the kitchen with the door closed. "Wait," she said quietly, "I'll light a lamp."

"No!" Pansy grabbed her arm. "It will see us."

"Snowmen can't see, you twerp." She reached for the lamp on the shelf and pulled it down. As long as she kept telling Pansy she was seeing things, she could almost convince herself the whole thing was in her imagination.

"It can walk, can't it?"

"So you blinking say." She reached for the box of matches, her fingers shaking so hard the matches rattled as she took them down from the shelf.

"Well, if it can walk, it must be able to see to move about, mustn't it?"

Gertie pulled in a sharp breath. Carefully she set the matches down on the kitchen table next to the lamp. "All right, then. Where is the bloody thing?"

Pansy pointed a finger at the window. "Over there."

Gertie moved forward, swearing as her hip collided with the corner of the table. Limping, she reached the window and peered out. "I can't see nothing."

Pansy crept up to stand next to her. "It was out there, I swear. It was right there in front of the coal shed."

"Well, it ain't there right now, is it."

"It must have walked off." Pansy turned her face toward

Gertie, her cheeks pale in the moonlight. "I bet if we go around to the dining room or the ballroom, we'll see it."

Gertie drew back from the window. "If you think I'm going dragging around the bleeding hotel in the middle of the night to look for a flipping snowman what ain't there you *are* bleeding bonkers, that's what. I'm blinking freezing, and I'm going back to bed. The sheets'll be like ice by now. I'll be lucky if I get any sleep tonight, thanks to you."

"I tell you I saw it. It was there and it was walking about. You're just afraid to go and look. I . . . oh!"

For a second Gertie thought Pansy's shriek was because she'd seen the snowman. She whirled toward the window but at that moment a shrill voice cut across the room.

"Gertie? Is that you? What in blazes are you doing in here in the dead of night?"

Groaning, Gertie turned to face Mrs. Chubb. She looked like a ghost herself in her billowing white night gown. Standing in the doorway, she held a lamp high above her head. Her silver hair was tied up in little bunches bound in red ribbons and any other time Gertie would have laughed at the sight.

One look at the housekeeper's face, however, warned her this was no time for laughter. "Pansy and me thought we heard a noise outside," she mumbled, "so we came to look."

Pansy made a small, desperate sound.

Gertie shook her head at her and she clapped a hand over her mouth.

Mrs. Chubb advanced into the kitchen. "Pansy, too? A noise? What sort of noise?"

"Dunno. It was more n'likely alley cats." Gertie wandered over to the window. "Nothing out there now, though."

"I hope you're not going to tell me it was that walking snowman again."

Pansy whimpered.

Sighing, Gertie faced Mrs. Chubb. "All right. Pansy says she saw it out in the back yard."

"I did see it, and it was walking!"

Pansy's voice had risen on the last word and Mrs. Chubb hurried toward her. "There, there, it's all right." She put a motherly arm around Pansy's shaking shoulders. "It's just someone playing tricks on us all, that's all."

Gertie prayed that she was right. She really wanted to believe that it was someone playing about, but part of her mind, the part she kept pushing away, kept telling her that it was a ghost come back to haunt her. A ghost that whistled a tune her ex-boyfriend kept whistling when he'd worked at the Pennyfoot years ago.

Somehow she had to find out if Ian Rossiter was dead and buried. Because if he was, then it was his ghost out there, and knowing Ian, it was there to cause them all a lot of trouble.

# CHAPTER
## ❁ 12 ❁

"This is *so* nice." Madeline hooked a finger in her hair and tucked the strands behind her ear. "We haven't had tea in Dolly's in simply months."

"Yes, I've really missed Dolly's delicious scones." Cecily leaned back in her chair and let her gaze roam around the tiny tearoom. Summer or winter, this room always seemed warm and welcoming. Right now the flames leapt high in the huge brick fireplace, their glow reflecting in the brass coal scuttle and fire irons.

Bright copper kettles and brass pitchers crowded the wide picture rail above her head, amid an assortment of china platters and jugs. Dolly had recently had the walls freshly papered in a design of pastoral scenes that Cecily found quite charming.

Matching curtains hung at the thick, leaded windows, muffling the clip-clopping of horses' hooves along the road outside. Even the occasional harsh blare of a motor horn failed to interrupt the quiet murmur of conversation from Dolly's many patrons.

"I have to say," Madeline said, reaching for her cup, "it is refreshing to enjoy the peace and quiet without Phoebe rattling off idiotically in my ear."

Cecily gave her a reproachful look. "Now you know you don't mean that."

"Of course I do." Madeline took a sip of the hot tea and replaced the cup in its saucer. "The woman prattles on about nothing at all. Always talking about dear Freddie this and dear Freddie that, or that impossibly effeminate son of hers. I don't know how she can fail to see that the man is a pansy."

Cecily paused with her cup hovering at her lips. "I'm not sure what you mean—"

Madeline leaned forward. "A pansy. Algie has homosexual tendencies."

Having never heard of the word, Cecily could only stare at her in confusion.

Madeline rolled her eyes. "For heaven's sake, Cecily. Algie is one of those men who prefers the company of men rather than women. Much prefers, in fact."

In the act of taking a sip of tea, Cecily choked, and hurriedly put down the cup. "I have never heard of such a thing."

Madeline raised a skeptical eyebrow. "Come now, Cecily, don't tell me you've never heard of such men? In your business you must have met at least one or two pansies."

Cecily could feel her cheeks burning and hurriedly fanned her face with her gloved hand. "It's not something we should be talking about in public, Madeline." She sent a furtive glance around at the other tables. Fortunately, the rest of Dolly's patrons seemed too absorbed in their own conversations to be paying attention to Madeline's embarrassing comments.

"Pish. It's common knowledge nowadays. I was reading an article about it just the other day in the *Daily News*." Madeline grinned, apparently enjoying her friend's discomfort.

Cecily cleared her throat. "That's as may be, but may I remind you that we are talking about a vicar—a man of God—and one who will be marrying you in three days, I might add."

She hadn't intended to bring up the subject quite so soon, but now that the wedding had been mentioned, she intended to get a firm commitment from Madeline. According to Kevin, she was still waffling about whether or not she would marry him.

It had taken Cecily three days to arrange this meeting with her friend, and would almost certainly be the last before the wedding day. There would be no further opportunity to talk sense into the mercurial woman.

Madeline's grin had vanished. "That's a matter of debate," she said shortly.

Cecily chose to deliberately misunderstand. "What is?"

"The wedding." She picked up her spoon and stirred her tea viciously enough that the liquid whirled around and sloshed into the saucer. "I don't know if I want to marry Kevin. He absolutely refuses to recognize my skills, and is far too demanding for my liking."

"Madeline, as long as I have known you I have never seen you succumb to orders from anyone. Just because you will be Kevin's wife doesn't mean that will change."

"Doesn't it?" Madeline's lovely eyes clouded. "Isn't that what a man expects when he takes a wife? That she will obey him in everything he says?"

"Ordinarily, perhaps, but Kevin knows you are anything but ordinary. That's the reason he adores you so."

Madeline's spoon clattered in the saucer. "I wish I could be certain of that."

"Well, I am certain of that." Cecily reached out and covered Madeline's hand with her own. "You love him, too. Don't you?"

"Of course. I'm just not convinced that it's enough."

"Would you prefer to live the rest of your life without him?"

Madeline stared at her teacup for so long Cecily grew seriously worried. Then she sighed. "No," she said softly. "I don't think I would."

"Then there's your answer. Marry him, and make the marriage what you want it to be. If the two of you love each other enough, and I believe you do, you will have a wonderful life together."

"As wonderful as you and Baxter?"

Cecily smiled. "Every bit."

"Then how can I not take your advice. Though I warn you, I absolutely refuse to promise to obey the man. In fact, I am considering writing my own vows."

Far too relieved that her friend had relented, Cecily ignored that particular piece of sacrilege. "Then you will go ahead with the wedding?"

Madeline's smile was pure mischief. "I always intended to go through with it, Cecily dear. Even with my doubts. I just wanted to give Kevin something to think about in his last days of freedom. I can't have him taking me for granted."

Cecily wished she could believe her. Madeline was utterly unpredictable at the best of times and in spite of her assurances, Cecily couldn't help wondering if there was a false ring to her words.

Brushing aside her doubts, Cecily laughed out loud. "I pity anyone who tries to take you for granted. You will keep Kevin on his toes, no doubt, and that will be good for both of you."

"My sentiments exactly." Madeline sighed. "Though I must admit, I'm not relishing the thought of the actual wedding. All that pomp and propriety."

"A traditional ceremony will help still vicious tongues. It's a sign of respectability."

"Well, you know what I think of respectability. Especially

when it means putting up with Phoebe twittering about like an agitated sparrow, a vicar putting everyone to sleep and the stuck-up doctor's wife for a bridesmaid. Thank heavens you and Grace will be there, too, or I swear, I'd drag Kevin off to Deep Willow Pond and marry him out there with only the birds and wild creatures as witnesses."

Cecily broke off a piece of scone and popped it into her mouth. She hadn't forgotten that if Dr. Winchester had indeed murdered the Hethertons, the wedding would have one less bridesmaid and no best man.

That possibility had kept her from pursuing her investigation for the past three days. She was torn between seeing a cruel killer brought to justice and making sure her friend's long-awaited wedding went off without a hitch.

"Is something worrying you?"

Madeline's question brought up Cecily's chin. "No, no, I was just thinking about Grace. I have to say, I'm curious how you became such close friends with someone like her. She's such a meek little person."

Madeline laughed. "Most of the time. Though I have seen her bare her teeth once in a while. I felt sorry for her, at first. She seemed so vulnerable and you know I can't resist that. Besides, she's one of the few people I know who actually understands my skills. I find that refreshing."

"I didn't realize she's a herbalist."

"She isn't." Madeline picked up her cup and drained it. "She a horticulturist. Roses, mostly. She grows hybrids. She's quite well known in London. That's where I met her, at the Royal Horticultural Spring Show in Chelsea. We don't see a lot of each other, but I usually make a point of visiting her whenever I go to London."

"Roses." Cecily closed her eyes. "My favorite flowers. How I adore strolling through the rose garden on a hot summer afternoon. I can smell the fragrance of the blossoms now."

"Well, Grace is quite an expert on the subject of roses.

She actually produced a brand new hybrid a few years ago. She named it 'Pure Grace' and was going to present it at the Royal flower show. If it hadn't been for the accident, it would have made her famous and put her name at the head of the horticultural society."

Fascinated, Cecily forgot about the rest of her tea cooling in her cup. "Accident? What happened?"

"One of the judges swept it off the table with her elbow as she walked by. Totally destroyed the planter. Grace couldn't find another empty planter, and by the time she did get the rose replanted it had died."

"Couldn't she have grown another one?"

"Apparently she found the crossbreed by accident. That's usually the way it happens. She's spent years trying to reproduce the hybrid but so far she's failed." Madeline shook her head. "It's sad, really. It was her life's dream to have a rose named after her. To come that close and lose by such a cruel stroke of fate must be heartbreaking."

"No wonder she always looks so downtrodden." Cecily picked up her cup. "I feel more charitable toward her now that I know the reason for her glum disposition."

Madeline laughed. "You are always charitable, Cecily dear. Which is one of the reasons I'm so fond of you. You try to find the best in everyone."

"I'm not sure I deserve the compliment, but thank you." She put down her cup. "Now I really must get back to the Pennyfoot. Baxter will be pacing the floor wondering where I am."

"You didn't tell him we were having tea at Dolly's?"

"Well, yes, but he doesn't always pay attention." Cecily eased her chair back and stood. "You will soon find that out, once you are married to that handsome doctor of yours. After a while a husband tends to answer you without having the slightest idea what it is you said."

Madeline pulled a face. "I have an idea I'll be finding out a whole lot of vexing things about being a wife."

Cecily smiled. "Ah, but there are many pleasurable surprises in store as well."

"Then I shall go forth to my wedding with a positive attitude, albeit with a fierce determination to maintain my independence, as our sisters in the cause have so zealously dictated."

Cecily winced. "I'm all in favor of women's rights," she said, as she followed Madeline out into the busy High Street, "but I sometimes wonder if by asserting ourselves so religiously we are inviting more than we are prepared to handle."

Madeline's answer was smothered by the clatter of horses hooves and the rattling of a passing carriage's wheels.

Perhaps it was just as well, Cecily thought, as she climbed up into the carriage waiting for them at the curb. The subject of women's rights not only raised arguments between the opposite genders, it also caused hot debates among its proponents as well as its foes.

So much of the world was changing, and there were times when she feared for the worst. Too many countries were gaining power, threatening to overwhelm the island she called home. Not the least of them was the burgeoning country across the Atlantic. So many aristocrats were taking American brides, she was afraid their culture would eventually take over the ideals that made England great, altering forever its destiny.

"You look exceedingly solemn," Madeline commented, the leather seat creaking as she settled herself next to Cecily. "What worries you so?"

Cecily shook off her apprehension. "Only that your wedding day be the most perfect day of your life."

"Well, don't count on it," Madeline said dryly. "With the entire ceremony in the hands of Phoebe, I'm sure you'll agree that just about anything can happen."

"That is the most beautiful cake I've ever seen." Leaning against the kitchen sink, Gertie watched in admiration as

Mrs. Chubb twirled a cone-shaped waxed paper bag around the edge of the cake, leaving behind an intricate white swirl of royal icing.

"It's not finished yet." Mrs. Chubb paused. "This is only the bottom tier. I still have three more tiers to ice, then all the pillars have to go on to hold them up, then I have to put on all them sugar ornaments."

She nodded at a tray on the dresser and Gertie went over to look. Glittering sugar leaves, bells and roses lay in tempting rows, making her mouth water. "Ooo! Can I have one?"

"No you can't." Mrs. Chubb finished decorating the border and laid down the bag. "Hand me over those silver balls. I have to set them in this icing before it gets too hard."

Gertie picked up a bottle full of tiny silver sugar balls and handed it to the housekeeper. "It's going to look smashing by the time it's finished."

"That is if I don't knock it off the table or something." She sounded cross. "I wish madam had ordered it from the bakery. I don't mind decorating Christmas cakes but a wedding cake is special. It makes me nervous."

"Your cakes are always special." Gertie wandered over to the table and picked up the bag. "Madeline's bloody lucky to have such a beautiful wedding cake." She squirted some of the icing onto her finger and stuck it in her mouth.

"Put that down!" Mrs. Chubb scowled as she picked up a silvery sugar ball with a pair of tweezers and dropped it exactly into the center of each swirl. "Go and polish the silver if you want something to do. Why aren't you with the twins, anyway? Isn't this your free time?"

"Yeah, but they're out with Daisy. Trying out their new sled. It's too bloody cold to be out there watching them. That's why I pay Daisy to do it."

Mrs. Chubb dropped another ball into the icing. "You should spend more time with them. They'll be grown up before you know it and then you'll never see them."

Gertie snorted. "With my luck they'll still be flipping hanging on to me in their old age."

Mrs. Chubb straightened. "Gertie McBride! How can you say such a thing. Lillian is such a pretty little girl. She'll be married before she's twenty, you mark my words. As for James, he's so clever and quick, he'll be working in London and making lots of money so he can look after you in your old age. I don't have a single doubt."

Gertie grinned. "Got it all worked out, Chubby, haven't you. I'll remind you of that when I'm old and gray and my kids are bloody eating me out of house and home."

"You should have more faith in your children." Mrs. Chubb went back to dropping the silver balls. "And don't call me, Chubby. If I've told you once I've told you more than a hundred times, I—"

She broke off as the kitchen door flew open. The young woman standing in the doorway wore a heavy wool coat and a bright blue woolen scarf tied over her hat. Strands of brown hair hung damply against her red cheeks, and her eyes were wide with apprehension.

Gertie took one look at her and dropped the icing bag. "Daisy? What's bloody happened now?"

Daisy took a deep breath, then blurted out, "It's the children. I can't find them."

Ignoring the stab of fear, Gertie managed to keep her voice calm. "Whatcha mean, you can't find them? Where did you last see them?"

Daisy gulped, and clutched the collar of her coat. "They took the sled out. I've told them and told them not to go near the woods and they've been really, really good about it. It's so cold out there, I've been watching them from inside the ballroom. I can see them from the French windows there and if I need to go after them I can be outside in a flash."

"So what happened?" Gertie demanded, her voice rising.

"Now, Gertie." Mrs. Chubb screwed the cap back on the

bottle of silver balls. "I'm sure they're just out of sight, that's all. They won't have gone far."

"I was watching them," Daisy said, her voice trembling, "and I saw this dog running across the lawns toward them. Must have been a stray. I got worried that it might bite them or something, so I ran outside and shouted out to them to come in. I must have frightened the dog, 'cos it ran off."

She paused for breath and losing patience, Gertie snapped, "What bloody happened, for gawd's sake?"

"They followed the dog on the sled." Daisy's voice rose to a wail. "I shouted and shouted at them to stop but the sled was going too fast down the slope and they went into the woods. I ran after them but . . . but . . ." She ended on a sob.

"But what?" Gertie walked up to her and shook her shoulder. "Bloody *what*, Daisy?"

"I can't find them. They're *gone*!" Daisy collapsed into tears.

Gertie flung herself around and grabbed her shawl from the peg. "I'm going out there. Get Samuel and as many footmen as you can find and send them out after me."

"Get your coat first," Mrs. Chubb called out as Gertie threw open the door. "You'll freeze out there without it."

"I haven't got time!" Gertie charged out into the hallway and made for the stairs at a full run.

Lumbering up the steps she prayed as hard as she could. *Not the twins.* She'd do anything God asked if He just kept them safe.

People scattered right and left as she burst into the lobby and tore across the thick carpet to the front doors. Outside, a cold blast of wind snatched at her shawl and she grabbed it, holding on to it as she flew down the stairs.

Her feet sunk into the snow on the lawns and slowed her down. She spotted the trail the sled had made and followed it, sliding and slipping on the flattened, icy surface.

"James? Lillian!" Her shouts, weakened by lack of breath,

died on the wind. A sharp pain stabbed her under the ribs and she swore, stumbling once more in the deep snow. She found the trail again, but now she was too winded to run.

Limping, panting, and praying like mad, she reached the edge of the forest. Looking at all those dark shadows lurking beneath the snow-laden branches filled her with dread. A flash of red caught her eye and she struggled toward it, trying to remember what the twins were wearing that morning.

The dread intensified into sharp, agonizing panic when she saw the sled, overturned against a tree.

"Lillian? Where are you?" She cupped her hands to her mouth and yelled again and again. Only the distant echoes answered her. Violent shudders shook her body, and only then did she realize that she'd lost her shawl. The cold was so intense it hurt.

She was about to move farther into the forest when a movement caught her eye. "James? Is that you?" She turned, and then froze. Moving slowly toward her from the direction of the rockery, complete with hat, scarf and gleaming coal buttons, was the snowman.

# CHAPTER
## 13

Cecily sat at her desk, absently tapping her blotter with the nib of her pen. She was no closer to finding out who had killed the Hethertons.

A hasty search of the Winchesters' room had turned up nothing. The second cracker was still missing and presumably in the hands of the murderer. Worse, it seemed likely he might well get away with the two murders.

Part of her wanted very much to leave matters as they stood, rather than run the risk of ruining Madeline's wedding day. As the precious time ticked away, however, her conscience jabbed at her more and more.

The thought of a vicious killer going scot-free was just too unconscionable to bear. Baxter had avoided the subject, perhaps knowing how muddled she felt about the entire situation and wary of starting an argument.

She thought back to their last conversation about the murder. *Short of actually asking Crossley and Winchester where they*

*were, I can't think of any way we can know for certain where either
of them went that day, or for that matter, what they were doing.*

Maybe that's what she should do. Just simply ask them
point blank, and hope she could tell if they were lying. But
what if she discovered Dr. Winchester was the killer?

Laying down her pen, she got to her feet. She'd cross that
bridge when she came to it. Right now her scruples were
troubling her so severely she needed to do something constructive. At least make an effort to find out who had wanted
Sir Walter Hetherton out of the way badly enough to kill
him and his wife along with him.

Heading for the door, she rehearsed the questions she
would ask. She would have to use extreme caution not to
sound accusing. Just try to introduce the subject in ordinary
conversation.

Praying she was up to the task, she closed the door of her
office and hurried down the hallway.

Hot, burning rage tore through Gertie, and she charged toward the snowman, her arms flailing the air as she screamed
at him. "What have you bleeding done with my kiddies? If
you've hurt them I'll smash your bloody head to pieces!"

Intent on getting her hands on the monster ahead of her,
she ploughed through the snow. The echo of her shrieks re-
bounded through the woods behind her.

The snowman halted, and for a moment she wondered if
she'd imagined it moving. It looked so harmless and peaceful, just a mound of snow with a hat and scarf. An ordinary
snowman, nothing more.

She slowed her stumbling run, and as she did so, she
heard a high-pitched voice carried on the wind behind her.
"Mummy! Mum-eee!"

Whimpering, she spun around, almost losing her balance.
There, emerging from the edge of the woods was Clive, each
hand clasping one of her children's.

Gulping back tears, Gertie staggered toward them. They let go of the maintenance man's hands and ran to meet her, both calling out in wailing voices.

She knelt in the snow, shivering so hard her teeth rattled. Heedless of the cold, she held the two warm, precious bodies close to her and buried her face in between theirs.

"Mummy, you're shaking," James complained, and pulled out of her grasp. "Where's your coat?"

"I forgot to bring it with me." Gertie's stuttering words made both twins laugh. She hugged them again. "What happened to you? Didn't Daisy tell you not to go into the woods?"

"We didn't mean to!" Lillian shoved her brother. "*He* wanted to catch the dog, and then we couldn't stop the sled and it hit a tree and we got lost . . . and then Mr. Clive found us and led us back out and then we heard you screaming." She paused for breath.

Belatedly, Gertie raised her head to thank Clive, but he must have left, since she couldn't see him anywhere. She'd have to thank him later, she told herself.

"Mummy? Why were you yelling so loud?" Without waiting for her answer, James shoved his sister so hard she stumbled and fell.

"Here, stop that! Don't you dare push your sister about like that." Gertie cuffed him around the ear and helped her daughter climb to her feet. Steeling herself, she turned around to look behind her.

The snowman had disappeared.

Cecily was fortunate enough to corner Dr. Winchester on his way to the card rooms. His wife, he told her, had retreated to their room for a nap, and he was about to enjoy a spot of gambling.

Cecily had thought long and hard about how to open the conversation. She'd spotted the doctor crossing the lobby and had called out to him, catching up with him before he reached the front doors.

"I wanted to ask your advice," she said, as the doctor attempted to end the conversation. "It concerns my stable manager, Samuel. I believe you've met him?"

Dr. Winchester nodded. "Nice chap. Very accommodating. I must congratulate you on your staff, Mrs. Baxter. They are most considerate and helpful."

"Well, thank you, doctor." Cecily beamed at him. "I would like to ask you something that might help Samuel. If you have a minute?"

The doctor's expression told her he was impatient to get to the gaming tables, but she wasn't about to let him slip away. "It won't take a minute," she added. "It is, however, rather a private matter. If you wouldn't mind stepping into my office for a moment?"

Winchester's eyes turned from impatience to wariness. "What's this all about?"

"I'll explain the moment we have some privacy." She turned, beckoning with her finger. "This way, doctor, if you don't mind."

He hesitated, and she thought he might refuse, but then he gave a slight shake of his head and followed her down the corridor to her office.

She closed the door and edged around her desk to take a seat, beckoning him to a chair.

"I hope this won't take long." He flipped his coattails and sat down opposite her.

"I promise I won't keep you more than a moment or two." She considered offering to order him a shot of brandy from the bar, then thought better of it. "It's about Samuel." She leaned back and folded her hands across her stomach.

"So I assumed. How can I help?"

"He has a problem with his hands. Some sort of rash. He keeps scratching them and I can see they are tormenting

him. I was wondering if you could suggest a remedy to help
with the itching."

In actual fact Samuel's rash had all but disappeared, but
since she could think of no other excuse to kidnap the doctor's attention long enough to question him, she saw no reason to mention that.

"Rash?" Winchester frowned. "How long has he had the
irritation?"

"About a week, I think."

"Well, it's hard to say without looking at it, but it sounds
like some sort of reaction to something."

Which was exactly what she expected him to say. What
she hadn't expected was his next words.

"I understand he was responsible for cleaning up the
Hethertons' room after that unfortunate explosion."

He had caught her unawares, and at first she could only
stare at him. Obviously, if he had talked to Kevin about it, he
knew that Kevin was aware the deaths were no accident. If he
was the killer, he was being remarkably calm about it. Carefully, she answered him. "Yes, Samuel cleaned up the room for
me."

"Well, that's most likely what has caused the problem.
The silver fulminate used in the explosive is an irritant. It can
cause a rather nasty rash with a maddening itch. Scratching it
only makes it worse."

"I see." She paused, then added, "Is there anything you
can suggest to remedy it?"

"Sodium bicarbonate should relieve the itching. Mix a
little baking soda with water and slap it on. Tell him not to
scratch and it should most likely clear up in a few days."

Cecily struggled to clear her mind. Out of nowhere, a so-
lution to her problem had been presented to her. She had
been looking for a way to open up the subject of the murder
and the doctor had managed it for her. Now all she had to
do was take advantage of it.

"Well, thank you, doctor. I truly appreciate your excellent advice."

"Good. Well, if that's all . . ."

He started to rise and she halted him with a raised hand. "There is one more thing, if you don't mind."

Sitting down again, his eyes were once more wary.

"I was wondering if you would possibly settle an argument for me." She smiled at him, hoping to allay any doubts he might have as to her intentions.

"I'll do my best," Charles said carefully.

"Well, it's not really an argument, just a little difference of opinion, really. Your reference to the explosion reminded me. Your wife happened to mention that you returned to London the day before the Hethertons died. Yet I thought I saw you that afternoon in the lobby. I was quite sure at the time, but Emily insisted you were gone for the entire day. Perhaps I was mistaken?"

The doctor dropped his gaze, and stared down at his hands resting on his knees. For a long moment he was silent, while the sound of music from the ballroom drifted down the hallway outside. Apparently the afternoon tea dance had begun.

Just when Cecily had become nervous enough to think about pulling the bell rope, Charles began to speak. "You were not mistaken at all, Cecily. I was indeed in the lobby that afternoon."

Her heart skipped a beat. "Well, it's none of my business, but—"

"But it is your business." He looked up, and his gaze was steady on her face. "Kevin told me the cause of the explosion, suggesting that the deaths were not an accident. Since you spotted me that afternoon when I was supposed to be seventy miles away in London, it's reasonable to believe that you are considering whether or not I killed Sir Walter and his wife, are you not?"

Again he'd surprised her. Floundering a little, she said

weakly, "Well, yes, I suppose, since you lied to your wife, I was wondering why you would do that."

His lips thinned. "I lied to my wife because I wanted her to think I'd left Badgers End for the day. I was under the impression that Emily was engaged in a romantic liaison with Sir Walter. Instead of taking the train to London, I secretly followed her around all day, hoping she would attempt to see Sir Walter and enable me to catch them red-handed."

"I see." Cecily watched his face. "And did you? Catch them red-handed, I mean."

"No." Again Charles dropped his gaze. "Emily didn't go anywhere near the man for the entire day."

Cecily's shoulders sagged in relief. "So you were mistaken about her."

"Not necessarily. I still think there was something going on between them. But I don't suppose I'll ever know for sure." He looked up again. "I didn't kill the Hethertons, Cecily. Even if I had caught them together, I wouldn't have attacked the man. I would simply have divorced my wife, naming Hetherton for the cad he was, and therefore destroying his credibility in the House of Lords. I most certainly would never have killed him or his wife. That poor woman's death was so utterly pointless and cruel."

"I couldn't agree more." Somewhat reassured, Cecily rose to her feet. "Well, Charles, I won't keep you any longer. Thank you for being so frank with me. Rest assured I shall not repeat a word of our conversation to anyone."

"I appreciate that, Cecily. Thank you."

"By the same token, I'd appreciate it if you would not repeat to anyone what Kevin told you."

"I've already given my promise to him to keep quiet on the subject."

"Then we are in agreement." She smiled brightly as she led him to the door. "I shall look forward to seeing you and your wife at the wedding."

"As will I." He nodded affably enough, though he looked none too happy as he left.

Cecily closed the door, feeling immensely sorry for the man. How could he possibly be happy in his marriage, suspecting that his wife had been unfaithful to him? It would take a strong and forgiving man to overcome that hurdle.

It did seem, however, that he was innocent of the crime. His explanation had been wholly feasible, and she believed him. Which left Roland Crossley as her lone suspect. Somehow she would have to manufacture an excuse to meet with him alone. Not an easy task. She had the feeling that the MP would be far less obliging than Charles Winchester had been.

Not that such setbacks had ever stopped her before.

Gertie sat on the kitchen chair, shaking so hard the hot milk and brandy in the cup she held between her frozen hands spilled onto her lap.

"You'll catch your death of cold, going out there like that." Mrs. Chubb fetched a shawl from behind the pantry door and draped it over Gertie's shuddering shoulders.

"I was f-frightened for my k-kiddies." Gertie took a sip of the hot toddy. "I don't know what I'd do if anything happened to them. Honest, I don't."

"Well, they're safe and warm now." Mrs. Chubb went back to jotting down the list of supplies on her notepad. "A lot warmer than you by the looks of it."

Gertie tilted the cup and gulped down more milk and brandy. She could feel it sliding down her throat and warming her stomach. Already she felt better. Even her teeth had stopped their chattering, though her lips still felt numb when she talked. "I'm all right. As long as my babies are safe and well, I'll be all right."

"Thank heavens Clive found them." Mrs. Chubb scribbled something down, then frowned at the list. "Lucky for them he came along. They could have wandered deep into the woods and taken hours to be found."

Gertie shuddered again, and this time, not from the cold. "Or that bloody snowman could have got to 'em."

Mrs. Chubb raised her chin. "Don't tell me someone's still playing that prank on you."

"I'm not so sure it is a prank." Gertie struggled with her doubts for a moment, then burst out, "I think that thing's a bleeding ghost, come back to haunt me."

Mrs. Chubb stared at her for a moment openmouthed, then burst out laughing. "Get on with you, Gertie. You know there's no such things as ghosts."

"Do I?" She put the empty cup down on the edge of the table. "Remember when I first met Ross, when all them Scots pipers were here? There was a real ghost then."

Mrs. Chubb's amusement vanished. "That was different."

"How? I wasn't the only one to see that ghost, now was I? Even madam saw that one."

"Well, I suppose, but we never knew for certain."

"I knew for certain." Gertie shivered, and drew the shawl closer around her shoulders.

"Well, I think it's someone trying to frighten the guests, like I said." Mrs. Chubb pressed so hard on the notepad the end of her pencil snapped off. She clicked her tongue in annoyance. "Now I'll have to sharpen this thing again."

"Then why haven't none of the guests seen it, then? Why didn't no one see it in the ballroom that day, with its face pressed right up against the window?"

"It must have ducked out of sight when you screamed." Mrs. Chubb opened the drawer under the table and picked out a sharp paring knife.

Gertie snorted. "Have you ever in your life seen a bloody snowman *duck*?"

"Well, we're not exactly talking about an ordinary snowman, are we."

"Too bloody right, we're not." Gertie slumped back in

her chair. "All I know is that thing is evil. The next time I see it I'm going to chop off its flipping head with a shovel. Then we'll see if it's a blinking ghost or not."

Mrs. Chubb began rapidly slicing the end of her pencil. "I'm just as sure as I can be that if you went out and looked in the snow where you last saw it, you'd see wheel marks or sled marks where someone is moving that thing around."

Gertie looked up. "You know, that's a bloody good idea. I'll go right now before it snows again."

Mrs. Chubb looked up in alarm. "You're not going out there again in that cold. You've just got warm again."

Gertie stood up, wrapping the shawl tighter around her. "It won't take me more'n a minute to go and look out there. At least I'll satisfy myself that it's not a bleeding ghost following me around."

She started for the door, ignoring the housekeeper's warning.

"Gertie . . . for heaven's sake take your coat with you."

"I'll be back in a minute." She let the door swing shut behind her and headed for the stairs.

A few minutes later she was once more trudging through the snow in the direction of the rockery. She could see the trail her footsteps had left and the churned-up snow where she had knelt to hug her twins.

If the snowman was a ghost, he would have vanished, leaving no trace behind. On the other hand, he could have come from behind the rockery, then gone back there while her back was turned.

Then again, her kiddies hadn't seen it when it was right behind her. Or at least they hadn't said anything about it. Of course, in all the excitement of hugging her and everything, they might not have noticed it.

She had almost reached the spot where she had seen the snowman. At first she couldn't be sure what had disturbed the snow, but as she drew nearer there was no mistaking the markings. The tracks came from behind the rockery and out to where she now stood. Then they turned in a half circle and trailed back to the rockery.

They weren't wheel marks or sled marks, after all. They were footprints, clear and distinct in the snow. One set of footprints, that was all. Gertie stared at them in disbelief. Ghosts didn't leave footprints behind, she was quite sure of that. Then again, since when did a snowman walk all by himself? Something very peculiar was going on, and she had a horrible feeling it wasn't anything good.

# CHAPTER
## 14

"So how are the wedding plans coming along?" Baxter lowered the evening paper and peered over the top of it. "You haven't mentioned anything about it for the last two days."

Cecily laid a bookmark in between the pages of her novel and reluctantly set it down beside her. Much as she loved participating in a conversation with her husband, the chance to relax in their suite with a good book was a rare pleasure too often interrupted by her duties. "I didn't think you were all that interested in the wedding."

"I'm not, other than wondering if it is still to take place. After all, I am supposed to be giving the bride away." Baxter folded his newspaper and dropped it on the small table at his elbow. "I believe there is some doubt about that?"

"Not anymore. Madeline has assured me she will marry Kevin on New Year's Eve." Again she felt a quiver of apprehension, and prayed she was worrying unnecessarily.

"Drat. I was hoping she'd given up on the whole thing."

Cecily sighed. "Now, Hugh, darling, you know you don't mean that. I'm quite sure you will be as happy as I am to see Madeline settled down and happily married."

"Hmmph. It if means we will see less of her, I suppose I can suffer through the ceremony."

"So that's it. You are not happy about having to go to church."

"I don't object to going to church. I do object having to listen to that idiot, Reverend Carter-Holmes, stuttering all through the service. Takes him twice as long to get through with it, and half the congregation are asleep by the time he's finished."

Cecily had to admit, his comments were well founded. She wondered what he'd say if she repeated Madeline's comments about the vicar. He'd most likely be as shocked as she had been. It had never occurred to her that Algie could be so inclined. She wasn't sure she could ever look him in the face again.

Then again, she was no expert on the subject, and in any case, it was definitely not something she could discuss with her husband. "Well, this is a wedding, a joyful, romantic event, so I'm sure no one will be falling asleep."

"Except me." Baxter stretched out his feet and gloomily contemplated his slippers.

"Just be happy you're not the best man. At least you won't have to stand up at the altar."

Baxter grunted. "Prestwick would never have picked me to be his best man. We can't stand each other."

"Piffle." Cecily narrowed her eyes. "Why, Bax, I do believe you're disappointed Kevin didn't pick you to be his best man."

"Not at all. I'm just somewhat surprised he picked that Winchester chap. He told me himself they hadn't seen each other in years."

"Well, I do think they kept in touch fairly often." She

wrestled with her conscience for a full ten seconds before blurting out, "At least we know he didn't murder the Het-hertons. At least I don't think he did."

Baxter raised his eyebrows. "Ah, I was wondering how long it would be before you brought up that subject again. "I'd hoped that the preparations for the wedding would keep your mind off the murders."

Cecily shook her head. "I'm afraid not even the wedding of my best friend could erase that problem. I'm just relieved that Charles doesn't appear to be the killer."

Baxter's eyebrows drew together. "And how, may I ask, did you arrive at that assumption? Or for that matter, why did you suspect him in the first place? I was under the distinct impression you were convinced that Crossley fellow had something to do with it."

"Well, yes, I did. I do." Cecily hesitated for a moment, remembering her promise to Charles. "It's the fact that the killer would most likely have some scientific knowledge," she said at last. "That included Charles as a suspect."

"That could include any number of people. Even that little friend of Madeline's. Didn't you say she was a biologist, or something?"

"Horticulturist. Not really anything to do with explo-sives."

"Well, neither is a doctor or a motorcar designer."

Cecily puffed out her breath in frustration. "Grace Dan-bury didn't even know Sir Walter. But you are quite right, of course. I admit I'm grasping at straws. The killer could be any one of our guests, I suppose. Or even someone from outside. I just think it's more likely to be Roland Crossley, because he had a strong motive to be rid of Sir Walter."

"Then again, there could be other people who benefitted from his death. His wife, for instance. She could have wanted to be free of him."

"Enough to die with him? Really, Bax, that makes no sense at all."

"Perhaps she didn't intend to get hurt. She may have underestimated the power of the explosive. Perhaps she simply wanted to frighten him, or something."

"It's a possibility, I suppose. One I hadn't considered, I must say. If that's the case, however, we shall never know for certain."

"You still haven't told me why you are so sure Winchester is innocent."

"I talked to him." Much as she longed to tell Baxter everything, she was bound by her promise to say nothing about Charles's suspicions concerning his wife. "He convinced me he couldn't have killed two people in cold blood. After all, he's a doctor. Dedicated to saving lives, not destroying them."

"So was Dr. Jekyll."

"That's fiction."

"I'm just trying to point out the holes in your logic. In any case, I thought you wanted to keep the murders a secret from everyone."

"I do. Kevin, however, confided in Charles, though I'm still not sure why he did that."

"I knew that chap couldn't be trusted."

Cecily decided to ignore that. "Well, anyway, let's just say I trust my intuition. I don't think Charles Winchester killed the Hethertons."

"And this Crossley chap?"

"I don't know." What's more, she told herself, she was unlikely to know for certain, unless she had a chance to talk to him. Even then, it was highly unlikely he'd confess to a double murder. It seemed inevitable that she would have to hand the case over to the inspector after all, or at the very least, P.C. Northcott, and hope that somehow the killer would be brought to justice.

The trouble was, as each day passed, the likelihood of that appeared to be fading. This was one murder that might very well remain unsolved. She wasn't sure how she could live with that.

* * *

Upstairs in a guest room, Gertie picked up the pillow off the bed and gave it a good shake. "Look at this bed. Looks as if these two were fighting each other all night. The sheets are all pulled out from the bottom."

Pansy giggled. "I can't imagine what they were doing. They're both too old and fat to do much."

Gertie threw the pillow at her. "That's no way to talk about our guests. Don't you let Chubby hear you talk like that. She'll put you through the wringer and hang you out to dry, that she will."

"You talk like that all the time."

"Not about the guests. Not in front of Chubby, anyhow. Besides, I'm the blinking head housemaid. I can get away with it."

Pansy tugged at the blankets to straighten them. "Strikes me you get away with a lot more than any of us, especially with Mrs. Chubb."

Gertie grinned. "You have to know how to get around her. She's got a loud mouth on her, but she's a softie inside. Do anything for you, she would."

"Except give us time off when we want it."

"Well, she can't, can she. She has to have us here when we're needed. You get your weekly afternoon off, and one whole day a month, just like we all do."

"Yeah, but they're different days than what Samuel gets, so we don't have much time to spend together."

Gertie pursed her lips. "You and Samuel are going strong, then, are you?"

Pansy's cheeks warmed. "Yes, I s'pose we are. I really, really like him a lot, and he says he likes me, too."

Gertie frowned. "Not thinking of getting bleeding married, are you?"

"Why? What's wrong with that?"

"Too blinking young, you are, that's what."

"I know lots of girls my age that get married."

"Are they happy?"

Pansy shrugged. "How do I know?" She gave Gertie a sly look. "Were you happy, married to Ross?"

Gertie lifted the edge of the eiderdown and pulled it across the bed. "I s'pose I was. Ross was a lot older than me, but he was kind to me and the twins. Treated them like his own, he did."

"But did you love him?" Pansy clasped her hands across her chest. "You know, like the deep down, warm inside, aching kind of love?"

Gertie paused, the eiderdown in her hand. "No, not really. I loved him, all right, but it was more like a friendship sort of love."

"What about Ian, the twins' father? I know you weren't married to him, but did you love him like that?"

Gertie threw down the eiderdown. "Whatcha talking about him for? You don't know nothing about him. Ian Rossiter was a bloody liar and a cheat. He kept saying we'd get married but then I found out he already had a wife. There I was, carrying his two babies, and it was the worst time in my life, so don't you never mention his bleeding name to me again, all right?"

"All right, all right. I'm sorry. I didn't know. You never told me the whole story until now." Pansy backed away from the bed. "I didn't know it would upset you so."

"Well, it does. Go and empty the slops. I'll finish making the bed."

Pansy pulled a face. "That's the job I hate the most." She bent down and pulled the chamber pot out from under the bed. "I wish everyone would use the lavatory at night, instead of piddling in this thing."

Gertie snorted. "Then we'd have all these people wandering up and down the stairs in the dark in their nightshirts looking for the lav."

"Well, then, I wish we had lavatories in every room, like

madam has in her suite. Then they wouldn't have to go nowhere in the dark."

"Are you blinking daft? Even Buckingham Palace doesn't have lavatories in the bedrooms."

"How do you know?"

" 'Cos I know, that's how." Gertie put on her best imitation of Mrs. Chubb's voice. "Now get downstairs with them slops before the guests start coming back from breakfast. And don't forget to cover up the pot with a towel, just in case you meet someone on the way."

"Why is it always me what has to empty the slops?" Carrying the chamber pot with both hands, Pansy headed for the door. "One day I'll be head housemaid, and then I won't have to do it no more."

"You won't be an ordinary housemaid much longer if you don't get a bleeding move on." Gertie shook her head as Pansy went out the door. She felt sorry for the girl, though she wasn't about to let on. Carrying the slops downstairs was a nasty job, but someone had to do it. She'd certainly done her share. How she'd hated it.

Gertie grinned to herself when she remembered how tempted she was to throw the lot out the bedroom window, like they did in the old days. She might have done it and all, if she hadn't been scared of hitting someone over the head with the stinking mess. That would have caused a row all right.

Giving the eiderdown a final pat, she moved over to the dresser to tidy up the brushes, combs and pins that lay in a heap. She had just picked up a silver-backed comb when she heard from somewhere outside the room the most bone-chilling shriek, followed by an almighty crash.

Heart thumping, she dropped the comb and leapt for the door. Dragging it open, she saw Pansy, halfway down the corridor, crouched against the wall with her hands over her face. Lying on the carpet in front of her were pieces of white china in the middle of a spreading pool of yellow liquid.

"You blithering idiot!" Gertie rushed toward her. "Look at that bleeding mess. We'll have to get it all cleaned up and the guests will be back from breakfast any minute. How could you be so blinking clumsy?"

"H-has it gone?"

Gertie stared at her, noticing for the first time that the young girl was shaking from head to toe. Bewildered, she looked down the hallway both ways but could see nothing but empty walls. "Has what gone? What are you flipping talking about?"

Pansy slowly lowered her hands and looked fearfully down the corridor toward the stairs. "It was there. Right at the top of the stairs. I saw it."

Gertie's heart started thumping uncomfortably again. "What did you see?"

Pansy's lips moved, but no sound came out.

"What?" Gertie leaned forward. "Tell me what you saw, Pansy."

The frightened girl mouthed something again, and this time Gertie heard the faint whisper. "It was the snowman. It was right here, creeping down the hallway." She shuddered. "It's alive, Gertie. I tell you, the snowman's come alive."


Determined to have a word with Roland Crossley, Cecily had feigned an excuse to go down to her office early that morning, leaving Baxter to enjoy his morning newspaper in peace.

She'd had breakfast sent up to the suite for him, and had made do in her office with fried herring roe on toast and fried tomatoes.

After finishing the pot of tea that had come with her breakfast, she left her office and headed for the lobby, where she engaged Philip in conversation until the guests started to leave the dining room.

Roland was one of the last to leave, talking in his grating voice to a fellow guest as he strode into the lobby. Sarah

Crossley trailed behind him, a discontented frown adding furrows to her forehead.

She wore a white chiffon scarf tied over her hat, and a warm shawl covered her shoulders. Apparently she intended to brave the cold winds outside for a breath of fresh air.

Cecily called out as the couple passed by her. "Good morning, Mr. Crossley! Mrs. Crossley!"

Sarah merely nodded and kept walking, but Roland paused, ignoring his male companion's latest comment.

"Mrs. Baxter! Excellent breakfast. Superb. Must congratulate your accomplished chef. The sausage, tripe, and onions were delicious." He rubbed his protruding belly with thick fingers.

"Well, thank you, Mr. Crossley. I must pass on your very kind comments to Michel, our chef. I know he will be most appreciative."

Crossley nodded and started to move on, and Cecily raised a hand. "I wonder if you have a moment? I have a question I'd like to ask."

"Certainly, my dear." Crossley beamed. "Always ready to oblige. That's my motto."

"It concerns the library. I'm thinking of adding some classic literature, and I was wondering if you could recommend some suitable books."

Crossley looked taken aback, as well he might. In her desire to hold his attention, Cecily had said the first thing that had popped into her head. She had no idea if the man even read the newspaper, much less was informed on classic literature.

"Well, I really don't . . ." The MP ran a finger around the inside of his starched collar, reminding Cecily of her husband. Baxter often did the same thing whenever he was flustered, or trying to avoid answering an awkward question.

"Oh, well, never mind." She gave him a bright smile. "I'm sure I can find something in Wellercombe. They have some very good bookstores there, you know."

Still looking baffled, Crossley nodded. "Yes, the shops

there are excellent. I did some Christmas shopping there and found some very good bargains."

"I'm happy to hear that." Cecily searched desperately for a way to guide the conversation in the direction she wanted it to go. The lobby had emptied out, and only she and Crossley remained. Philip had buried himself behind the reception desk as usual.

This was probably the only opportunity she would get to talk to Crossley alone, and she couldn't come up with a single idea on how to ask him where he was the day he was supposed to have gone hunting, without arousing his suspicion.

"I imagine Mrs. Crossley must have enjoyed the shopping as well," she said, grasping at straws as Crossley gave every indication of walking away.

To her surprise, the man sent a startled look over his shoulder, as if he were afraid someone else would overhear her comment.

Apparently noticing Cecily's raised eyebrows, he said quickly, "I don't want my wife to know I was in Wellercombe. She thinks I bought her Christmas present in London a month ago."

Cecily stared at him in bewilderment.

"You don't know my wife," Crossley said, his face grim. "If she knew I waited until the very last minute again to shop for her I wouldn't hear the last of it. She made my life miserable last year when I went out on Christmas Eve to get her presents. Never mind that I spent a fortune on the ungrateful woman."

"Oh." Cecily was beginning to understand and was not quite certain how to answer. "Well, I'm sure if—"

"It's not only that." Again Crossley glanced over his shoulder. "I told her I was going hunting. If she knew I'd lied to her she'd never trust me again. I have a hard enough time now convincing her I'm not doing anything underhanded when I'm late getting home. That woman knows more ways to put me through hell than you can ever imagine."

Intrigued to discover that the blustering braggart was so

thoroughly henpecked, Cecily could only nod weakly. "Rest assured, Mr. Crossley, I shall not mention a word to her about this."

"Thank you, Mrs. Baxter. Much obliged, I'm sure. I tell you, I nearly had a heart attack when I saw that woman, what's her name, Miss Danbury, coming out of a building in Weller-combe. I thought for certain she'd seen me and would mention it at the dinner table that night. All that fuss about the gas explosion must have taken her mind off it. Lucky for me, what?"

He backed away, bowing and nodding, then turned and hurried toward the stairs.

Cecily watched him go, her spirits deflating. By sheer chance she had the answer she was looking for, and it wasn't at all what she'd expected.

It seemed that Roland Crossley was not the killer after all. Which meant she had to start all over again. Unless either he or Charles Winchester had lied to her about what they were actually doing that fateful day before the explosion.

If that were so, she had no idea how to find the truth and reveal the killer. There was nothing left for her to do now but wait for P.C. Northcott to return, by which time, both the doctor and the MP would be back in London.

How she hated the thought that a ruthless killer could evade justice, after perpetrating such a brutal crime in her establishment. She felt responsible, somehow, and mortified that she was unable to solve a murder that had happened right under her nose. Her inability eroded her confidence and made her feel helpless and incapable—not something she accepted lightly.

Underlying it all was a deep, intense anger at the man who had got the better of her, and was most likely laughing up his sleeve at his cleverness in deceiving her.

She had vowed to bring him to justice and she had failed. It was not a good ending to the Christmas season.

# CHAPTER

## ❧ 15 ❧

"I don't know what to think." Mrs. Chubb stood in the kitchen shaking her head, her fingers plucking the folds of her apron. "I really don't know."

Gertie looked at Pansy, who sat on a chair, her face as white as the flour on the housekeeper's pastry board. "I can't believe you saw the snowman indoors. How did it get upstairs? Why wasn't it melting? There was no water on the carpet." She glanced at Mrs. Chubb. "Except for what spilled out of the chamber pot, anyway."

The housekeeper turned on her. "What? You spilled a chamber pot? Gertie, how could you?"

"It weren't me!" Gertie nodded at Pansy. "She was carrying it down the hallway when she saw the snowman. Or so she says. She dropped the chamber pot and it smashed into pieces."

"I did see it. I *did*!" Pansy burst into tears.

"Never mind that for now." Mrs. Chubb patted her

shoulder. "If you say you saw it then you did. The important thing is, did you clear up the mess?"

Gertie sighed. "Course we did. I made her clean it up while I kept watch. We had to hurry because the guests were coming back from breakfast but we got it all mopped up and we scrubbed the carpet with carbolic soap so it don't smell any more. Not much, anyway."

"You mean *I* mopped and scrubbed the carpet," Pansy said tearfully.

"Yeah, well, I helped."

"It was all that snowman's fault." Pansy sniffed, and rubbed her nose with the hem of her apron. "Scared me half to death, it did."

"So why. didn't it melt?" Gertie shoved a stray strand of hair out of her eyes. "If it's made of snow it should have melted. That's what I don't bleeding understand."

"I'd like to know how it got inside the Pennyfoot in the first place, and why no one else has seen it." Mrs. Chubb gave Pansy a stern look. "Was it on its own or was someone carrying it?"

Pansy shuddered. "It were on its own. *Walking* on its own. Evil it was."

"Yeah, I saw footprints, too." Gertie hugged herself to ward off the cold chill attacking her spine. "Out there in the snow. There was only one set, and all. Pansy's right. That snowman walks all by hisself."

"That's impossible." Mrs. Chubb sat down heavily on a chair. "I refuse to believe that there's a snowman walking around out there. Unless . . ."

Pansy looked hopefully at her, while Gertie demanded, "Unless what?"

What if it's someone dressed up as a snowman come to rob the guests?" She jumped up from her chair. "We must tell madam about this. Right away."

"I'll go." Gertie scrambled to get out the door before Mrs. Chubb could stop her. Any excuse to get out of that kitchen for a while. The whole business of the snowman was really getting on her nerves. She'd just like to get her hands on whoever was doing this.

Hurrying up the steps, she narrowly missed colliding with Samuel, who was on his way down.

"Here," he said, slapping her behind with his cap, "what's yer flipping hurry?"

"Never you mind." She paused as he ran by her. "Pansy says you two are going strong."

Samuel halted at the foot of the steps. "Yeah? What of it?"

"Just make sure you don't say or do nothing to her you don't mean. She's young, our Pansy. I don't want to see her get bleeding hurt."

He looked at her for a long moment, then said quietly, "You don't have to worry about me and Pansy. My name's not Ian Rossiter."

She smiled. "Yeah. I know that."

"Good." He nodded at her, then continued on his way.

Reaching the lobby, she hurried across to the stairs, keeping a sharp eye out for any sign of the snowman. Not that she really expected to see it.

Part of her still wanted to believe that Pansy had imagined it. She didn't want to think about that thing creeping down the hallway where she could bump into it any minute.

She reached the first landing and quickened her step as she made the turn for the second flight of stairs. As she did so, she heard a faint sound from down the hallway.

Someone was whistling the tune that turned her blood cold. The same tune that Ian used to whistle in the halls of the Pennyfoot years ago.

Slapping her hands over her ears, Gertie fled up the stairs and arrived panting and shivering at madam's suite. Frantically she rapped on the door, until it abruptly opened and she stumbled inside.

"Good Lord, whatever's happened now?"

Struggling for breath, she looked up into Baxter's outraged

face. "The snowman," she said, her voice sounding strange to her ears. "It's here inside the building and Mrs. Chubb thinks it's someone come to steal from the guests."

"What the blazes are you talking about?"

Gertie winced as Baxter took hold of her arm in a firm grip and led her across the room to the davenport. "Here. Sit down and start from the beginning. Slowly."

She obeyed the curt command, sinking onto the soft surface and wishing she could bury herself right down inside it.

"Now, what's all this rubbish about a ghost?"

Gulping, Gertie told him the whole story. How they first saw the snowman in different places, and how James heard it whistling Ian's tune, and how it turned up when she thought the twins were lost and then it disappeared, and how she saw the footprints in the snow. When she got to the part about Pansy seeing it in the hallway, Baxter held up his hand.

"Are you trying to tell me there's an actual snowman in the hallway?"

"Well, it's not there now." Gertie pulled in a deep breath. Talking about it all at once like that, she had to admit it all sounded pretty daft.

"I imagine not. I would assume, however, that there's a large pool of dirty water staining the carpet."

"Well, that's it, isn't it. There ain't."

Baxter looked baffled. "There ain't . . . *isn't* what?"

"Water. That's what I'm trying to tell you. I heard it whistling. Just now. If it had been made of snow, it would have melted by now, wouldn't it."

Baxter rubbed his chin. "You say both you and Pansy saw this . . . uh . . . snowman, both outside and inside the Pennyfoot?"

"Yes, sir. Both of us saw it."

"At the same time?"

"Yes, sir. It was moving from place to place. Course, we didn't actually see it moving. Not then, anyhow. Pansy saw it moving in the yard first, then I saw it moving out on the lawn and—"

"I'd say someone is playing pranks. Probably some of the footmen. They tend to get bored after Christmas and end up looking for mischief."

Gertie let out her breath in frustration. "But what about the whistling? And Mrs. Chubb says as how she thinks it's someone dressed up as a snowman and he's trying to rob the guests. That's what she sent me up here to tell madam."

"I think Mrs. Chubb may have had a spot too much of Michel's brandy." Baxter marched to the door and held it open. "Tell her I will look into the matter. Meanwhile, let's get everyone back to paying attention to their duties instead of worrying about snowmen or any other such nonsense."

"Yes, sir." Gertie dragged herself to the door. "You will tell madam what I said?"

"Yes, I will inform Mrs. Baxter that someone on her staff is playing tricks and upsetting everyone."

"I s'pose that will have to do." Gertie crept out into the hallway, afraid she'd hear the creepy whistling again. The door snapped shut behind her, making her jump.

Muttering to herself, she started down the stairs. Her nerves were all in pieces, thanks to that bloody snowman. The next time she saw it, she was going to attack it with whatever she could lay her hands on. Then she'd find out once and for all if it was someone playing pranks, or someone out to rob the rooms, or even a ghost seeking vengeance on her for cutting Ian out of his babies' lives.


Cecily looked up in surprise from her desk when her husband tapped on the door and walked into her office. She could see at once something was troubling him, and quickly closed the ledger so she could give him her full attention.

"Gertie just came to see me." He sat down on the chair opposite her, and leaned his elbows on the desk.

"Is she not well?" Cecily felt guilty. Having been so occupied with the Hethertons' killer lately, she had quite forgotten that Gertie was having an emotional problem of some kind.

"She was babbling about a snowman." He frowned. "I seem to remember you saying something about her seeing a snowman a few days ago."

"Yes, I was telling Kevin about it." Cecily shook her head. "Apparently Gertie keeps seeing an imaginary snowman that moves about. How could I have forgotten. I meant to speak to her about it."

"Yes, well, it might not be so imaginary. Gertie said Pansy had seen this snowman as well." He leaned back in his chair. "If you ask me some of the footmen are playing pranks again. They can be a dratted nuisance, upsetting everyone. We need to give them some extra duties, keep them occupied."

"Oh, that's right. I remember now. Oh, dear, do you really think it's the footmen playing around? I suppose we shall have to reprimand them."

"I'll have a word with them." He paused, then added, "Mrs. Chubb apparently has formed the conclusion that this snowman person is someone in a costume attempting to rob the guest rooms. I doubt that, of course. Still, it's disturbing that it was actually seen inside the building."

Cecily sat up straight. "The snowman was inside? In here? When? Where?"

Baxter leaned forward again. "Now, now, Cecily, there's no need to be agitated. As I said, I'm quite sure the footmen have a hand in this and as soon as I find out who—"

"Did Gertie see it? Where did she see it?"

"Actually I think it was Pansy who saw it in the Pennyfoot, but—" He broke off. "What are you doing?"

"I'm ringing for someone to come up from the kitchen." Cecily tugged hard on the bell pull, then let it go. "I want to question both Gertie and Pansy, and try to get to the bottom of this."

"What about the footmen?"

"By all means talk to them. As soon as possible. I'll need to know what they say."

"I'll go now." Baxter shoved himself off the chair. "If I find out those brats have caused all this trouble . . ."

"You'd better hope it *is* the footmen playing tricks."

"What does that mean?"

"It means that Mrs. Chubb may well be right. It could be someone in disguise trying to rob the rooms. It wouldn't be the first time someone disguised himself in a costume and scared everyone half to death."

Baxter nodded. "I'll tell Clive to keep an eye out for anything suspicious. If the footmen are not involved, I'll have them keep watch as well. Though I can't imagine why no one else has seen the blasted thing."

"Well, even if someone had, he would probably assume it had something to do with the Christmas festivities. It's not unusual to have people dressed in fancy costumes during the Christmas season. Especially here at the Pennyfoot, when we put on so many revues."

"I suppose not. Still, you would have thought someone would have mentioned seeing a snowman wandering around the place, for heaven's sake."

Cold with apprehension, she watched him leave the room. There was one other possibility—one she wasn't yet ready to voice to her husband. If neither Charles Winchester nor Roland Crossley were responsible for the deaths of the Hethertons, could it be possible that this mysterious person dressed as a snowman had killed them? If so, why would he still be lurking about the Pennyfoot, unless he planned to use the second cracker on someone else?

The thought chilled her to the bone. What should she do? The wedding was tomorrow. The rehearsal that very evening. Dare she wait another day to allow Madeline's wedding to proceed without incident? Or should she heed the warning and ring the inspector right away?

If only she could be sure the risk was real, and not just a

figment of an overactive imagination, or as Baxter seemed to think, the work of bored, mischievous footmen.

A tap on the door disturbed her thoughts. In answer to her response, Gertie edged into the room. "You rang, m'm?"

"Yes, I did." Cecily waved a hand at the chair. "Sit down, Gertie."

She waited until the young woman was settled, which took some time since Gertie fidgeted a good deal before finally giving her an expectant look.

"Baxter tells me that you and Pansy have been seeing your rather unusual snowman quite a lot on the grounds of the Pennyfoot."

"Yes, m'm. And not just outside, neither." Gertie leaned forward and lowered her voice. "Pansy saw it upstairs this morning. On the top landing."

"You didn't see it, too?"

"No, m'm. I was inside one of the rooms. But I heard it. Just now, when I went up to your suite. I heard it whistling."

"Whistling?"

"Yes, m'm. It were that tune. The one that Ian always used to whistle."

"Great heavens." Cecily stared at her. "Ian Rossiter. I haven't thought about him in years."

"Nor me, m'm. At least, not that often anyway. But I am now. What with that whistling and all. I kept thinking he was dead and it was his ghost coming after me. Only ghosts don't leave footprints in the snow, do they, m'm?"

Cecily drew a sharp breath. "No, Gertie, they don't. Now I want you to go back to the kitchen and try to put this ghost business right out of your mind. Obviously someone is playing a joke on all of us, and in very poor taste, I might add. Mr. Baxter and Clive will do their best to find this person and put a stop to all this nonsense."

"Yes, m'm. Thank you, m'm." Gertie got up and dropped a small curtsey. "I'll be going now, then."

Cecily nodded. "Very well. Please send Pansy to me when

you get back to the kitchen. I'd like to talk to her as well."
She waited until the door had closed behind the housemaid
before reaching for the telephone. The safety of her guests
was more important that a perfect wedding. Madeline
would just have to understand.

The operator's voice answered her and she asked to be put
through to Inspector Cranshaw. While she waited, she rehearsed what she would tell him. She would have to explain
that P.C. Northcott had concluded that the deaths were an
accident, whereas evidence suggested otherwise.

He would doubt her word at first, until she explained
about the missing cracker and the mysterious snowman.
Though, now she really thought about it, the whole thing
sounded like a particularly poor fairy tale.

While she was still debating on whether or not to replace
the receiver, the operator spoke in her ear.

"Inspector Cranshaw is away on a case, Mrs. Baxter. He's
not expected back until the first of the year. If it's an emergency I can contact the constabulary in Wellercombe?"

Cecily hesitated, then said firmly, "That won't be necessary. Thank you, operator. I will contact the inspector myself
when he returns." With a small sigh of relief, she replaced the
receiver.

The decision had been made for her. Now all she could
do was hope that her staff would be able to catch whoever
was prowling the hallways of the Pennyfoot in a snowman's
suit before he gave someone a heart attack. Or worse.


"What did madam want?" Mrs. Chubb asked, when Gertie
charged into the kitchen.

"She wanted to ask me about the snowman." Gertie picked
up the apron she'd thrown down when she'd heard the bell
summoning her to madam's office. "Mr. Baxter told her what
I told him and she wanted to hear it from us. Not that I could
tell her much.

Mrs. Chubb bent down to pick up the milk urn from under the table. "What did she say, then?"

"She said Mr. Baxter and Clive were going to find the snowman and stop him from running around like that. Though if you ask me, that Clive is as bad, shuffling around the way he does, staring and all." She tied the apron strings firmly behind her back. "If I hadn't seen him in one place at the same time I saw the snowman in the other, I'd have sworn it were him trying to get a rise out of me."

She paused as a thought occurred to her. "You know, it's a funny thing, but every time I've seen that snowman, Clive is somewhere close by. I wouldn't be surprised if he don't have something to do with it somehow."

Mrs. Chubb poured some milk into a jug, then returned the heavy urn to its place under the table. "Go on with you, Gertie. Always saying nasty things about that man. Just because he's quiet and keeps his place. Not a bit like your Ian used to be. That lad was always swaggering about and talking about himself all the time."

"Shut up about Ian." Gertie picked up a tray of silverware from the sink and brought it over to the table. "Why does everyone keep talking about him lately? I'm sick of thinking about bloody Ian. I've spent the last few years trying to forget all about him. I hope he *is* dead, then he can't bother me or my twins no more."

"Gertie McBride! What a horrible thing to say. Say you don't mean it. Right this minute."

"All right, all right. Don't get your knickers in a twist. It just slipped out, that's all. Course I didn't mean it." Though deep down inside she knew she had meant it.

Although she never said so out loud, she lived with a constant dread that one day Ian Rossiter would turn up and try to take her twins away from her. If that ever happened, so help her, she'd take a knife to him before she'd let him take her babies away.

# CHAPTER
## ❀ 16 ❀

Cecily smiled at the young maid who sat fidgeting in front of her desk. Pansy always looked as if she were ready to run away the moment anyone said anything to her. "There's no need to be alarmed," she said. "I simply wanted to ask you about the snowman you saw upstairs this morning."

Her bottom lip trembling, Pansy clutched her knees. "I'm sorry I smashed up the chamber pot, m'm, really I am. I couldn't help it, what with that thing walking about and all. I know I'll have to pay for the chamber pot out of me wages but . . ." She smacked a hand over her mouth as tears started spilling down her face.

Cecily stared at her in bewilderment. "Chamber pot?"

Pansy nodded, the bottom half of her face still covered by her hand.

"Pansy, I have no idea what you're talking about. Perhaps you'd better tell me about it."

Cecily waited while the young girl choked back sobs, then struggled to get her voice under control.

"I dropped it . . . when I saw that *thing*."

"Oh, my," Cecily said faintly. "You dropped a chamber pot? Was it . . . er . . . full?"

"Yes, m'm." Pansy choked back a sob. "But you don't have to worry, m'm. We cleaned it all up. At least, I did. I scrubbed the carpet with carbolic soap. It don't smell no more now."

"Well, that's a blessing at least." Cecily leaned back. "So now tell me about the snowman. Where was it going? What did it look like?"

Pansy appeared to think about it. "It looked like a snowman, m'm."

"Perhaps you can describe exactly what it looked like," Cecily said gently.

"Oh! Well, it had a hat on its head, and a red scarf around its neck. I can't think of anything else, 'cos it was all snow. Except . . ." Her voice trailed off.

"Except what?"

Pansy leaned forward, her words dropping to a whisper. "His eyes, m'm. Weird they was. Black like coal and staring. Like he was blind. Only how could he see to walk about if he was blind?"

"Are you quite sure he was made of snow?"

Pansy's brows drew together. "I think so. He were all white, anyway, and sort of . . . fuzzy. Though he weren't melting or nothing." Her face cleared. "Now I come to think of it, m'm, it could have been cotton wool."

"Ah!" Cecily leaned forward. "Now think hard, Pansy. Did you see his feet?"

Pansy sat with furrowed brow for several seconds, then shook her head. "I don't remember, m'm. I was so scared and he was staring right at me and yet he wasn't, if you know what I mean. Then he sort of turned around in a clumsy sort of way and disappeared down the hallway."

"Toward the steps to the roof garden?"

"Yes, m'm." She caught her breath. "You think he went up on the roof?"

"It's possible." Cecily gave her an encouraging smile. "Don't worry, I'm quite sure someone is playing a joke on us. We'll catch him sooner or later and put a stop to all this nonsense."

"Yes, m'm."

"You can go now, Pansy."

"Yes, m'm." Pansy got up and dropped an awkward curtsey. "Thank you, m'm." She started for the door.

"Oh, and Pansy?" Cecily waited for her to turn around. "There's no need to worry about the chamber pot. You won't have to pay for it."

For the first time since she'd entered the room, Pansy's shy smile appeared. "Thank you, m'm. I'm very much obliged, I'm sure." She fled out the door, leaving Cecily to contemplate once more the sinister implications of the chilling unknown visitor.

Madeline arrived later that afternoon to decorate the ball-room. Carrying large bouquets of flowers, she sailed across the lobby, while her future husband followed, laden down with two large boxes.

Cecily met them at the reception desk, where she'd been asking Philip if he'd noticed a snowman wandering about the place. It had taken some time to explain to him that she was not testing him on his powers of observation, or his attention to his duties, but that there really had been a snow-man sighted inside the walls of the Pennyfoot.

Seeing Madeline floating toward her, Cecily decided that her friend would be the perfect person to ask about the intruder who was causing so much commotion among her staff. Madeline could see things others couldn't. Maybe she could help catch the culprit.

"Those flowers are magnificent," she exclaimed, when

Madeline reached her. "It always amazes me that you can find roses in the dead of winter."

"I have good friends at Covent Garden." Madeline buried her face in the fragrant blossoms. "I was unable to get white roses, though. Most disappointing. I had hoped that the roses I ordered for Lady Clara would still be fresh enough to use, since she has no use of them now, but they have faded and I had to throw them out."

"How sad. White roses would have looked wonderful for the wedding reception."

"Well, pink ones will have to do." She smiled at Cecily. "They will blend very nicely with the Christmas fir, which still looks fresh enough to leave up, though if I don't get these flowers into water soon, they will lose their vibrancy and will look very sad by tomorrow."

"Of course. Come along, then." Cecily started down the hallway to the ballroom. She waited until Kevin had deposited the boxes on a table and Madeline had laid down the flowers before saying to the doctor, "Do you remember Gertie's fainting fit the other day, and her mention of a snowman whom she said frightened her?"

Kevin nodded. He seemed tired, and out of sorts. His eyes looked heavy lidded and his tie was askew . . . most unusual for the usually impeccable doctor. "Of course I remember. I've been expecting her to pay me a visit."

"Oh dear, I'm afraid I forgot to pass on your message." Cecily watched Madeline arrange a bouquet of roses in the stone vase on one of the ballroom's pillars. "As it happens, however, Gertie wasn't having hallucinations after all. There really is a snowman running around the Pennyfoot."

In the act of lifting white ribbon garlands out of a box, Kevin froze. "I beg your pardon?"

"I'm sorry, I know it sounds ludicrous, but apparently someone is dressed as a snowman and is prowling about the hallways."

Madeline turned, a pink blossom waving about in her hand. "How positively ridiculous."

"Well, yes, I certainly thought so." Cecily gave her what she hoped was a meaningful look. "The problem is, so far no one else has seen it. Or at least, no one has mentioned seeing it. So I really don't know too much about it."

"Ah." Madeline finished fitting the blossoms into the vase. "Kevin, darling. Do be a dear and fetch me a large urn of water for these flowers, if you please. If I don't get them wet soon they will fade and die before the reception tomorrow."

"Right." Kevin looked relieved as he dropped the garlands back into the box and hurried out through the doors.

"He'll take his time." Madeline approached the table. "He offered to help me decorate, which surprised me. I know he loathed the idea."

"It was nice of him to offer." Cecily glanced at the door to make sure the doctor had left. "Is he all right? He looks a little under the weather."

"He's perfectly well. Just a little apprehensive. It isn't every day one marries a witch."

Looking at Madeline's pinched expression, Cecily murmured, "I hope you two haven't been arguing about the difference in your professions again."

"We'll always argue about it." Madeline sighed. "He refuses to accept the fact that my potions work, yet he won't allow me to prove it. But enough about that. Tell me about the snowman."

Cecily recounted everything that Gertie and Pansy had told her.

Madeline looked thoughtful, but much to Cecily's disappointment, she did not go into a trance. "If I were you, Cecily dear," she said, when Cecily had finished her tale, "I'd send every able-bodied man in the place out looking for that prankster."

"So you do think it's someone playing tricks?"

Madeline raised a delicate eyebrow. "What else would it be?"

Cecily hesitated. "Well, I did think it might have something to do with the Hethertons' deaths."

"Oh, well, it's possible I suppose." Her frown cleared. "Oh, you thought I'd be able to tell you . . . I'm sorry, Cecily. I don't have any perceptions concerning your snowman, though I must say—"

She broke off as Kevin entered the ballroom, carrying a large urn. "Oh, there you are, darling. Could you pour water into these vases for me?"

While Kevin obliged, Madeline lifted the garlands from the table and thrust her face close to Cecily. "I don't think you have anything to worry about from your snowman," she whispered. "I'm sure he means no harm." Raising her voice for Kevin's benefit, she added, "I should remove all the Christmas decorations before I hang the garlands. Could you help me, Kevin, dear?"

With that she sailed away across the ballroom to the stairs that led to the balcony.

Cecily was left to wonder if her reassuring comments were based on opinion, or one of Madeline's sudden insights.

Phoebe arrived just as Madeline had finished draping the white ribbon garlands over the balcony railings. "I left Freddie in the bar," she announced, as Madeline descended the stairs. "I thought he'd get in the way if I let him in here."

"Thank the Lord for small mercies," Madeline murmured.

Kevin grinned, while Phoebe sent her a suspicious look. "I hope you will be on time for the rehearsal this evening," she said, in her prim voice. "Algie doesn't care to be kept waiting, you know."

Madeline sniffed. "I just hope he remembers his lines. The last time I attended one of his weddings he forgot the bride's name and dropped the wedding rings on the floor. As I remember, they rolled out of reach and had to be retrieved with a candle snuffer."

Phoebe tossed her head. "The poor dear had a bad case of the sniffles that day and happened to sneeze at the wrong moment. Hardly his fault, I'd say."

Kevin stepped forward and laid his hand on Madeline's shoulder. "I think I shall join the colonel in the bar, if you'll excuse me, ladies." He nodded at Phoebe. "Until this evening, Mrs. Fortescue. I look forward to the occasion with great pleasure." He strode off, leaving Phoebe staring after him.

"Such a well-mannered man." She turned to Madeline. "You are so lucky to be marrying such a gentleman."

For once, Madeline didn't argue.

"I'm so excited about the wedding tomorrow." Gertie gathered up a stack of dishes from the kitchen draining board and laid them on a large silver tray. "I can hardly wait. I do love weddings. And the twins are excited, as well. They've never been to a wedding before."

Mrs. Chubb looked at her in surprise. "They were at your wedding to Ross McBride!"

"Well, yes, but they were a lot younger then. I don't think they remember it." Gertie shook her head. "Sometimes I don't even remember it. It all seems such a long time ago." She picked up the tray. "You know, sometimes I have trouble remembering what Ross looked like. I try to picture him in me head, but it's all fuzzy, like the photographs in that magazine you're always reading."

Mrs. Chubb nodded. "I know what you mean. It's been a long time since I could picture my hubby in my mind. Been dead and gone for more than twenty years, he has. All that time just flown by. Doesn't seem possible."

Gertie was about to answer when the door burst open and Pansy rushed in. Her cap had slid to one side and she was panting so hard she couldn't get any words out that anyone could understand.

"What's the blinking matter with you?" Gertie demanded, then caught her breath. "You've seen it again?"

Pansy nodded.

Mrs. Chubb gasped. "Not the snowman?"

Pansy nodded again.

"Where?" Gertie demanded.

Pansy threw an arm up in the air and frantically flapped her hand.

"Come on." Gertie grabbed the startled maid by the arm. "I'm going after it," she told Mrs. Chubb. "Tell whoever you can get hold of to come and help me."

The housekeeper started to protest, but Gertie was past listening to her advice. She was sick and tired of the snowman and she was going to put an end to it, one way or another.

Dragging a squealing Pansy behind her, she charged down the hallway to the stairs. Halfway up them she paused to give Pansy time to catch her breath. "Now," she said, when Pansy's panting slowed a little. "Exactly where did you see it?"

"Outside the ballroom."

The words were still breathless, but Gertie understood them. "Right. Come on."

"What are you going to do?"

Gertie gritted her teeth. "I'm going to knock its bleeding block off, that's what."

"Can't we wait until someone comes to help?"

"No, we bloody can't. It will be gone again and we'll have to wait for another day for it to come back. It's now or nothing."

"I'd rather it was nothing."

Pansy held back and Gertie took a firmer grip on her arm. "Come *on*. I want you to show me exactly where you saw the bugger."

Fortunately most of the guests had retired to their rooms for a late afternoon rest, and the lobby was empty when the maids reached the top of the stairs.

Holding tight to Pansy's arm, Gertie hurried across to the

hallway. Philip was nowhere to be seen, much to her dismay. She was hoping to ask for his help. Not that the frail desk clerk could do much, but any help was better than none.

Stopping just long enough to grab a mop and a broom from the closet, Gertie handed the mop to Pansy. "If we see it," she said, "bash it as hard as you can with this."

Pansy took the mop in hands that visibly trembled. "What if it bashes me back?"

"It will have to take on two of us," Gertie said grimly. "If we keep hitting it and yelling as loud as we can, someone's bound to get here sooner or later."

Praying that Mrs. Chubb had managed to summon help, Gertie crept down the hallway. She could hear voices in the bar at the other end and thought about going down there to ask for help. On the other hand, madam would be really cross with her if she told everyone about the snowman.

While she was still dithering, Pansy gave her a hefty nudge in her back, whispering fiercely, "There it is!"

Nerves jolting, Gertie looked around the corner and down toward the ballroom. There it stood, a huge, white menacing presence. One of its hands gripped the door handle to the library. A very human hand.

Gertie didn't stop to think, she charged like a knight on horseback, her broom held like a lance. Galloping forward, she yelled and yelled. Vaguely she could hear Pansy squealing behind her, but she was too infuriated to pay attention to her.

The snowman had turned as she started her charge, and its coal black eyes seemed to fix on her face. For a moment she faltered, chilled by the staring, expressionless gaze. Then, with a supreme effort of will, she closed her eyes and lunged with her broom.

She heard a muffled exclamation, and felt the broom jump in her hand as it struck its target. Behind her Pansy screamed, so loud the screech of it hurt her ears. Seconds later, muffled shouts drifted down the hallway behind them.

Gertie opened her eyes, and saw something round and white rolling toward her. It took a moment to realize what it was, and now it was her turn to let out a bloodcurdling yell. The snowman's head, its mouth gaping, black eyes staring, came to a rest at her feet.

With a shout of horror, Gertie jumped back, dropping the broom on her toes. She barely felt the pain. She was staring at the headless snowman. Only it wasn't exactly headless.

Another head poked up from its neck. With a face she recognized.

Gertie's knees gave way and she slid down the wall to the floor. She found her voice, and it sounded shaky and weird. "What the bloody hell are you doing here?"

"I came to see my kids." Ian Rossiter shook his head, then did something to the front of the snowman's chest. The whole body divided down the middle and swung back on hinges. Ian stepped out of it, and let it fall to the floor with a crash.


Inside the ballroom, Cecily had just fitted white candles into a candelabra when she heard the ruckus outside. Phoebe and Madeline halted their bickering long enough to stare in the direction of the doors.

"Good grief," Madeline muttered. "Whatever's going on out there?"

"Oh, my." Phoebe clutched her lace-covered throat. "I do hope it's not Freddie battling the Boers again."

"There's one way to find out." Cecily set the candelabra down on a white-clothed table and marched toward the doors. "Stay here, both of you. If there's trouble we don't need all of us to get involved."

"I'm coming with you." Madeline thrust a bunch of ribbon bows into Phoebe's arms and ran after Cecily. They reached the door together, just as a thump shook the wall, followed by a loud thud.

Cecily hauled open the door and stepped out into the

hallway. The first thing she saw was Gertie, sitting on the floor with her back against the wall. Obviously the source of the first thump. The second apparently was the head of a snowman and what appeared to be an open casket of sorts.

Stunned, Cecily stared at the face of the man standing over Gertie. "Ian? Ian Rossiter! What in heaven's name are you doing here?"

"That's exactly what I asked him," Gertie said, climbing awkwardly to her feet. "He says he's come for my twins. She took a threatening step toward her ex-boyfriend. "Over my bloody dead body. I'll kill him first."

"Let's not talk about killing anyone," Cecily said sharply. "Ian, what on earth were you doing skulking around in that ridiculous snowman suit? Don't you realize you scared everyone half to death? Explain yourself!"

Ian lifted his hands. "I just—"

"What the blue blazes is going on here?"

The thunderous voice turned Cecily's head. Baxter stood behind her, breathing rather heavily. Samuel peered over his shoulder, brandishing a large rake from the stables.

At the sight of him, Pansy threw herself at him, clutching his coat, much to his obvious embarrassment. "I thought I was going to die!" she sobbed.

"Oh, put a bleeding sock in it," Gertie snapped. "It was nothing but a nasty little weasel who didn't have the guts to show hisself."

"Here!" Ian took a threatening step forward.

"Good Lord! Is that Ian Rossiter?" Baxter pushed past Cecily and took a firm grip on Ian's arm. "That's enough of that. You have a lot of explaining to do, young man."

Cecily noticed the small crowd of onlookers gathering at the end of the hallway. "Everyone in my office," she said briskly. "Right now." She glanced at Samuel, who was attempting to disengage himself from Pansy's clutches. "Samuel, you take Pansy back to the kitchen and ask Mrs. Chubb to give her a drop of brandy. She's had a nasty shock."

"Yes, m'm." Looking greatly relieved, Samuel led the still sobbing Pansy down the hallway.

Following them, Cecily hurried toward her guests, who were talking anxiously amongst themselves. "It's nothing to worry about," she assured them. "Just a little misunderstanding. If you'd like to return to the bar with Baxter, he'll see that you all get a free drink."

"Except for Colonel Fortescue!" a thin voice called out. Phoebe stepped up to Cecily's side. "He's probably had quite enough," she added in a soft whisper so that only Cecily could hear her.

"Quite." Cecily looked up at Baxter, who had also joined them.

He nodded. "I'll see to it." Turning to the curious group, he beckoned with his finger. "Come along, we'll keep that bartender busy for a while."

Still throwing backward glances at the empty snowman suit, the group of men moved off with him.

Cecily waited until they'd moved out of earshot before drawing a deep breath. Now she had to deal with two embittered antagonists with a delicate and complex problem. She could only hope she was up to the challenge.

# CHAPTER
## ❀ 17 ❀

Cecily turned back just in time to see Gertie raise a hand in an attempt to slap Ian's face. "Gertie!" She rushed toward them as Ian blocked the slap, grabbing Gertie's wrist and twisting it enough to make her cry out in pain.

"Let her go." Madeline, who had said nothing at all until now, raised her own hand. "Or I'll turn you into something quite nasty."

Ian relaxed his grip on Gertie's wrist. "Tell her to bloody lay off me, will you? I didn't say I was going to take the twins. I only wanted to see them, that's all."

"Then why couldn't you come and ask me, like a normal person?" Gertie dug her fists into her hips. "Why did you have to go sneaking around like a bleeding criminal?"

"Because you wouldn't have let me see them if I'd asked, that's what." Ian scowled at her. "I asked enough times in the past, didn't I."

"You don't deserve to see 'em. Besides, they don't know who you are. They won't understand."

"They know me as the snowman, though."

Ian started to whistle, and Gertie put her hands over her ears. "Stop it, before I slap that silly grin right off your bloody face."

"All right. That's enough." Cecily glanced over her shoulder. "We'll finish this conversation in my office. Right now." She looked at Madeline, and then at Phoebe hovering nervously in the background. "Perhaps you and Madeline could finish decorating the ballroom, Phoebe, and if you wouldn't mind taking this mess with you?" She poked the snowman's head with her foot. "I'll be right there as soon as I've sorted out this predicament."

Phoebe started to say something, but Madeline interrupted her. "Please, Phoebe. I could really use your help. I'd be so grateful if you could spare the time."

Looking flustered at this totally unfamiliar attitude from Madeline, Phoebe raised her hands and settled her hat more firmly on her head. "Oh, well . . . if you really need me . . . of course!" She bent over and gingerly took hold of the head. Carrying it with the very tips of her gloved fingers, she headed for the ballroom.

Madeline rolled her eyes at Cecily, bent over to pick up the suit and glided after her.

"Now," Cecily said firmly, "come with me." She led Ian and Gertie to her office and ushered them inside.

Gertie slumped down on a chair, her face drawn and creased in worry lines.

Ian hovered near the door, his hands dug into his pockets, his chin on his chest.

Cecily took her seat behind the desk. "Now," she said, "Ian, start from the beginning. Please explain why you felt it necessary to disguise yourself."

"She wouldn't let me see the twins," he began, but Gertie butted in.

"I don't want him near my kiddies. They don't know who he is."

"I'm their father. I—"

"Fat lot of good as a father you were. Promised to marry me, then I find out you're already married."

"But we weren't together no more. She was living in London and I was here."

"But you weren't divorced, neither." Gertie glared at him. "Why couldn't you have told me all about her before I . . . before we . . ."

"That's all water under the bridge," Cecily said hastily. "All in the past. What I want to know, Ian, is why you couldn't just come and talk to Gertie instead of disrupting my staff with your ridiculous antics."

Ian's face burned. "I told you, she wouldn't let me see my kids."

"They're not—" Gertie began, but Cecily cut in, effectively shutting off her words.

"Enough, Gertie! Please allow Ian to have his say, then we'll hear your side of it."

Gertie slumped back on her chair.

"Well, as I was saying"—Ian glowered at the housemaid— "I wanted to see my children. I've been wanting to for a long time, but she never answered my letters, and I had to take things into my own hands."

Gertie looked as if she would say something, then bit her lip and sat back.

"Anyhow, I saw this snowman suit, it was in a sale of stage costumes. I thought, if I dressed up in it so no one would recognize me, I could stand around in the snow and see the twins when they came out to play." He glanced at Gertie. "That way, I could get to see them, only they wouldn't know it was me."

Cecily glanced at Gertie. At least he'd been willing to hide his identity from them. That was one thing in his favor, surely?

"You mean you hid inside that bleeding thing so's no one would recognize you and throw you out." Gertie's expression remained belligerent, and Cecily sighed.

"So you did see the children?"

"Yes, m'm. I whistled, and they heard me and came running over to me. We talked. A lot." He smiled for the first time. "It was really nice."

Gertie fidgeted on her chair.

"I'm sure it was," Cecily said, sending a warning glance at her housemaid. "But that wasn't enough, was it."

Ian shuffled his feet. "No, m'm. It wasn't. It was cold standing out there all the time, and I wanted to see where the twins lived, and what sort of toys they had—"

Unable to keep quiet, Gertie burst out, "You had no bleeding right to spy on us!"

"I'm their bloody father!"

"No you're bloody not!"

Once more Cecily had to intervene. "Gertie, I think this is something you will have to work out with Ian yourself. But you both need to calm down first. Ian, I suggest you leave for now. Come back in a few days when Gertie has had a chance to think about what she wants to do."

"I know what I want to do," Gertie muttered. "I don't want him to come back. He's evil. I don't want him anywhere near my twins."

"If she still feels the same way when you come back," Cecily went on, as if she hadn't heard the housemaid, "then you will have to accept her decision. Meanwhile, Gertie, I want you to think about what is right and what is fair. Do you think you can do that?"

Gertie's dark eyes flashed defiance, but she nodded. "Yes, m'm."

"Very well." Cecily rose to her feet. "You may leave now, Ian, and be thankful I didn't call the constable to have you arrested for trespassing."

"I appreciate that, m'm." Ian touched his forehead with his fingers, then sent Gertie a dark look. "I'll be back." With that, he pulled the door open and left.

Gertie shivered, rubbing her arms as if she was cold. "I don't trust him, m'm. Honest, I don't. He's a liar and a cheat, and he'll do or say anything to get his way. I don't believe he just wants to see the twins. He wants to take them away from me. I know he does. He doesn't want them because they're his, he just wants to get back at me."

"Hush, Gertie. I'm sure that's not true. As I said, think about it for a few days, and if you don't want to see him when he comes back, then I'll see that he leaves peacefully."

Gertie looked up, her eyes brimming with rare tears. "Thank you, m'm. I'd be much obliged."

"Now go back to the kitchen and tell Mrs. Chubb you're to have a spot of that brandy, too."

"Yes, m'm." Gertie trudged to the door, her shoulders hunched.

"And Gertie?"

"Yes, m'm?"

"Try not to worry. Tomorrow we have a wedding to look forward to, so think about that, and let everything else rest until after that."

"Yes, m'm." Gertie managed a wavering smile. "Thank you, m'm."

Cecily waited for the door to close, then sank back on her chair. Poor Gertie. She had to admit, she was concerned for the feisty housemaid. She seemed so certain that Ian was up to no good, and might have good reason to feel that way.

Cecily couldn't help remembering Ian as a young lad, however, when he worked for her at the Pennyfoot. He'd been likeable, cheerful and willing, and a responsible worker. Not at all like the bitter, unpredictable man he'd become.

How sad that life could change someone so drastically.

Still, it was nice to finally have the snowman puzzle

cleared up. It left yet another puzzle to be solved, however. It seemed quite obvious that Ian wasn't responsible for the death of the Hethertons.

That meant the killer was still at large, and still unidentified. Not to mention the fact that he was armed with a possibly lethal Christmas cracker.

When Cecily arrived with Baxter at St. Bartholomew's that evening, she could hear Phoebe screeching before she entered the church.

Baxter paused at the door, rolling his eyes toward heaven. "Do we really have to go through with this preposterous business?"

"Yes, we do. You're an important part of the ceremony and you need to know what to do."

"I think I can walk down the aisle with the bride on my arm quite well without any guidance, particularly Phoebe's insufferable directions."

"Nevertheless, we are all going to rehearse the ceremony." She touched his arm. "Please, Bax, don't be tiresome about this."

"Oh, very well. I will do this for you, my dear. No one else."

"Thank you, my love. We shall all appreciate your sacrifice." Cecily waited for him to open the door for her, then stepped inside.

Phoebe stood near the altar, waving her arms about, while her son, the Reverend Algernon Carter-Holmes, stood meekly with head bowed, listening to her rampage.

Cecily hurried forward, and caught sight of the colonel apparently asleep in the front pew. Behind him sat Charles and Emily Winchester, while Grace Danbury sat in the pew behind them at the opposite end. Madeline and Kevin apparently had not yet arrived.

Phoebe, it seemed, was most displeased with the hapless

Algie, who made no attempt to protest the browbeating his mother gave him.

Upon catching sight of Cecily, Phoebe halted her tirade. "Oh, there you are, Cecily. Where, pray is that infuriating woman? I expressly asked her not to be late."

"I assume you are speaking of Madeline." Cecily drew closer, adding in a whisper, "You have a problem? Is there something I can do to help?"

"Yes," Phoebe hissed back, "You can tell my son to stop badgering my husband."

She'd said it loud enough for Algie to hear. He shook the folds of his surplice and raised his head. "I m-m-m-merely pointed out, m-m-mother d-d-dear, that your husband is in-n-neb . . . in-n-nebri . . . He's plastered."

Phoebe glanced over at the colonel, whose loud snoring now echoed to the rafters. "He is not *plastered*, as you so crudely phrased it. Freddie has had an exhausting day. He's taking a little nap."

She stepped down and marched over to her husband. Leaning over him, she lightly boxed his ear. "Wake up, dearest! The rehearsal is about to begin."

The colonel grunted, blinked rapidly for a moment, then leapt to his feet. "Great Scott! We are under attack! Fetch me my sword. Where is my blasted horse?"

Phoebe took hold of his coat's lapels and shook him. "Freddie. You are in the church. Do sit down and please, be *quiet*."

Cecily held her breath as the colonel's wild gaze swept up and down the pew. Then, muttering something that was mercifully unintelligible, he slumped down on his seat.

A tinkling laugh echoed up to the rafters. "It's good to see you still hold the reins, Phoebe dear." Madeline floated down the aisle, followed by her husband-to-be, who looked none too happy for a man about to claim his bride.

"Madeline!" Phoebe's strident tones clearly expressed her

exasperation. "You're late, as usual. We have been waiting simply ages. You know the reverend doesn't like to be kept waiting."

The reverend, it seemed was having trouble locating his spectacles. He stood staring vacantly into space, one hand patting around the edges of the font where he apparently assumed he'd left them.

Phoebe clicked her tongue in irritation, plucked the spectacles from the pocket of his surplice and jammed them on his nose. "For heaven's sake, let's get on with it, or we'll be here all night." She glared at Madeline. "You and Kevin, come with me. The rest of you please take a seat until I request your presence."

Cecily exchanged a resigned look with Madeline, both of them rolling their eyes, then took a seat next to Emily Winchester. Baxter sat down next to her, his thunderous expression rejecting any attempt at conversation.

Deciding to let him simmer down on his own, Cecily turned to Emily. Phoebe's attention was on the bridal couple while Algie stumbled through his instructions. Deciding it was safe to talk, Cecily leaned toward Emily. "I think this will be a very nice wedding tomorrow, don't you?"

"Oh, I'm sure of it." Emily made an attempt at a smile. "The ballroom looks magnificent. I peeked in for a look before we left the Pennyfoot."

"Madeline always works magic with her decorating. She loves it so. This must have been especially enjoyable for her, decorating for her own wedding. Though she was a little put out that she couldn't find white roses."

Emily sat back with a little sigh. "White roses. I remember Lady Clara always ordered white roses. They were her favorite flowers." She was quiet for a moment, then added softly, "How she loved roses. She never missed the flower show in Chelsea. She was quite an expert on roses, you know."

With one eye on Madeline and Kevin, Cecily murmured, "Really? No, I didn't know that."

"Oh, yes, she was one of the judges—" Emily broke off as Phoebe charged down the steps toward them. "Come on, come on, I need you all in your places. Bridesmaids, please go with Madeline to the dressing room and wait for my signal. Dr. Winchester, I need you up here next to Kevin. Mr. Baxter, since you will be giving the bride away, I need you to wait in the foyer until you hear the opening chords on the organ."

"There's no one playing the organ," Baxter said, his voice gruff with the effort to sound marginally civil.

Cecily hid a grin as Phoebe tossed her head, then grabbed the wide brim of her hat to steady it. "Of course there's no musician. She won't be here until the wedding. When I raise my hand, that means the opening chords are playing and it's your signal to tap on the door of the dressing room."

"I see. I have to imagine the dulcet tones of the organ playing, then?"

Phoebe gave him a suspicious look while Cecily dug him in the ribs with her elbow.

"Behave," she muttered.

"Why?" he muttered back, but to her relief, rose to his feet and trudged up the aisle to the foyer.

"Good." Phoebe turned her attention to Cecily. "Matron of honor, when you hear the signal, please marshal your bridesmaids into the proper order and then follow Madeline and Mr. Baxter down the aisle at the proper distance. And ladies!" Her imperious gaze swept up and down the pew. "Slowly, *please*. One . . . step . . . at . . . a . . . time."

Resisting the urge to salute, Cecily stepped out into the aisle. Grace Danbury stepped out in front of her, as if anxious to get the ordeal over with. Not that Cecily could blame her. Phoebe could be overbearing at the best of times, but when she was supervising an event of any kind, she could be quite unbearable.

Grace trotted up the aisle, rubbing her hands. Cecily felt a deep sympathy for her. The poor woman apparently suffered from cold hands, even though she wore gloves. Most likely due to a flaw in her circulation.

Cecily knew how uncomfortable that could be, since her feet were constantly freezing due to the same problem. At least they used to be, until Madeline had made up an herbal medication for her that had wonderful results.

She made a mental note to mention the fact to Grace, though she wasn't sure if Grace's interest in horticulture and herbalism stretched to actually taking one of Madeline's unconventional remedies.

They might have much in common, but somehow Cecily couldn't quite see the two of them brewing up those unorthodox potions together.

Madeline's relationship with Grace Danbury, however, was the least of Cecily's worries. She couldn't help feeling there was a distinct rift between Madeline and her future husband. That worried her far more.

The relief Cecily had felt at seeing Madeline arrive at the church that evening was an indication of the uncertainty she harbored. It remained to be seen whether or not Madeline would actually attend the wedding ceremony tomorrow.

Much as she hated to admit it, Cecily was afraid that at the very last minute, Madeline would have some kind of premonition, decide that marriage was not for her, and simply forgo the ceremony. If that happened, she would break Kevin's heart and forever lose any chance of happiness with him. That would be tragic, indeed.

# CHAPTER

# ❀ 18 ❀

The morning of Madeline's wedding day Cecily awoke early, with an urgent feeling that she had forgotten something important.

Lying warm and snug under the eiderdown, she fought to clear the fog of sleep from her mind. What could she have forgotten? Everything was ready for the reception that evening. She'd talked to Mrs. Chubb and Michel last night and made the final arrangements.

The wedding was scheduled to begin at three, and the reception was due to begin in the ballroom as soon as the guests started arriving back from the church.

Phoebe had arranged a short revue before the banquet was to be served, and after the dinner the tables would be cleared away for dancing and the orchestra Phoebe had hired would play until after midnight. Refreshments would be available all evening and champagne would be served to welcome in the New Year.

Altogether it made a fitting wedding for the town's esteemed doctor, though Cecily was quite sure Madeline would not agree. It was a measure of how much she really loved him for her to consent to all this pomp and pageantry, when all she really wanted was a private wedding in some quiet hideaway.

Thinking of Madeline made Cecily sit up in bed. Was that why she had this peculiar feeling? Had she been worrying about Madeline in her sleep, afraid her friend's reservations would destroy her chance of happiness?

Or was it something else, something far more insidious gnawing in the back of her mind? Something she should remember, but couldn't quite grasp.

Hunching her shoulders, she dragged the eiderdown up to her neck. The fire had long ago died in the fireplace, allowing the warmth in the room to flow up the chimney. The cold shiver she'd felt, however, had little to do with the chill air invading the boudoir.

She'd had this feeling before. While in pursuit of a killer. When she'd had the knowledge she'd needed to bring him to justice and yet hadn't recognized it as such.

Could she possibly be that close to solving the Hethertons' murders? What could it be that she knew—something important—yet didn't know it was significant?

She frowned, going over her conversations with both Charles Winchester and Roland Crossley. Both of them had perfectly good explanations for lying. By the same token, it was quite feasible that either of them could have been lying to her about that as well. All she'd had to go on were her instincts. She'd trusted them enough to believe both men.

And yet, here she was, with this feeling that she had the answer to the puzzle, if only she could straighten it out in her mind. Somewhere in the last few days, someone had said something important, something that could lead her to the killer. *What was it?*

"How much longer are you going to sit there hugging that blasted eiderdown while my shoulders turn to ice?"

With a violent start, Cecily swung her head around to look at her husband. She'd dragged the covers off him down to his waist, and he lay there shivering in the thin nightshirt.

"I'm so sorry, my love." She snuggled down beside him, covering him up with the eiderdown. "There, does that feel better?"

"I'll feel better when this confounded wedding business is over with." Baxter pulled the feather-filled cover up under his chin. "It's got everyone in a such a flap—you, the staff, even the bridal couple themselves. I could feel Madeline's hand shaking so hard on my arm as I led her down the aisle last night I thought she was trying to warn me that I was making some terrible faux pas or something."

"Just wedding day nerves, that's all."

He squinted at her in the cold, gray dawn light. "Did you shake like that when you married me?"

"All the way to the altar."

"Good Lord."

She debated for a moment or two whether or not to tell him that it wasn't the wedding occupying her thoughts so intensely. But then she thought better of it. There was enough to do and think about on this happy day. She would not spoil it by bringing up the subject of the Hethertons' deaths.

This was a day for new beginnings, not grisly endings. She would leave whatever was bothering her in the back of her mind, until she could think more clearly about it.

Meanwhile, she had a wedding to help prepare, and dozens of tasks to be completed before the service that afternoon. As for Madeline, all she could do was hope that her friend would find the courage to follow her heart. For there was not one single doubt in her mind that Madeline and Kevin belonged together. All they really needed was time to get to know each other more intimately, and eventually they would take care of their differences.

May the good Lord help Madeline to know that, too.

Gertie picked up the heavy tray of dishes and glanced across the dining room to see what Pansy was doing. The young girl had been moping about all morning. Instead of clearing the tables she was standing at the window, gazing out at the lawns.

Gertie's stomach lurched. "Whatcha staring at? Not a bloody snowman again, I hope."

Pansy swung around to face her. "No, course not. I was just looking out there, that's all."

"Well, get a bloody move on." Gertie turned her back on her, talking over her shoulder. "We've got to get this bleeding lot cleared away and washed up before we can get dressed for the wedding, and we've only got an hour or so before we leave. We can't be late to the church."

"All right, I'm coming."

The rattle of dishes assured Gertie that Pansy had picked up her tray and headed for the door. Daisy had promised to have the twins dressed and ready to leave in plenty of time, so all she had to do was get the dishes put away and she'd be free to go and enjoy the wedding.

After loading her dishes on the dumbwaiter, she waited for Pansy to load hers. The girl took so long Gertie ran out of patience. "Here." She pushed her aside. "Let me do it. They'll all fall over on the way down if you flipping load 'em like that."

Stacking the plates securely, she glanced at the young girl. "What's the matter with you, anyway? You look like you swallowed a worm."

Pansy shuddered. "A worm? Ugh! That's horrid."

"I know. That's what I meant, wasn't it. So what's the matter then?"

"Me and Samuel had a row last night. Now he's not speaking to me."

Gertie was never shy about poking her nose into other people's business. "What was it about?"

Pansy shrugged. "He told me I was too young to get married."

Gertie laughed. "He's right. What did you do? Ask him to marry you?"

"All I said was how I was looking forward to getting married and having babies to look after."

"I can just imagine how our Samuel took to that. He's never been one for settling down. I thought when he went to London with Daisy's twin sister, he might finally get settled, but then Doris went on the stage and got successful. So he left her and came back here without her."

"He must not have really loved her then, or he would never have gone and left her behind."

Gertie bit her lip as once more pain stabbed her heart. She'd believed that when she'd told Dan she couldn't live in the city. She'd hoped he would stay in Badgers End, to be with her. Foolish thinking. That's what she got for letting a bloke get close to her again. Men. She was better off without them, that she was.

"What's she like?"

Startled, Gertie looked at Pansy. "What's who like?"

"Doris, Daisy's twin sister."

Gertie closed the latch on the dumbwaiter and lowered it to the floor below. "She's tiny, and really pretty. Looks exactly like Daisy, except . . . softer . . . if you know what I mean. She's doing really well on the stage—got a voice like an angel. You should hear her sing. Makes you cry, she does."

Pansy looked even more miserable. "She sounds like a very special person. It must have been hard for Samuel to leave someone like that."

Gertie could have kicked herself for describing Doris in such glowing terms. That's not what Pansy wanted to hear, especially when she was on the outs with Samuel. "Everyone's special in their own way. You're just as special."

Pansy managed a wan smile. "Thank you, Gertie. I'm glad someone thinks so."

"In any case, Doris and Samuel were never meant to be together. They belong to two different worlds." Gertie swallowed hard. "Just like me and Dan."

"Daisy must miss her sister. 'Specially since she's her twin."

"We all miss her."

"But there's a special bond between twins." Pansy nudged her. "You should know. Your twins act like they're joined at the hip. Never see one without the other."

"Yeah. I think it would kill them to be separated. I don't know what they'll do when they grow up and have to live separate lives."

"Well, they'll sort it out by then."

"Yeah." Gertie started down the hallway. "Come on, let's get these bleeding dishes done with. We have to get cracking if we want to be at the church on time."

With Pansy scuffling along behind her, Gertie rushed through the lobby and down the steps to the kitchen.

Mrs. Chubb was already unloading the dishes from the waiter, and Gertie gave her a grateful smile. "Ta, ever so. We're a bit behind, thanks to Moping Minnie over there." She nodded at Pansy, who stood at the sink, running water into a large cast iron pot.

Mrs. Chubb raised her eyebrows and tipped her head in Pansy's direction.

Understanding the unspoken question, Gertie whispered, "She had a row with Samuel."

"Ah. It'll blow over." Mrs. Chubb carried an armful of dishes over to the sink. "Here you are, luv. Give me the pot, I'll put it on the stove." She took the pot from Pansy's unresisting hands and heaved it onto the top of the oven.

Gertie pulled a tray of glasses toward her and turned to

take them to the sink. As she did so, she caught sight of a movement through the window overlooking the yard. A flash of dark red—the color of Lillian's coat.

Gertie swore, earning a shocked exclamation from Mrs. Chubb. "Sorry, but I think that's my twins out there. They must have given Daisy the slip. She'd never let them out in the yard dressed in their best clothes."

She dumped the glasses on the sink, rattling them together so hard they were in danger of breaking. Leaning forward across the sink to get a better view, she peered out the window. What she saw shut off her breath.

Ian had Lillian by the hand and was dragging her across the yard, while the little girl struggled and kicked to get away from him.

"Bloody hell!" Without waiting to grab her shawl, Gertie dove across the kitchen and hauled open the back door. "Get Samuel!" she yelled. "Get madam and Mr. Baxter. It's Ian, and he's stealing my Lillian!"

Heart pounding, she flew out the door, yelling at the top of her voice. "You let go of her, you bloody rotter! I'll feed your bleeding innards to the wolves when I bleeding get hold of you!"

Ian had almost reached the back gate, and Lillian's terrified screams rang in Gertie's ears. Filled with rage she pounded forward, but Ian's hand was already dragging open the gate.

It took all her strength to close the gap before he could drag Lillian outside. Reaching him, she lunged, clawing her nails down the side of his face.

He yelped, and loosened his hold on Lillian's hand. The little girl pulled away and ran screaming for the back door, where Mrs. Chubb waited to gather her up in her arms.

"I'll kill you, you miserable coward. How dare you hurt my baby!" Gertie lunged again.

Ian caught her flailing arm and closed his fingers around her wrist. It was the same wrist he'd grabbed before, and the bruise hadn't quite healed. She cried out in pain, and he forced her down onto her knees.

"You got two of 'em," he snarled. "Why shouldn't I have one of 'em? They're mine, too. Share and share alike, that's what I say."

Holding back tears, Gertie choked out words. "You'll never have either one of them. I'll see you dead first."

"Yeah? I'd like to see you try."

Gertie barely heard the thundering feet behind her until the figure was upon them. She heard a thud, a crack and Ian's yelp of pain as he let go of his cruel hold on her wrist.

She fell back, staring up in amazement as Clive caught Ian under the chin with another savage blow to the jaw. He went down like a sack of rotten potatoes.

Scrambling to her feet, Gertie stood shivering with cold and shock as Clive leaned over the fallen man, one fist held close to Ian's face.

"If I see you anywhere near Miss Gertie or her little ones again," he said, his deep voice soft with controlled menace, "I'll give you what you *really* deserve. Next time you won't get off so easy."

Ian dragged himself up until he could lean against the wall. Blood dripped down the side of his chin, and he wiped it away with the back of his sleeve. Clive stood solidly in his path, and he had to stumble around him to reach the gate.

He turned back, one hand steadying himself, and glared at Gertie with such a diabolical look in his eyes she felt her stomach churn.

What had happened to the happy-go-lucky young man she had fallen for so long ago? She hardly recognized this ruffian for the man she once thought of marrying.

Clive made a threatening move toward the enraged man at the gate. "Go! Get the blazes out of here if you know what's good for you!"

"All right, all right, I'm going." Ian wiped his mouth

again, and his expression was pure evil. "But you haven't seen the last of me. None of you. That's a promise."

Gertie was speechless with fear, but Clive answered for her. "Then you'd better hope and pray you don't run into me again."

Ian took one look at Clive's raised fist and swung through the gate. It closed behind him with a loud bang that seemed to vibrate all through Gertie's body.

She started to thank Clive, and only then did she realize that tears soaked her cheeks.

The big man drew a creased and grubby handkerchief from his pocket and with an awkward gesture offered it to her. A day ago she would have turned her nose up at it. Today she took it, and loudly blew her nose.

"Thank you," she said, as she handed it back to him. "I don't know what I would have done if you hadn't been there to help me."

Taking the handkerchief, Clive tucked it in his pocket. He avoided her gaze and stared at the ground as he mumbled, "I don't like to see women and children manhandled like that."

"I was really scared." Gertie swallowed. "He was trying to take off with my Lillian."

Clive nodded. "I know. I'll keep an eye on both of them from now on, if you like."

Gertie managed a weak smile. "I'd like that a lot. Thank you, Clive."

"I'll watch out for you, too, miss." He looked up quickly, as if to gauge her reaction, then added, "Just to keep an eye out, in case he comes back."

"Thank you, Clive. Me and the kiddies will be very much obliged to you, I'm sure."

Clive touched his forehead with his fingers. "My pleasure, indeed, miss."

She watched him shuffle off, and the chill in her stomach

started to fade. She'd never make fun of him again. He was a good man. A friend. A bodyguard. She liked the thought of that.

Mrs. Chubb stood in the doorway as Gertie tramped back to the kitchen. The housekeeper still held Lillian, though now the little girl's howls had quietened to a loud sniffling.

Gertie folded her arms around her daughter and pulled her close. Leaning her chin on her soft hair, she murmured, "There, there, Lilly. It's all over now. The nasty man has gone."

"He f-frightened me!" Lillian hugged her tight around the hips.

Gertie straightened. "Well, he won't frighten you no more. Mr. Clive will see to that."

Mrs. Chubb raised her eyebrows. "Clive?"

Gertie shrugged. "He said he'd keep an eye out for them. Just in case."

"Told you he was a nice man."

She sounded smug, and Gertie sniffed. "So you were bloody right for once." She took hold of Lillian's hand. "Now I'm going to find out why Daisy let that bleeding sod take my child away."

"Gertie! Such language in front of the little one!"

Ignoring her, Gertie marched across the kitchen, dragging Lillian behind her.

She found Daisy in her room, helping James to line up his toy soldiers ready for battle. Daisy scrambled to her feet when she saw Gertie's face. "What's happened?"

Being careful not to sound too frightening in front of the children, Gertie told her everything.

Daisy's hands covered her face by the time Gertie had finished. "I'm sorry, really I am. He said you'd sent him to fetch Lillian to you. I thought . . . I mean he said he was her father and all and he seemed so nice. . . ." Her face was wet with tears when she lowered her hands. "I didn't know he was going to take her away. I'd never forgive myself if he hurt either one of them. Or you, either. I'm so sorry, Gertie."

"Don't you never let anyone take them anywhere. Not without talking to me first." Gertie's voice shook. "If I hadn't seen him out the window . . ." She pulled in a deep breath.

Daisy sank onto her bed, gulping back tears. "I'll never let anyone near them again. Honest I won't."

"All right." Gertie made herself smile at the twins, who were both watching her with wary eyes. "I'm going to get ready for the wedding now, so you two behave until I get back. All right?"

Lillian nodded, still looking a little fearful, while James went back to lining up his soldiers. Gertie gave each of them a hug and left the room.

Her stomach still felt as if something was eating away at it. She kept hearing Ian's last words. *You haven't seen the last of me. That's a promise.*

Her children would never be safe as long as that man was hanging about. It wasn't a comforting thought to take with her into the new year.

# CHAPTER
## ❀ 19 ❀

"You look absolutely stunning, my dear."

Cecily smiled at Baxter's reflection in the mirror above her dressing table. "Thank you, darling. You look quite dapper yourself. That coat fits you to perfection. I have always been partial to a man in tails."

She gazed at him in silent admiration for a moment or two. She'd always thought him handsome, with his square cut face and piercing gray eyes. Now that his hair had turned completely white, she could add distinguished to the list.

He had added some inches to his waist over the years, but he was still a fine figure of a man, and she was proud and blessed to be his wife.

"What are you smiling at me for?" Baxter passed a hand self-consciously over his hair. "Have I forgotten something? Is my tie straight?"

Her smile widened. "Perfectly straight, my love. I was just

thinking how lucky I am to have such a divine escort at my side."

"I'm the lucky one." He bent over her shoulder to kiss her cheek. "You will outshine the bride, my dear."

"Heavens. I sincerely hope not." Pleased with the compliment, she regarded her own image with a critical eye. The lilac silk gown had a deep yolk in white lace that covered her throat.

The pearl buttons marching down the front glowed in the light from the gas lamp. The full gathers in the back flattered her mature figure, and she adored the white fur cape that would ward off the cold winter wind. Phoebe had done her work well.

Seated in the carriage later, she was glad of the cape's warmth. Although the sun had chased away the clouds, the ocean breeze chilled everything it touched. She could see steam rising from the nostrils of the horses as they trotted down the Esplanade.

Outside the church a curious crowd waited for a glimpse of the bride. Cecily suspected that many of Kevin's patients had come to mourn the capture of Badgers End's most eligible bachelor.

Emily and Grace were already in the dressing room when Cecily pushed open the door. Leaving her husband to stand outside, she closed the door behind her and hurried over to the fireplace, where flames leapt greedily up the chimney.

Noticing the awkward silence between the two women, Cecily remarked brightly, "I see Madeline hasn't arrived yet. I do hope she wears something warm about her shoulders. The air outside is positively frigid."

Emily still wore her cape, while Grace had discarded hers. She stood by the window, some distance from Emily, and seemed intent on whatever was outside.

"The weather is quite chilly," Emily observed. "Though it's rather warm in here." She slipped off her cape and glanced at Grace, who stood absently rubbing her hands.

"Come and stand by the fire, Grace." Emily gazed anxiously at the other woman. "You will need warm hands to carry your bouquet."

"My hands are quite warm, thank you." Grace lifted her hands to look at them. "It's these prickly georgette gloves. They are irritating my rash."

About to comment, Cecily froze. She heard Charles Winchester's voice quite clearly in her mind. *The silver fulminate used in the explosive is an irritant. It can cause a rather nasty rash with a maddening itch.*

How many times had she seen Grace Danbury rubbing her hands? She hadn't been cold at all. She'd been scratching a rash. A rash, perhaps, caused by the silver fulminate in an exploding Christmas cracker?

As if matching the pieces of a broken vase, questions formed in Cecily's mind in quick succession.

Just last night Emily had told her that Lady Clara was one of the judges at the flower show. Could she possibly be the same judge who had knocked Grace's prize hybrid to the ground? Had Lady Clara been the person who had dashed Grace's chances of becoming a celebrity and a cherished member of the horticultural society?

Was Sir Walter not the intended victim after all? Could he have been the innocent victim of a plot to kill his wife?

She could be wrong. She had to be wrong. Grace Danbury just didn't fit her idea of a cold-blooded murderer. Madeline would be devastated.

"Cecily? Are you not well?"

With a start Cecily realized that Emily and Grace were staring at her—one with concern, and the other with speculation.

"I do beg your pardon." She cleared her throat. "Did you say something?"

Emily looked worried. "I asked if you were feeling poorly. You appeared to be in a trance of some sort."

"Oh, goodness." Cecily forced a laugh. "I was trying to

remember if I had asked my coachman to bring in the bags of confetti."

"Oh." Emily looked relieved. "I thought perhaps you were worrying that your friend might not make an appearance."

Well, that, too, Cecily thought wryly. "Oh, I'm sure she'll be here. Madeline has never been one to arrive for anything on time." Aware that Grace was watching her, Cecily uttered another forced laugh. "Not even her own wedding." She turned to Grace. "I'm sure you'll agree, Miss Danbury."

"Quite." Grace hunched her shoulders and rubbed her hands against her hips. "The few times we've met, Madeline has always arrived late. I do believe it's simply a matter of habit for her."

"Well, it was so very nice of her to invite me to be one of her attendants at the wedding." Emily touched a nervous hand to her hair. "Considering we had never met when she kindly made the offer. It isn't often a bride chooses a complete stranger to be her bridesmaid."

"Madeline thought it would please Kevin, since your husband is his best man." Cecily refrained from mentioning that Madeline was a firm believer in threes in order to bring good fortune, and had no one else to ask to be her third attendant. Well, there was Phoebe, but Madeline was thoroughly convinced that having Phoebe as a third bridesmaid would invite disaster rather than prevent it.

"Well, you don't have to worry about whether or not Madeline will be here anymore." Grace gestured at the window. "Her carriage just arrived a moment ago."

"Oh, thank goodness." Cecily was relieved on more than one count. Having worried all this time that her friend might change her mind at the very last minute, it was most gratifying to see her hurrying up the pathway.

What's more, the arrival of the bride prevented her from pursuing any theories she might have as to who had killed the Hethertons. The matter was out of her hands for the time being and she could do nothing else now but concentrate fully on the wedding.

Once that was over, she'd have to delve further into her investigation. Perhaps snatch an opportunity to search Grace's room before the woman departed. If not, she might very well hand the entire matter over to the constabulary and let P.C. Northcott or Inspector Cranshaw bring the murderer to justice. Much as it would vex her to do so.

The door opened and Madeline swept in, looking unusually dignified in a white lawn gown trimmed with lace and tiny white ribbon daisies. "I absolutely refuse to wear a veil," she declared, before anyone could speak. "So, please, do not ask me to do so."

Grace looked amused, while Emily's aghast expression made Cecily smile.

"But you absolutely, positively have to wear a veil," Emily protested.

"Why?" Madeline had bound her heavy black hair into a knot on top of her head, surrounding the mound with a ring of daisies. Even so, strands escaped and floated across her forehead, and she brushed them back with an impatient hand.

On anyone else the stray hair would have looked out of keeping with the elegant, yet simple gown she wore. On Madeline, it merely looked enchanting.

"It's expected. It's tradition. It would be sacrilege to go without!" Emily looked from Cecily to Grace for help.

Grace shrugged and walked over to Madeline. "I really can't see that it matters. Madeline will make a beautiful bride, with or without a veil."

Madeline rolled her eyes. "Thank you, Grace. I'm happy you agree. Hiding one's face is a sign of submission. I, Madeline Pengrath, submit to no one."

"Not even your husband?" Emily looked horrified.

"Especially not to my husband," Madeline said grimly. "Now, will someone please help me with this dratted train.

I can't see behind me and I'm sure it's not sitting the way it should. I don't know why I bothered with it."

"Nonsense. It will look wonderful once we have it set right." Grace moved around behind her and started fussing with the train, while Cecily drew Emily aside.

"Madeline is not exactly a conventional person," she said quietly. "It's a miracle she's here at all. Let's not give her reasons to start doubting the wisdom of her choices."

Emily pouted. "I was only trying to help."

"I'm sure you were, and I know she appreciates it, but the best way you can help is by accepting things the way they are without question."

"I suppose you're right, though it troubles me that a bride marrying in a church doesn't observe the protocol."

Cecily couldn't help wondering what Emily would think when Madeline and her new husband disposed with the traditional vows for ones they had composed themselves.

It had taken a good deal of argument between Madeline and Algie before he had agreed to accept her decision. Even then, he had warned her that the Lord might take a dim view of someone usurping the holy tradition with a common substitute. No matter how tasteful and exquisite it might be.

She had no time to ponder further, since a sharp rap on the door indicated that the organist had begun the opening chords of "Here Comes the Bride." At least Madeline had agreed to that much.

Cecily hurried over to the anxious bride, and put her arms around her frail shoulders. "Be happy, my good friend," she whispered in Madeline's ear. "Be good to each other."

"We will certainly try."

To Cecily's surprise, she thought she saw a tear form in Madeline's eye before it was quickly blinked away.

"I must go now," Madeline said, her voice husky. "Before that harridan Phoebe descends on us with nostrils flaming."

Laughing, Cecily turned to the bridesmaids. "Ladies? I do believe this is our cue. Just follow me down the aisle at the appropriate distance and do, please, remember . . ." she assumed a fair imitation of Phoebe's voice, ". . . slowly. *Please.* One . . . step . . . at . . . a . . . time."

Even Grace smiled as both she and Emily hugged Madeline, then followed her out the door.

The ceremony proceeded without a major disaster. Baxter remembered where he'd put the rings, and Algie managed to get them handed over without dropping them.

When he went rambling on far too long with the sermon, the organist, a fragile woman with the longest fingernails Cecily had ever seen, struck up a few chords to drown out his words, much to everyone's relief.

Phoebe fluttered around like a fretful bird in the third pew, but mercifully kept quiet until Algie proclaimed the happy couple to be man and wife. Just before the organist struck up the chorus of the wedding march, Phoebe's voice could be clearly heard declaring, "Oh, thank heavens that's over!"

Outside the church the photographer busily pushed and pulled and ordered everyone around until Madeline finally announced she'd had enough primping in front of the camera.

Kevin helped her up into the carriage, amid a burst of applause from the appreciative crowd, and the horses started forward, white ribbons streaming from their manes.

Cecily followed closely behind in her own carriage, with Baxter at her side and Charles and Emily Winchester opposite her. As the horses drew away from the church, she spotted Grace Danbury climbing up into a waiting carriage.

She wondered briefly if the woman intended to return to the hotel. If she were guilty of murder, it seemed feasible that she would leave at the earliest possible moment. Of course, if she wanted to avoid putting suspicion on herself, she would have had to stay for the wedding, since that was the reason she was in Badgers End in the first place. How long would she stay after that, however? Would she make some excuse not to attend the reception, or stay for the New Year's Eve celebrations?

That's if she was guilty in the first place, of course. Cecily sighed. She had been wrong on so many counts over this tragic situation. She was beginning to doubt every single thought that popped into her mind.

Listening with only half an ear to Baxter's conversation with Charles, Cecily thought about Grace's rash. It was possible, of course, that something else could have caused it. She could hardly accuse the woman of murder simply because she had itchy hands.

There was the incident of the destroyed rose, of course, but just because Lady Clara was a judge at the flower show did not necessarily mean she was the one who had knocked the plant to the floor. Furthermore, it seemed such a flimsy reason to take two lives.

In any case, Grace would have had little opportunity to buy the chemicals and tamper with the cracker. All that would have taken time, and except for the day she had spent shopping with her friend, Grace had remained inside the hotel, to the best of Cecily's knowledge.

Yet, there was something about the woman that made Cecily uneasy—glimpses of a nature unlike the one she presented to the public. Still, it would be most remiss of her to base her suspicions on the fact that she didn't like the woman. Most unprofessional, indeed.

With an effort she made herself concentrate on her husband's comments.

"Then again," Baxter was saying, "Wellercombe isn't exactly a hub of industrial activity. I admit, traveling to and fro to work in London can get tedious, but there simply isn't enough business in this area. Apart from shops and restaurants, there's hardly any other kind of enterprise."

Cecily sat up with a start. Shops and restaurants. Roland

Crossley had mentioned that he'd seen Grace in Wellercombe leaving a building. A building—not a shop or a restaurant, as one would expect—but a building. Could it have been a chemical company, perhaps?

She would have to search Grace's room, Cecily decided. As soon as possible. Tonight, perhaps, during the reception, while Grace was occupied with the celebrations. By the morning it would be too late. Everyone would be leaving and she'd have no opportunity to do anything constructive.

She sent a worried look at her husband. He would want to know why she was leaving the reception. She would have to take him into her confidence and ask for his help. With any luck, he would agree to come to her aid, rather than argue about it in front of everyone.

Arriving back at the Pennyfoot, she went immediately to the ballroom to make sure everything had been prepared according to her orders.

She was relieved to see that chairs had been arranged in front of the stage for the revue, which Cecily hoped was as short as Phoebe had promised.

One lady had been most put out that there had been no Christmas revue, although Cecily had explained there simply would not be time with the preparations for the wedding.

Phoebe had then proposed a much shortened version at the wedding reception. One, hopefully, in good taste as befitting the occasion.

She had promised nothing more raucous than a few songs from a local vocalist, a competent juggler and her own dance troupe in a gentle ballet. They would be depicting the promise of a new beginning, she had assured Cecily.

Cecily wasn't quite sure what that meant, but had reluctantly agreed. Then wished she hadn't when she learned she would have no time to preview the performance, since rehearsals would have to take place at the church hall.

All she could hope was that Phoebe's presentation was

free of the kind of catastrophe that usually accompanied such questionable events.

Putting aside her worries for now, Cecily concentrated on the task at hand. The guests had begun to arrive, with Grace Danbury entering on her own with the first group.

Standing in front of the stage with Baxter, Cecily watched her drift over to the far side of the room and take a seat in the back row.

It had to be hard for the woman, being alone in a country club full of couples. Cecily wasn't at all sure she could attend something like that if she didn't have her beloved husband by her side.

"I hope this blasted revue thing of Phoebe's doesn't end up in disaster as usual," Baxter muttered in her ear.

"I'm sure it will turn out perfectly well this time," Cecily assured him, being sure of no such thing. "Phoebe tells me the girls have rehearsed really hard and have their performance perfected, so I'm confident all will be well."

When he didn't answer right away she glanced up at him, and found him staring down at her with the quizzical expression that always irritated her. "What is that look for?"

"It never fails to amaze me," he said lazily, "how you can harbor such unmitigated optimism when you know quite well you are doomed to disappointment."

"One of these days Phoebe will surprise us all. Let us hope that this is the day."

"A forlorn hope at best."

"Well, if you are bound and determined to be such a grouch, I shall seek out more enlivening company." She had caught sight of the Crossleys across the room, and Baxter had just given her the perfect excuse to leave his side for a while. "Please save me a seat in the front row, there's a dear. I shan't be more than a moment or two." She hurried off before he had time to protest.

Sarah Crossley gave her a lukewarm smile when she approached the couple, but Roland was his usual effusive self.

"Mrs. Baxter!" he boomed, as she reached him. "Lovely wedding, was it not? All this is magnificent." He waved an arm at the decorations floating above his head. "Marvelous. Must have taken hours."

"Thank you, Mr. Crossley. This is all the work of the bride. I'm sure she would be most gratified to hear your compliments."

"The bride, h'mmm? She's a clever little filly, is she not?"

His wife gave him a furious glare, which he appeared not to notice. "I'm going to take my seat," she told him, tossing her head. "I shall expect you to join me forthwith." She sailed off toward the rows of chairs.

"Of course, my dear." Crossley gave Cecily an apologetic smile. "Must be off. We are really looking forward to the revue."

"Before you go"—Cecily laid a gloved hand on his arm—"I've been meaning to ask you. You mentioned that you saw Miss Danbury in Wellercombe the other day."

Crossley snatched an alarmed look over his shoulder, then relaxed when he saw his wife was out of earshot. "Yes, yes, I did. Mum's the word, though, right?"

"Oh, I won't say anything to anyone." Cecily leaned forward and in a whisper added, "It's just that Miss Danbury was telling me about a marvelous new drapers she saw in Wellercombe, but she couldn't remember the name of it. I was wondering if you remembered where you saw her?"

Crossley frowned. "Drapers? Oh, no, it wasn't anywhere near the shops. I was coming out of the public house, you see. No, it was a building of some sort. A factory, by the look of it."

"I see. Well, thank you, Mr. Crossley. I suppose I shall just have to go looking all over the town myself."

" 'Fraid so, madam." Crossley glanced at the chairs. "Now, if you'll excuse me . . ."

"Of course." She waited until he'd turned, then added, "Mr. Crossley?"

He looked back at her, obviously impatient. "Yes? What is it?"

"I was wondering. Did you happen to notice Miss Danbury's friend, by any chance?"

"Friend?" Crossley shook his head. "Oh, no, Mrs. Baxter. Miss Danbury was quite alone. I saw her crossing the street and there was no one with her."

Cecily let out her breath on a small sigh. "Thank you, Mr. Crossley. Perhaps you should join your wife. She appears rather agitated."

Crossley muttered something under his breath then touched his forehead before slinking over to the chairs.

Cecily walked slowly back to the front row and took her seat next to Baxter. It looked very much as if Grace had lied about visiting Wellercombe with a friend. No wonder she had seemed so unsettled when her shopping trip was mentioned.

She felt reasonably certain now that Grace Danbury had gone into Wellercombe, not to do some Christmas shopping as she'd maintained, but to purchase the chemicals she needed to turn an innocuous Christmas cracker into a lethal explosive.

Now all that was left was to prove it.

# CHAPTER
# ❀ 20 ❀

The revue started out well, with some lovely songs sung by a competent vocalist, followed by a juggler who performed remarkable feats with plates spinning on poles. Unfortunately, while responding to enthusiastic applause, his flamboyant bow resulted in his elbow contacting the pile of the dishes stacked on the table.

Cecily winced as the china plates crashed to the floor, and the curtains were hurriedly drawn. The ensuing noises of pieces of china being swept up were accompanied by Phoebe's shrill tones as she lambasted the hapless juggler for his clumsiness.

Just as the audience showed visible signs of becoming restless, the curtains parted again to reveal Phoebe's dance troupe. Dressed in filmy ragged-looking costumes, they pranced about the stage in a rather ungainly rendition of what Cecily assumed to be part of the "Swan Lake" ballet, though what part she couldn't be certain.

Two of the dancers ran out of breath before the end, due most likely to their excess weight, and had to be propped up for the final arabesque. Nevertheless, the audience was generous with the applause, and the dancers, puffing and panting, trudged off the stage with satisfied smiles.

Phoebe waltzed on to center stage and thanked the audience for its indulgence. As she disappeared behind the curtains to more sporadic applause, Baxter muttered, "Heaven preserve us from any more of that rubbish. Utterly dismal, as usual."

"Just be thankful nothing earthshaking happened." Cecily rose to her feet. "Everyone has emerged unscathed and Phoebe kept her promise to present a brief event. All things considered, taking into account her past disasters, I think we can count this one as an unprecedented success. Even her dance troupe managed to get through an acceptable performance for once."

Baxter raised an eyebrow. "Obviously you have not attended too many renditions of 'Swan Lake.'"

"Ah, I thought that might be what it was supposed to be." Hurriedly changing the subject, she glanced at the door, where two footmen waited to announce the arrival of the bridal couple. "Madeline and Kevin should be here any minute. As soon as they arrive I'll signal for the food to be brought in."

She had to raise her voice as maids and footmen hustled to drag the chairs back to the tables surrounding the dance floor. Up on the stage Gertie, Pansy, and Samuel were setting up a long table for the bridal party.

Cecily sighed. She had been justified in doubting the wisdom of allowing Phoebe to hold a revue before the wedding banquet. The scramble to rearrange the room was most distracting.

When Madeline had insisted, however, on going home to change her wedding gown for something more comfortable before attending the reception, Phoebe had stoutly maintained that a revue would be just the thing to entertain the guests while waiting for Madeline and Kevin to arrive. After all, she'd argued, no one could begin eating until the bride was seated.

There was some merit to that, Cecily had to allow, though she wished there had been another way to get things organized other than dragging chair legs across her precious sprung parquet floor.

Glancing at the window, she noticed a light rain beginning to fall. A welcome sight after the heavy snowfalls they had endured over the Christmas week. Rain should wash the muddy slush away, thereby saving her from lifting her skirts every time she stepped outside.

As it was the hem of her bridesmaid gown had been stained by the grimy snow churned up by the horses' hooves. Not that she planned to wear it again. A bridesmaid's gown, like a wedding gown, should only be worn once. She planned to donate it to the Salvation Army. Baxter would take it with him when he returned to London.

A disturbance at the door caught her attention. "Here they are," she exclaimed, and laying her hand on Baxter's arm, she prepared to greet the happy couple.

Madeline looked more like herself now that she wore a primrose yellow gown that floated around her feet as she walked. Gold open-toed sandals peeked out from under her hem, and she had let down her hair, catching it back behind her ears with a gold ribbon.

Her eyes sparkled with humor as she gazed up at her brand new husband, and the look in Kevin's eyes took Cecily's breath away. How wonderful to be gazed upon with such ardor!

She could still remember Baxter looking at her like that. Those times were few and far between now, but on the rare occasion he did so, it meant all the more to her that he still could make her heart beat faster.

Glancing at the stage, Cecily was pleased to see that the

table was now ready. Gertie waited at the door for her signal, and Cecily raised her hand to indicate the food should now be served.

As Baxter led the way to the stage, the footmen announced that everyone should take their seats. Watching the guests take their places at the tables, Cecily let out her breath on a sigh of satisfaction.

Everything was moving along smoothly. After all the worrying, the planning, the organizing, and issuing orders, it seemed that Madeline's long awaited wedding was a resounding success.

As if reading her thoughts, Madeline's gaze met hers across the table. Her lips moved, mouthing the words. "Thank you, Cecily."

Three simple words, but Cecily appreciated the heartfelt meaning behind them. She nodded, her heart full for her dear friend, who had finally found the happiness that had always eluded her.

*May you always be this happy,* she silently prayed. *May you always be this blessed.*



"Gawd, those people know how to eat." Gertie piled dirty dishes into the sink. "They'll all be fat as bleeding pigs by the time they get through this lot."

Mrs. Chubb clicked her tongue. "That's no way to talk about the guests, Gertie McBride. Just be thankful they are enjoying Michel's wonderful cooking."

"And Mrs. Chubb's fantastic baking, *non?*" Michel waved a wooden spoon at Gertie. "You should be proud to serve such a *magnifique* feast, *n'est-ce pas?*"

Gertie spun around. "Crikey, what's got into you two? Why all this lovey-dovey stuff all of a sudden? Been at the brandy again, I suppose."

Mrs. Chubb looked guilty. "Just a drop. It is New Year's Eve, after all."

"Time to celebrate!" Michel brandished the spoon with such a flourish it flew out of his hand and smacked Gertie on the side of the head.

"You bleeding twerp!" Gertie picked the spoon up off the floor and flung it back at him. "That flipping hurt."

The spoon hit Michel on the nose, making him howl. Promptly forgetting his French accent, he yelled, "Bloody hell, Gertie! Put a sock in it!"

Mrs. Chubb threw up her hands. "For goodness sake, you two. Gertie, go and fetch some coal for the stove. It's nearly out and I have cheese sticks baking in the oven."

Gertie scowled at her. "Why me? Why can't one of the other maids get the bleeding coal? I'm supposed to be in the ballroom filling up the champagne glasses."

Mrs. Chubb glanced at the clock. "It's another hour until midnight. You're the only one here right now and if I don't get coal in the stove soon my cheese sticks will be ruined."

"Oh, all right." Gertie reached for her shawl and pulled it off its peg. "But I want a drop of that brandy when I get back. It's cold out there."

"I'll have a drop or two waiting for you," Mrs. Chubb promised.

Gertie stomped across the kitchen, swung the coal scuttle off the floor and dragged open the back door. "It's always me what has to go out in the cold, dark night," she muttered. "Always poor old Gertie."

Stepping out into the yard, she closed the door. Cold rain dripped on her head and down her neck, and she dragged the shawl tighter around her shoulders.

One more night and she could put this Christmas behind her. She'd done her best to enjoy it for the sake of the twins, but it hadn't been easy. If only she didn't keep thinking about Dan and how much she missed him. If only she could forget him and get on with her life.

After all, they were only together a few months. Not like her and Ross, being married and everything. She hated to admit it, in fact, she felt guilty just thinking about it, but she missed Dan more than she'd missed Ross that first year after he'd died.

Sloshing through the slushy melting snow, Gertie tried to remember exactly how she'd felt when Ross passed away. It was all a blur—a painful blur, but none of it seemed real now. She'd loved Ross more like a friend. She'd leaned on him, depended on him, enjoyed being with him, but she'd never felt about him the way she'd felt about Dan.

The hardest thing she'd ever done in her life was to refuse to move to London. Maybe if he'd proposed marriage, she might have thought about it more. But he hadn't. All he'd asked was that she move back to the city so they could see more of each other.

Then again, it was probably for the best. Being married to him would only make things harder. She'd managed to convince herself that it was better to make a clean break and face the pain now, rather than watch him slowly turn from her when he realized she wouldn't fit into his life.

After all, she had her twins to think about. They'd loved Dan, too. She couldn't bear to see them lose another father figure. No, she'd done the right thing. Only why did it have to hurt so much?

She hadn't realized just how bad the pain would be. How many nights she'd lie awake wondering if she'd made the biggest mistake of her life.

Reaching the door of the coal shed, she took hold of the handle. She was about to pull open the door when she heard something move behind her—a quiet shuffling somewhere in the yard.

Nerves jumping, she swung around. Holding her breath, she listened, but all she could hear was the thudding of her heartbeat echoing in her ears.

The memory of Ian's face sprang into her mind. *You haven't seen the last of me. That's a promise.*

No, it couldn't be.

Her voice sounded weak and shaky when she called out. "Clive? Is that you?"

The shuffling sounded again. Closer this time.

Panic shut off her breath. A rat, maybe. Or a mole. Maybe a fox looking for food. "Hello? Who's there?" She took a step forward. "If that's you out there, Ian, you can bloody well bugger off."

At that moment, two brawny arms closed around her from behind. Her scream seemed to fill the yard, echoing all the way to the sea.

Cecily leaned back in her chair with a sigh of relief. The banquet had been quite spectacular. Michel, Mrs. Chubb, and the kitchen staff had done a magnificent job.

The pigeon soup had been followed by delicate Dover sole, then platters of ham and roast beef surrounded by Cornish game hens had been placed on each table. Bowls of mashed potatoes, beetroots, and pickled onions accompanied the platters, together with grated turnips and carrots.

An enormous sherry trifle followed, glistening with candied peel and cherries buried in the whipped cream, after which the maids had served an assortment of cheeses with pieces of apple and pear.

Now all that was left was for Madeline and Kevin to cut the cake, whereupon the maids would deliver slices of it to the already satiated guests.

Soon the floor would be cleared for dancing. Already the orchestra members waited in the wings to take the stage once the bridal table had been cleared away.

Cecily glanced down the table, to where Grace Danbury actually seemed to be enjoying her conversation with the Winchesters.

It remained to be seen whether or not Madeline's friend would stay for the rest of the evening to celebrate the New Year, or retire early.

Cecily intended to keep an eye on her, and at the very first opportunity, slip upstairs to search Grace's room. She hoped she'd be able to talk Baxter into standing guard. At the moment he seemed rather mellow, thanks to the excellent cognac he had consumed.

Charles Winchester stood at that moment, and tapped his glass with a fork. His speech was short and to the point, wishing the happy couple a long and prosperous life together.

Kevin responded with a few brief words, then it was time to cut the cake. Madeline's hand was quite steady as she and Kevin held the knife and made the first cut. Then they toasted each other, then the guests, and then kissed, to a roar of approval from their audience.

Minutes later, when everyone had been given more than enough time to eat the cake, the flurry of activity began again as the maids and footmen went to work.

Cecily descended from the stage to find Madeline waiting for her.

"This has been the most beautiful and enjoyable wedding," Madeline said, linking her arm though Cecily's. "I'm so glad you persuaded me to do things this way. Everyone has been so nice to me. It really has been a most wonderful, pleasurable experience. Thank you so much for everything."

Cecily smiled. "I'm so happy you enjoyed it. I know it wasn't what you wanted, but I was hoping that it would all turn out well for you. I just couldn't picture you and Kevin getting married in the woods with everyone traipsing around in the soaking rain. I wanted to see you married in a proper ceremony in a church."

Madeline's eyes glinted with mischief. "What if I were to tell you I did both?"

Cecily stared at her in disbelief. "You did what?"

"I did both." Madeline looked over her shoulder, then drew Cecily closer. "Kevin made me swear I wouldn't tell anyone, but I'm sure he didn't include you in that. You are, after all, my very best friend. So I'll tell you." She drew in a breath, then whispered, "Kevin and I were married in a ceremony beside Deep Willow Pond this morning. That's why we were a little late at the church this afternoon."

Cecily didn't know whether to laugh or shake her. "Madeline! Who married you?"

"We married ourselves, by the laws of nature, with the wildlife as our witnesses." Madeline hugged Cecily's arm. "It was so beautiful, Cecily. I do wish you could have been there to see it."

That was one wish that Cecily was rather thankful hadn't been granted. "Well, I'm sure it was beautiful and meaningful to you both." Actually she was stunned that Kevin had agreed to such a primitive ceremony. Perhaps her fears for their happiness were unfounded after all.

Clasping Madeline's hand, she murmured, "At least you are now thoroughly married. With all those vows you should both be ecstatically happy."

"I'm quite sure we will be." Madeline glanced over at her husband. "Oh, dear, Phoebe has Kevin cornered. I had better rescue him. Thank you again, Cecily dear. You are a true friend."

She floated off to join her husband, and Cecily's smile was rueful as she watched her leave. It was hard to imagine that free spirit captured by anyone, much less by a logical scientist who refused to accept that there were some things about his wife that could not be slotted into conventional compartments.

The road would not be easy for them, but true love could overcome many boundaries, and one could only hope that their love for each other was strong enough.

Thinking of scientists reminded Cecily of Grace Danbury. Scanning the room, she caught sight of Grace over by the French windows. She appeared to be deep in conversation with Charles Winchester.

Cecily pulled in a breath. This would seem to be an opportune moment to slip upstairs. Baxter was still up on the stage, conversing with the leader of the orchestra. The musicians had finally taken their seats and were in the painful process of tuning their instruments.

Moving over to the front of the stage, Cecily caught her husband's eye and inclined her head.

Baxter immediately cut off whatever he was saying and excused himself.

Meeting him at the bottom of the stage steps, Cecily took his arm and led him over to the exit.

"Where are we going?" he demanded, as she waited for him to open the doors.

"I'll tell you in a moment."

He gave her a suspicious look, but pulled open the doors and waited for her to pass through before following her out into the hallway. "Is something wrong?"

"Not as far as I know." She waited until they were halfway down the hall, then making sure no one was around to overhear, she said quietly, "I want you to come to Grace Danbury's room with me."

He raised his eyebrows. "What the devil for?"

"I'll explain later."

She made to walk past him, but he held out his arm, blocking her progress. "You'll tell me now."

She didn't care for his proprietary tone, and her look told him so.

He sighed. "All right. I'm sorry. Please, Cecily, tell me now. I'd really like to know why you want to drag me up to that woman's room."

"I want to search it."

His face darkened. "That's what I was afraid you would say."

"I think that Grace Danbury might be involved in the Hethertons' murders."

His eyebrows flew up. "Good Lord! What on earth makes you think that?"

"I don't have time to explain now." She glanced back over

her shoulder. "I don't know how long Grace will remain in the ballroom. We need to hurry, so we can return before we arouse suspicion."

Baxter shook his head. "I don't know why I allow myself to go along with these preposterous shenanigans of yours. I really—" He broke off with a low curse as they entered the lobby and heard a hoarse voice calling out.

At the top of the kitchen stairs, Colonel Fortescue stood waving his arm in an urgent gesture for them to join him.

"Ignore him," Baxter muttered, and would have crossed the lobby to the stairs, had Cecily not detained him with a hand on his arm.

"We can't," she whispered. "He's likely to follow us all the way upstairs."

"Drat the man." Sighing heavily, Baxter strode over to him, with Cecily hurrying behind.

"What is it, Colonel? Baxter demanded, when he reached him. "Is something wrong?"

Fortescue's eyes looked glazed, and his glowing nose suggested he'd been heavily indulging in his favorite pastime in the bar. He swayed as he stared up at the ceiling, his eyes half-closed. "Spiders," he said, in a hushed voice. "Big as rats."

"I beg your pardon?" Cecily followed his gaze to the ceiling, but could see nothing but the white swirls of plaster gleaming in the gaslight from the chandelier.

"Saw them in India, you know. Pesky things would bite a hole in your leg."

"Yes, well, that was India." Cecily gave Baxter a pleading look. "We are in England now, Colonel. Our spiders are a lot more civilized."

The colonel's watery eyes did their best to focus on her. "Civilized? Not in India, old girl. Nothing's civilized there. Why, I remember when—"

Cecily frantically rolled her eyes at Baxter.

"I say, old chap." Baxter clapped him on the shoulder,

making him cough. "The barman has just opened a bottle of our best gin. He makes a devilish collins. Just the thing for a refresher before downing the midnight champagne, wouldn't you say?"

The colonel's eyelids blinked rapidly at him. "Collins? By Jove, I haven't had one of those blighters since the night I got into a brawl in a Shanghai nightclub. There I was—"

"Gin," Baxter said desperately. "Our very best."

"—trapped in a pesky corner, surrounded by a bunch of vicious scar-faced rogues armed with knives." Fortescue leaned forward so far he was in danger of toppling over. "All I had was a broken bottle, old boy." He swiped the back of his hand across his mouth. "Fought my way out of there, by George, but got my blasted tooth knocked out." Pulling his mouth into a ghastly grin, he jabbed a finger at it. " 'Ook, 'ight 'ere."

Cecily glared at Baxter. "Colonel," she said sternly, "I must insist you join your wife in the ballroom. She is quite concerned about your whereabouts. I really think you should let her know you are well."

Fortescue smacked his lips. "Always worrying, that woman. Still, wouldn't be without 'em, what? What?" He raised his hand to his head, apparently realized he had no hat to doff, then nodded instead and started down the steps.

"Ah, colonel?" Baxter grabbed his arm and turned him around. "That's the stairs to the kitchen. I believe you need to go down the hallway. Over here."

With a firm hand, Baxter led the mumbling gentleman over to the hallway where, to Cecily's heartfelt relief, he ambled off in search of the ballroom. Or more likely, the bar.

"Thank goodness." She sent a furtive look around the foyer, then beckoning Baxter to follow, headed for the stairs.

# CHAPTER

## ❃ 21 ❃

Having reached the top floor without bumping into anyone, Cecily hurried down the hallway to the closet and took out the keys. "Wait for me at the top of the stairs," she told Baxter, "and tap on the door if you see anyone coming up them."

Baxter frowned. "How are you going to explain our presence up here, when we are both supposed to be playing host in the ballroom?"

"I'll simply say I needed something from our suite and you accompanied me to get it."

He seemed unconvinced, but she had no time to reassure him. Leaving him on guard, she slipped farther down the hallway to Grace's door.

It opened silently and she stepped inside, closing it behind her. Pitch blackness filled the room and she crept forward, feeling her way to the bed stand, where she knew an oil lamp would be waiting.

Her fingers met the edge of the lamp's saucer, and she felt

around for the matches. The square box shifted away from her as she touched it, and she had to grope some more before she could close her fingers around it.

After fumbling in the dark for a few seconds, she managed to extract one of the matches. She closed the box and struck the match against the flint on the side of it.

The little stick flared, then settled into a flame. Light flickered across the glass globe as she reached for it. The moment she touched it, however, she snatched her hand back. The glass was hot.

It had been recently lit.

Very recently.

At that moment she sensed another presence in the room. Just for a second or two she glimpsed a figure moving toward her, and then the flame burned her fingers, forcing her to drop the match. It flickered and went out, leaving her to face the unknown in the deadly darkness.

Gertie's scream died away in the cold night air. The bulky figure behind her held her in a bear hug that imprisoned her arms. Rigid with fear, she lashed out with her foot. "Let go of me, you lousy, rotten sod! I'll—"

She broke off with a gasp as the arms turned her around, and a deep voice exclaimed, "Now is that any way to talk to a man who's come all the way down from London just to give you a New Year's Eve kiss?"

Her mouth dropped open, and she stared in disbelief. *"Dan?"* She shut her eyes, convinced she was seeing things in the dark shadows of the yard. When she opened them again he was still there—smiling at her the way he'd smiled in her memories for so long. Finally she found her voice. "What the bloody hell are you doing here?"

"I told you. I came for this." He leaned forward and planted a kiss on her stunned mouth.

Gathering her scattered thoughts together, she shoved

him away from her. "You bleeding scared me half to death. Who says I want you kissing me, anyway? I thought you was gone away for good."

"So did I."

She could barely see his face in the faint light from the kitchen window. It was hard to tell what he was thinking. "Well, all I can say is it's a long way to come just for a blinking kiss," she muttered.

"Well, to be honest I was hoping for a little more than that."

She backed away from him. "Here, I'm not that sort of girl. I told you that before."

She could hear laughter in his voice when he answered her. "I know you're not. That's not what I meant." He rubbed his arms. "Can we go somewhere and talk? Somewhere private and a whole lot warmer?"

She shook her head. "It's almost midnight. I have to get back to pour the flipping champagne."

"Oh."

She actually saw his shoulders sag. "I'm free after that," she added gruffly.

He didn't answer right away and she wondered frantically what he was thinking. She didn't dare hope for anything much, but he had come a long way and maybe, just maybe, he'd come to tell her something she really, really wanted to hear.

"I was hoping to see the New Year in with you," he said at last.

She let out her breath. "Well, I'm sure madam wouldn't mind if you came in and had a drop of champagne with us. After I get done in the ballroom I'll have a few minutes to get back down to the kitchen before twelve. Me and Mrs. Chubb and the others will be toasting the New Year but you can join us if you like."

"I like." Dan linked her arm through his. "And then we can talk, all right?"

Happily she smiled up at him. "All right." They were almost at the door when she remembered. "Bloody hell! Wait
a minute."

Dan halted. "What? What's the matter?"

"The bleeding coal. I have to go back and get it, or Mrs.
Chubb will have a bleeding cow."

Dan's laughter rang out across the yard. "Gertie, I've
missed you like crazy."

She beamed at him. "Me, too. Come on, you can help me
get the coal." Picking up her skirts, she dashed for the shed,
safe in the knowledge he was right behind her.

The voice that came out of the darkness was familiar, though
the sound of it did little to relieve Cecily of her anxiety. She
caught her breath as she recognized it.

"I thought it might be you, Mrs. Baxter. Do be so kind as
to light the lamp."

The box of matches rattled in Cecily's hand as she scrabbled for another match and struck it. This time she was
careful to remove the glass globe by holding the very tip of
the rim. She set it down, then turned the tiny brass wheel
on the side of the lamp to raise the wick.

The match wobbled precariously in her nervous fingers as
she set it on the oil soaked cotton. The flame flared into a
circle, and she turned to face Grace Danbury.

The woman stood by the bed, upon which lay a small
wooden trunk, the lid flung open to reveal folded clothing
inside. "I was hoping to leave without attracting too much
attention," Grace said pleasantly. "First thing in the morning. Which is why I'm packing tonight."

Cecily struggled to clear her mind. Grace must have
passed her and Baxter in the lobby while they were talking
to the colonel. They must have been too preoccupied to notice her going up the stairs.

"I assume you came looking for this." Grace bent her

knees and reached under the bed. "Ah, here it is." She rose, holding a bright golden tube in her hand.

Cecily stared at the cracker. It looked so harmless, just a pretty Christmas trinket to celebrate the season of peace and goodwill. Yet one just like it had caused the death of two people.

Remembering what she had learned about the explosive presumably packed inside the golden tube, fear trickled down Cecily's back like a melting icicle.

Despite the pleasant tone, it was obvious Grace Danbury was as unstable as the weapon she held. Cecily could see it in her eyes, in the way her hand shook, in the trembling of her lips. What would it take to make the cracker explode?

Obviously Grace would not pull it apart herself, since that would only result in her own death. Would it explode if she threw it? How far would the woman have to be from it to escape injury herself?

Aware of the oil lamp flickering away at her elbow, it was fairly obvious to Cecily that all Grace had to do was throw the cracker and dive under the bed. If the movement itself didn't set off the explosive, the bare flame from the lamp almost certainly would. How stupid of her. She should have replaced the globe.

The door seemed a long way away. *Where was Baxter?* How long would it be before he got nervous about the time she was taking and came looking for her? Even if he did, would he be able to stop the deadly impact of the cracker if Grace threw it at her?

She had to keep the woman talking long enough to arouse Baxter's impatience. Perhaps his arrival would throw Grace off guard long enough for her to snatch the cracker from her without it going off. It was a small hope, but it was all she could count on.

She jumped when Grace spoke again. "You did come into my room looking for this, didn't you?"

Cecily drew a deep breath. "I'm not sure I know what you

mean. My maids are busy with the reception downstairs, and I wanted to make sure they'd turned the covers down on all the beds."

Grace smiled. It was not a pleasant smile. "I find that hard to believe, Mrs. Baxter. You see, I saw your face when I mentioned the rash on my hands. I could tell you found it significant. I watched you work it all out in your head. That was a very stupid slip of my tongue. I should have known that you would have discovered one of the hazards of handling silver fulminate."

Cecily frowned. "I beg your pardon?"

"The explosive compound in a Christmas cracker. Please, Mrs. Baxter, don't bother to deny it. Your stable manager suffered the same rash. Did he not? I imagine his hands were affected when he cleaned up after the deaths of the Hethertons."

So that was why Grace was talking so earnestly with the doctor. To find out just how much Cecily knew about the compound.

"Oh, that," she said, taking the smallest step away from the lamp. "Yes, I believe he did mention something about it. I didn't pay much attention to him at the time."

Grace matched her step. "I didn't mean to kill them, you know. I only meant to mark the woman's face and hands a little. I thought a few scars would take her down a peg or two. I had no idea this stuff was so powerful. So deadly. It was a complete shock to me when I learned that both of them had died."

Realizing there was no point in pretense any longer, Cecily took another step in the direction of the door. "Why? Why did you want to hurt her?"

"She destroyed my rose." Her hand grasping the cracker lowered a little, as if she was tired of holding it up. "It was so beautiful. Pure white, with just a hint of pink on the edges. The only one of its kind in the world. And she destroyed it."

"I'm sorry. . . ."

"There it lay, my life's work in ruins on the floor at my feet. The only chance I ever had of my name going down in history."

Cecily shook her head. "I'm sorry, but I don't understand—"

Grace's harsh voice interrupted her. "The woman actually laughed. *Laughed* at me. She said the rose was quite unattractive and never would have been accepted as a valued hybrid." She studied the cracker, her expression thoughtful. "I found out later she was experimenting with hybrids as well. I have no doubt she destroyed my beautiful 'Pure Grace' rose in a fit of petty jealousy."

Cecily inched closer to the door. "So you came down here planning to hurt her."

Grace stepped toward her again. "Oh, no. Not at all. I had no idea the Hethertons would be staying here at the Pennyfoot. It was quite a shock when I saw them. I recognized Lady Clara, of course, the moment I saw her in the lobby. She was talking rather loudly about the special surprise in one of the Christmas crackers at the banquet. Someone had told her it was a pearl brooch. She didn't seem too impressed."

Grace rolled the cracker around in her fingers, causing Cecily's heart to flutter quite precariously. "I had a dream that night. I dreamt that abominable woman pulled a cracker and it blew up in her face. When I woke up I started wondering how much explosive one would need in a cracker to scar someone's face for life."

Carefully, Cecily shifted a little closer to the door. "So you went into Wellercombe to buy explosives."

"I called a friend of mine—a scientist—who was really quite helpful. It was a simple matter to locate a company who would sell me the chemicals. I borrowed two of your beautiful crackers—I wanted an extra one in case something happened to the first one—and I added the compound to the contents inside both of them."

She shrugged in such a callous way, Cecily's apprehension turned to outright fear. "I miscalculated," she said, her voice matter-of-fact. "I used too much. I didn't mean to kill them both. Sir Walter should never had died. He'd been punished enough in life being saddled with that shrew."

Her narrowed eyes glinted in the flickering light from the lamp. "At least now she'll never have her name on a hybrid rose."

Cecily risked a glance at the door. Perhaps, if she moved really quickly, she could get the door open and leap out before Grace had time to aim the cracker at her.

"It's really too bad, Mrs. Baxter, that you couldn't keep your nose out of my affairs." Grace took another step toward her.

Cecily couldn't imagine what the woman had in mind. She had no time to contemplate the matter, however, as the door flew open at that moment and Baxter stepped into the room.

"Cecily, what the devil—?" He broke off, his eyebrows shooting upward as he caught sight of Grace and the deadly weapon she held. "Good Lord."

Grace seemed uncertain what to do about this latest development. Her gaze darted from Baxter and back to Cecily, and then to the cracker she now held aloft again.

Cecily hoped the woman wasn't too deranged to realize that if she did anything at all with the cracker she would almost certainly be hurt herself in the process.

"Cecily!" Baxter's urgent tone revealed his apprehension. "Get behind me, now."

"I think it would be wise if neither of you moved." Grace jerked the cracker toward Cecily and she jumped backward, far enough to bump into Baxter's solid presence.

He wrapped his arms around her and swung her behind him. "Now," he said grimly, "give me that damn thing before it goes off and blows you apart."

"It won't go off unless it's pulled," Grace said, with a defiant scowl. "I made sure of that."

In view of the fact that Grace had miscalculated the amount of explosive she'd used, Cecily was not in the least reassured. "Just put it down on the bed," she said, peeking around Baxter's back. "Then we can talk about all this and decide what to do about it."

"I know what I'm going to do about it." Grace took hold of both ends of the cracker, as if she meant to pull it. "I'm going to walk out of here and you will stay right here until I'm gone. I'm not hanging for that loathsome woman. She ruined enough of my life. I will not allow her to have the last laugh."

"Just a minute—" Baxter began, but she cut him off with a vicious gesture of the cracker.

"No! Get out of my way, or I'll pull this and we'll all go up in flames."

Cecily stepped out from behind her husband. "Grace, I'm sure there's a better way—"

"Do what I say!" Grace held the cracker up in the air, still grasping both ends.

"Let her go," Baxter said gruffly. He grabbed Cecily's arm and pulled her away from the door.

Still brandishing the cracker above her head, Grace stepped over to the door. "Open it," she ordered.

Baxter complied, his face like stone.

Grace slipped through and disappeared.

"After her," Cecily said urgently. "We must warn people to stay out of her way."

"Let us hope everyone is still in the ballroom." Baxter went through the door first, pulling Cecily after him.

Together they raced to the top of the stairs. Cecily leaned over the bannisters, just in time to see Grace turn the corner. As she straightened up, yet another memory clicked in her mind. She grabbed Baxter's arm. "Is it still raining?"

He stared at her as if she'd gone mad. "Raining?" His voice rose to a falsetto. "What has rain got to do with any of this? What are you talking about?"

Cecily's stomach seemed to drop like a rock. "Oh, great heavens. Bax, we have to stop her." She started down the stairs, shouting at the top of her voice. "Grace! *Wait!* For heaven's sake, stop! It's *raining*!"

Ignoring Baxter's orders to wait for him, Cecily bounded down the stairs. With just a few steps to go to the foyer, she saw the front door closing. She paused, then turned back and threw herself into Baxter's arms.

He clutched her tight, demanding, "For heaven's sake, Cecily—"

He never finished the sentence. A thunderous boom shook the front door and Cecily clung tighter to him, her face buried in his coat.

"What the hell was that?"

Her eyes closed tight, she shook her head.

"Wait here, I'm going out there to see what happened." He sounded grim. "Though I can guess."

Cecily stayed where she was as he left, too shaken to move. The sound of pounding feet from the hallway finally lifted her chin. Samuel burst into the foyer, followed by two of her footmen.

"What's going on?" Samuel asked, as he rushed toward her, his face creased in concern.

"I'm not sure. Baxter has gone out there." She waved a hand at the door, and at that moment it opened and Baxter strode in.

She took one look at his face, and she knew. "She's dead, isn't she."

"I'm afraid so."

"Charles told me," she said. "I tried to stop her. I knew that one drop of water on that compound could blow it up."

Baxter put his arm around her and pulled her close. "Samuel, go and find Dr. Prestwick. Be as discreet as you can. Just tell him I'd like to speak to him in the foyer. Preferably without his wife."

"Yes, sir."

"You two. I'll need you to come with me." Baxter beckoned to the footmen, then put Cecily away from him. "Don't go out there. Go back to the ballroom and make some excuse for the noise. That's if anyone heard it back there."

Cecily nodded, too disturbed to answer. She had been terrified that Grace might blow her up, but she felt now that the woman had never intended to kill her. Nor had she intended to kill the Hethertons.

It had been a very nasty quest for vengeance that had got out of hand, and had resulted in the deaths of three people. And now she would have to tell Madeline that one of the very few friends she had was now dead. What a terribly sad ending to what should have been the happiest day of Madeline's life.

# CHAPTER

## ❀ 22 ❀

"Look who's here!" Gertie pulled Dan into the kitchen, grinning at Mrs. Chubb, who sat at the kitchen table. Michel sat opposite her, and was the first to speak.

"Sacre bleu, what have we here?" He flapped his eyebrows up and down in a comical gesture of surprise. "We thought we had seen the last of you, *mon ami*. Now perhaps Gertie will treat us all with smiles instead of curses, *oui*?"

For once Gertie ignored him. "He scared the bloomin' daylights out of me, he did. Didn't you hear me screaming? Loud enough to wake the dead, I was."

Mrs. Chubb looked alarmed. "You were screaming? Why, what happened?"

"He grabbed me in the dark, that's what happened." Gertie grinned at him. "Lucky he didn't get a bloody wallop on the nose."

Mrs. Chubb clicked her tongue. "Hello, Dan. It's nice to see you again."

Gertie let out a shaky sigh. "For a minute there I thought it was Ian coming back to get me."

Dan looked at her in surprise. "Ian? The father of your twins?"

"It's a long story. I'll tell you—"

A muffled boom cut her off mid sentence.

For a moment they all stared at each other, then Gertie said softly, "What the bleeding hell was that?"

"Oh, my." Mrs. Chubb clutched her chest. "I hope and pray it's not another gas leak."

Dan looked alarmed. "Gas leak?"

Gertie sighed. "That's another story I have to tell you later."

Mrs. Chubb got up from the table. "Michel, perhaps you'd better go and find out what that noise was all about."

Michel shook his head. "I do not go anywhere. I sit right here at this table until the clock strikes twelve and then voilà! I drink the bottle of brandy."

Mrs. Chubb looked down her nose at him. "And wake up with a sore head in the morning. Then we all have to put up with your rotten mood."

Michel nodded. "That is the sad price I pay for a good time."

"A price we all pay. What about that noise? What if it was a gas leak? We could all be blown up."

Michel shook his head. "We hear no more noise, *oui*? It is just people celebrating the New Year."

"Then they're a bit too quick off the mark, that's all I can say."

Gertie had been too wrapped up in the joy of seeing Dan again to pay much attention to the conversation, but the housekeeper's last words penetrated the fuzzy warmth in her head. She glanced at the clock. "Blimey, I'd better get along to the ballroom. It's ten minutes to midnight and I have to pour the champagne."

She turned to go, and Dan caught her about the waist. "You'll be back before twelve, I hope?"

She smiled with her whole face. "Just like flipping Cinderella," she promised, then fled through the door. She hadn't skipped in years, but she did so now—just a few quick steps to take her to the stairs. This was going to be the best New Year's Eve ever.

Cecily reached the ballroom without running into anyone, which meant everyone was probably waiting in the ballroom for midnight to strike.

Bracing herself, she threw open the doors, half expecting to see people milling about anxiously wondering what could have caused the explosion.

To her immense relief, no one seemed to have noticed anything amiss. The orchestra was playing a lively waltz, while couples whirled around the floor. Others sat at their tables, seemingly engrossed in conversation. Apparently the music, and the fact that the ballroom was at the opposite end of the building, had prevented anyone from hearing the effects of the explosion.

Cecily spotted Madeline at the far end of the room. She looked bored and ill at ease, while Charles Winchester seemed intent on engaging her in what appeared to be an earnest discussion.

Cecily was halfway across the floor when Madeline spied her, her face lighting up with relief. She seemed concerned, however, when Cecily reached her.

"Something's happened," she said, her voice sharp with anxiety. "Samuel just came to fetch Kevin a few minutes ago. He left with him. What's wrong?"

Cecily glanced up at Charles. "May I borrow your charming companion for a moment?"

Charles smiled. "If you must. I don't suppose you have seen my wife?"

Cecily nodded across the room. "She's over there, chatting with the Crossleys and their friends."

"Oh, well then, I suppose I had better rescue her." He inclined his head, then drifted toward the group surrounding his wife.

Without a word, Madeline followed as Cecily led the way across the floor to the balcony steps. Neither of them spoke as they mounted the stairs and emerged on the balcony overlooking the ballroom floor.

The sweet sounds of the orchestra soared to the rafters. Cecily looked down on the spectacle of the ladies in pastel gowns twirling around with their men in black coattails. Above the dancers, white ribbon garlands mingled with the fragrant fir and cedar that still hung from the railings and adorned the walls.

Flowers abounded everywhere, adding their own splash of muted colors. A festive sight, and not at all the background nor the occasion she would have chosen to impart the sad news to her friend.

"Something's happened to Grace," Madeline said, a little too quietly.

Cecily turned to face her friend, knowing her words were a statement rather than a question. "Yes, I'm afraid so." As gently as she could, she related the events that had happened in Grace's room.

"I tried to stop her from leaving," she added, when she was finished. "The moment I remembered that water could set off an explosion. But I was too late. Grace ran out into the rain, and then we heard the explosion." She drew a shaky breath. "I'm so sorry, Madeline. I know you were fond of her."

Madeline stared down at the glittering floor below, her knuckles white on the railings. "I had a feeling. Nothing definite, but something evil seemed to hover around her when we were together. I didn't try to find out why. I suppose I really didn't want to know."

It occurred to Cecily at that moment that she had never

seen Madeline cry. Even now, her friend's eyes were dry when she looked up.

"So sad. I wish I could have done something to prevent what happened. If only she'd confided in me. . . ." She paused, and drew a deep breath. "I'd like to see to the burial arrangements. Grace has—*had*—no family. One of the reasons we understood each other so well. I'm sure Kevin will agree that we should do this for her."

"Very well." Cecily took hold of her hand. It felt icy cold through the flimsy fabric of their gloves. "I see Gertie is down there filling up the champagne glasses. Do you feel you can celebrate the New Year, or is that asking too much of you right now?"

Madeline hesitated, then shook her head. "Grace wouldn't want her mistakes to interfere with my wedding. I just hope that Kevin returns in time to see the New Year in with me."

Cecily nodded at the dance floor. "He's just come in. I do believe he's looking for you."

"Then let us get down there, before the clock strikes twelve." Madeline's sad smile made Cecily's heart ache for her.

Together they descended the stairs to join the revelers on the floor.

Cecily was happy to see Baxter making his way toward her. It would have been a miserable start to the New Year had he not been by her side.

"Is . . . everything taken care of?"

He nodded. "Kevin will notify the constabulary in the morning. One of the footmen will be taking the body to the morgue."

"Thank you, darling." She reached for a glass of champagne. "I only hope the New Year starts out much better than the old one has ended." As the orchestra leader counted down the seconds, she raised her glass.

"To the New Year, and to us," Baxter said, touching her glass with his.

"To us." She sipped, then raised her glass again. "To Madeline and Kevin. May they be as happy as we are."

"Amen." He gave her an anxious look. "Are you all right, my dear?"

She nodded, then as the crowd broke out into cheers, she lifted her face for his kiss. As long as she had him by her side, all was well with her world.

The vast kitchen seemed to be bursting at the seams with people when Gertie pushed open the door. Maids and footmen were jammed in every corner.

Clive stood by the sink, a glass almost swallowed up in his big hand. He kept looking out the window as if wishing he were outside. Gertie felt sorry for him and was about to push through the crowd to speak to him when Dan appeared in front of her and thrust a glass of champagne in her hand.

"Here you are. I was worried you wouldn't get back in time. I'd hate to think I came all this way for a New Year's kiss for nothing."

She pulled a face at him. "You already got your kiss."

"Nah, that was just a peck."

"Well, that's all you're going to get with everyone looking on."

He grinned. "Then we'll just have to go somewhere else more private."

She raised her voice to be heard above the clamor of voices. "I have to get back to my twins. I don't like leaving them on their own."

"Then that's where we'll go."

She looked at him, trying to read his expression. "How long are you staying?"

"That depends on you."

She wasn't sure she'd heard him right with all the noise going on around her. "What?"

He bent his head so his mouth was close to her ear. "I'm thinking of moving back to Badgers End for good. If Mohammed won't come to the mountain . . ."

She caught Mrs. Chubb watching them and drew away from him. "Mountain? What mountain?"

He shook his head. "Would you like it, Gertie McBride, if I moved back here for good?"

She could feel her smile warming her whole body. "Of course I'd bloody like it."

The crowd began to chant, counting the seconds to midnight. For some reason, she thought again of Clive, and turned to see if he was counting, too. She was just in time to see him open the door and leave.

For a second or two she felt sorry for him again. Even in a crowd he was a lonely man.

Then, as Dan curled his arm around her waist, she forgot everything else.

"Three, two, one! Happy New Year!" Michel's voice could be heard above everyone else's.

Gertie smiled up at the man by her side. It was not only the best New Year's Eve. The whole bloody year was going to be the best ever. "Happy New Year!" she echoed, and knocked back the whole glass in one go.